Beneath the

Contents

This book is dedicated to three
great editors of weird fiction:

to Peter Haining

and in memory of August Derleth
and Karl Edward Wagner

INTRODUCTION
NO MAP AND NO GUIDE

SUPERNATURAL HORROR IS a literature of myths. It develops and renews the images already embedded in folklore to represent the terror and mystery of our lives. It's no surprise, therefore, that great works of supernatural horror have often taken their setting from a traditional source. According to myth, the underground is the realm in which the mysteries of death are made visible. It's where the dead live; where secrets are hidden; where the past is buried.

In H.P. Lovecraft's story 'The Rats in the Walls', a system of underground caverns reveals the history (and even prehistory) of a family's warped religion and haunted atrocities. The descent from the house to the lower pits is at once an historical journey and a metaphysical one. W.H. Auden's poem 'In Praise of Limestone' gives us another reason to view underground landscapes as symbolic: they are not permanent. Like the living world, the world of caverns and tunnels changes and evolves with time.

The thirteen stories in this anthology – ten of which are published here for the first time – were selected for their atmospheric and disturbing use of an underground setting. They show a range of styles and approaches: surreal, witty, grim, romantic. But they are all scary. Here are tube stations, disused mines, railway tunnels, bomb shelters. Here is the underground as distorted geography, domain of evil, place of lost memory. This book presents some of the best of new British writing in the field of supernatural horror – a genre that is still capable of telling us a great deal about ourselves and the world that we live in.

The stories fall into three groups. Firstly, several tales are concerned with the transition between our world and the underground realm: the step into the dark. In Ramsey Campbell's classic 'The End of a Summer's Day', a young couple take a guided tour of a cave system to discover that their world contains no map and no guide. Pauline E. Dungate's ironic story 'In the Tunnels' plays on our sense of the familiar and the unknown. Mike McKeown's 'Going Underground' is a supernatural urban myth in the *Unknown* vein: a warning about the dangers of commuting. D.F. Lewis spins a web of morbid rumour around the bomb shelters of the Second World War in 'From the Hearth'. And that master of understated paranoia, Nicholas Royle, discovers a staircase to a world of cinematic twilight in 'Empty Stations'.

A second group of stories portray the more terrible occupants of the underworld. David Sutton's chilling 'Tomb of the Janissaries' explores the complicity between modern-day and ancient hunger. Equally bitter is Tim Lebbon's 'The Empty Room', where a pit in a forest causes two children to make a grim discovery. Derek Fox's 'The Stone Man' shows a child trapped in the relentless grip of an incomprehensible trauma. And in 'Grendel's Lair', Paul Finch blends crime fiction with folklore to evoke an unforgettable subterranean horror. Be warned: this story takes no prisoners.

A third group of stories draw on the Orpheus myth, portraying the underground realm as the domain of a metaphysical quest. In '"Where Once I Did My Love Beguile"', John Howard links a haunted geography to the dark side of adolescence. The complex, subtly Lovecraftian narrative of Simon Avery's 'Lost and Found' weaves together the threads of madness, failed love and sounds from another world. In Jason Gould's 'Nights at the Regal', pornography and spiritualism form an alliance in the loneliness of a basement flat. Finally, Simon Bestwick's powerful novelette 'To Walk in Midnight's Realm' introduces us to the beauty and terror of the afterlife.

From outright horror to visionary myth-making, these stories link the unknown to our world. They show us how, in Auden's words, *the crack in the tea-cup opens / A lane to the land of the dead.* The starting-point may be familiar; but once the ground opens up, there is no map and no guide.

Be careful down there.

Joel Lane
Birmingham 2002

THE END OF A SUMMER'S DAY

Ramsey Campbell

"DON'T SIT THERE, missus," the guide shouted, "you'll get your knickers wet!"

Maria leapt up from the stone at the entrance to the cave. She felt degraded; she saw the others laugh at her and follow the guide – the boisterous couple whose laughter she'd heard the length of the bus, the weak pale spinster led by the bearded woman who'd scoffed at the faltering Chinese in front, the others anonymous as the murmur bouncing from the bus-roof like bees. She wouldn't follow; she'd preserve her dignity, hold herself apart from them. Then Tony gripped her hand, strengthening her. She glanced back once at the sunlight on the vast hillside tufted with trees, the birds cast down like leaves by the wind above the hamburger stall, and let him lead her.

Into blindness. The guide's torch was cut off around a corner. Below the railed walk they could sense the river rushing from the sunlight. Tony pulled her blouse aside and kissed her shoulder. Maria Thornton, she whispered as an invocation, Maria Thornton. Goodbye Maria West, goodbye forever. The river thrust into blind tunnels.

They hurried toward the echoing laughter. In a dark niche between two ridged stalactites they saw a couple: the girl's head was back, gulping as at water, their heads rotated on the axis of their mouths like planets in the darkness. For a moment Maria was chilled; it took her back to the coach – the pane through which she'd sometimes stared had been bleared by haircream from some past kiss. She touched what for a long time she couldn't bring herself to name: they'd finally decided on Tony's 'manhood'. On the bus she'd caressed him for reassurance, as the bearded woman's taunts and the Chinese gropings grew in her ears; nobody had noticed. "Tony Thornton," she intoned as a charm.

A light fanned out from the tunnel ahead; the tallow stalactites gleamed. "Come on, missus," the guide called, "slap him down!"

The party had gathered in a vault; someone lit a cigarette and threw the match into the river, where it hissed and died among hamburger-papers. "I am come here to holiday," the Chinese told anyone who'd listen.

"Isn't it marvellous?" the bearded woman chortled, ignoring the spinster pulling at her hand. "Listen, Chinky, you've come here on holiday, right? On holiday. You'd think English wasn't good enough for him," she shouted.

"Oh, Tony, I hate this," Maria whispered, hanging back.

"No need to, darling. She's compensating for fear of ridicule and he's temporarily rootless. He'll be back home soon," he said, squeezing her hand, strong as stone but not hard or cold.

"Come on, you lot," the guide urged them on, holding his torch high. "I don't want to lose you all. I brought up last week's party only yesterday."

"Oh, God! Oh, hoo hoo hoo!" shrieked the boisterous couple, spilling mirth. "Hey, mate, don't leave me alone with him!" screamed the wife.

The party was drawn forward by a shifting ring of light, torn by stalactites like tusks. Behind her Maria heard the couple from the niche whisper and embrace. She kissed Tony hungrily. One night they'd eaten in a dingy cafe; dog-eared tablecloths, congealed ketchup, waitresses wiping plates on serviettes. At another table she'd watched a couple eat, legs touching. "She's probably his mistress," Tony had said in her ear; gently he showed her such things, which previously she'd wanted to ignore. "Do you want me to be your mistress, Tony?" she'd said, half-laughing, half-yearning, instantly ashamed – but his face had opened: "No, Maria, I want you to be my wife."

Deep in shade a blind face with drooping lips of tallow mouthed. Peering upward, Maria saw them everywhere: the cave walls were like those childhood puzzle-pictures which once had frightened her, forests from whose trees faces formed like dryads. She clung to Tony's arm. When they were engaged she'd agreed to holiday with him; they'd settled for coach-trips, memories to which they had returned for their honeymoon. One day, nine months ago, they'd left the coach and found a tower above the sea; they'd run through the hot sand and climbed. At the top they'd gazed out on the sea on which gulls floated like leaves, and Tony had said: "I like the perfume." "It's lavender-water," she'd replied, and suddenly burst into tears. "Oh, Tony, lavender-water, like a spinster! I can't cook, I take ages to get ready, I'll be no good in bed – I'm meant to be a spinster!" But he'd raised her face and met her eyes; above them pigeons were shaken out from the tower like handkerchiefs. "Let me prove you're not a spinster," he'd said.

The guide carried his torch across a subterranean bridge; beneath in the black water, he strode like an inverted Christ. The faces of the party peered from the river and were swept glittering away. "Now, all of you just listen for a moment," the guide said on the other side. "I don't advise anyone to come down here without me. If it rains this river rises as far as that roof." He pointed. But now, when he should be grave, his voice still grinned. "I don't like him," Maria whispered. "You couldn't rely on him if anything happened. I'm glad you're here, Tony." His hand closed on hers. "It can't last for ever," he told her. She knew he was thinking of the hotel, and laid her head against his shoulder.

"So long as the roof doesn't cave in!" yelled the boisterous man.

"Cave in!" the guide shouted, resonating from the walls; the faces above gave no sign that they'd heard. "Ha, ha, very good! Must remember that one." He poured his torch-beam into a low tunnel and ushered them onward. Behind her on the bridge Maria heard the couple from the niche. She lifted her head from Tony's shoulder. Thinking of the hotel – the first pain had faded, but in the darkness of their bedroom Tony seemed to leave her; the weight on her body, the thrust inside her, the hands exploring blindly, were no longer Tony. Yet she wasn't ready to leave the light on. Even afterward, as they lay quiet, bodies touching trustingly, she never felt that peace which releases the tongue, enabling her to tell him what she felt. Often she dreamed of the tower above the sea; one day they'd return there and she'd be wholly his at last.

The vault was vast. The walls curved up like ribs, fanged with dislocated teeth about to salivate and close. Behind her, emerging from the tunnel, the other couple gasped. Stalactites thrust from the roof like inverted Oriental turrets or hung like giant candles ready to drip. The walls held back from the torch-beam; Maria sensed the faces. In the depths dripped laughter. The party clustered like moths around the exploring torch. "Come on, love-birds, come closer," the guide echoed. "I've brought thirty of you down and I don't want to have to fiddle my inventory." Maria thrust her fingers between Tony's and moved forward, staying at the edge of light.

"Now before we go on I want to warn you all," the guide said sinisterly. "Was anybody here in the blackout? Not you, missus, I don't believe it! That's your father you're with, isn't it, not your husband!" The boisterous woman spluttered. "Even if you were," the guide continued, "you've never seen complete darkness. There's no such thing on God's earth. Of course that doesn't apply down here. You see?" He switched off the torch.

Darkness caved in on them. Maria lost Tony's hand and groping, found it. "Oh, God! Where was Moses!" yelled the boisterous couple. The young girl from the niche giggled. Somewhere, it seemed across a universe, a cigarette glowed. Whispers settled through the blackness. Maria's hand clenched on Tony's; she was back in the bedroom, blind, yearning for the tower above the sea.

"I hope we haven't lost anyone," the guide's face said, lit from below like a waxwork. "That's it for today. I hope someone knows the way out, that's all." He waved the torch to draw the procession. Laughing silhouettes made for the tunnel. Maria still felt afraid of the figure in the dark; she pulled Tony toward the torch. Suddenly she was ashamed, and turned to kiss him. The man whose hand she was holding was not Tony.

Maria fell back. As the light's edge drew away, the face went out. "Tony!" she cried, and ran toward the tunnel.

"Wait," the man called. "Don't leave me. I can't see."

The guide returned; figures crawled from the tunnel like insects, drawn by the light. "Don't be too long, love-birds," he complained. "I've got another party in an hour."

"My husband," Maria said unevenly. "I've lost him. Please find him for me."

"Don't tell me he's run out on you!" Behind the guide the party had reformed within the vault; Maria searched the faces shaken by the roving torch-beam, but none of them was Tony's. "There he is, missus!" the guide said, pointing. "Were you going to leave him behind?"

Maria turned joyfully; he was pointing at the man behind her. The man was moving back and forth in shadow, arms outstretched. The torch-beam touched his face, and she saw why. He was blind.

"That's not my husband," Maria said, holding her voice in check.

"Looks like him to me, love. That your wife, mate?" Then he saw the man's eyes. His voice hardened. "Come on," he told Maria, "you'd better look after him."

"Is husband?" the Chinese said. "Is not husband? No."

"What's that, mate?" asked the guide – but the bearded woman shouted: "Don't listen to the Chink, he can't even speak our language! You saw them together, didn't you?" she prompted, gripping her companion's arm.

"I can't say I did," the spinster said.

"Of course you did! They were sitting right behind us!"

"Well, maybe I did," the spinster admitted.

"Just fancy," the boisterous woman said, "bringing a blind man on a trip like this! Cruel I call it."

Maria was surrounded by stone faces, mouthing words which her blood swept from her ears. She turned desperately to the vault, the man stumbling in a circle, the darkness beyond which anything might lie. "Please," she pleaded, "someone must have seen my husband? My Tony?" Faces gaped from the walls and ceiling, lines leading off into the depths. "You were behind us," she cried to the girl from the niche. "Didn't you see?"

"I don't know," the girl mused. "He doesn't look the right build to me."

"You know he isn't!" Maria cried, her hands grasping darkness. "His clothes are wrong! Please help me look for Tony!"

"Don't get involved," the girl's escort hissed. "You can see how she is."

"I think we've all had enough," the guide said. "Are you going to take care of him or not?"

"Just let me have your torch for a minute," Maria sobbed.

"Now I couldn't do that, could I? Suppose you dropped it?"

Maria stretched her hand toward the torch, still torn by hope, and a hand fumbled into hers. It was the blind man. "I don't like all this noise," he said. "Whoever you are, please help me."

"There you are," the guide rebuked, "now you've upset him. Show's over. Everybody out." And he lit up the gaping tunnel.

"Wonder what she'd have done with the torch?" "The blind leading the blind, if you ask me," voices chattered in the passage. The guide helped the blind man through the mouth. Maria, left inside the vault, began to walk into the darkness, arms outstretched to Tony, but immediately the dark was rent and the guide had caught her arm. "Now then, none of that," he threatened. "Listen, I brought thirty down and thirty's what I've got. Be a good girl and think about that."

He shoved her out of the tunnel. The blind man was surrounded. "Here she is," said someone. "Now you'll be all right." Maria shuddered. "I'll take him if you don't feel well," the guide said, suddenly solicitous. But they'd led the blind man forward and closed his hand on hers. The guide moved to the head of the party; the tunnel mouth darkened, was swallowed. "Tony!" Maria screamed, hearing only her own echo. "Don't," the blind man pleaded piteously.

She heard the river sweep beneath the bridge, choked with darkness, erasing Tony Thornton. For a moment she could have thrust the blind man into the gulf and run back to the vault. But his hand gripped hers with the ruthlessness of need. Around her faces laughed and melted as the torch passed. They'd conspired, she told herself, to make away with Tony and to bring this other forth. She must fall in with them; they could leave her dead in some side tunnel. She looked down into the river and saw the sightless eyes beside her, unaware of her.

The guide's torch failed. Daylight flooded down the hillside just beyond. Anonymous figures chewed and waited at the hamburger stall. "All right, let's make sure everybody's here," the guide said. "I don't like the look of that sky." He counted; faces turned to her; the guide's gaze passed over her and hurried onward. At her back the cave opened, inviting, protective. "Where are we?" the blind man asked feebly. "It feels like summer."

Maria thought of the coach trip ahead; the Chinese and the girl unsure but unwilling to speak, the bearded woman looking back to disapprove of her, the boisterous couple discussing her audibly – and deep in the caves Tony, perhaps unconscious, perhaps crawling over stone, calling out to her in darkness. She thought she heard him cry her name; it might have been a bird on the hill. The guide was waiting; the party shuffled, impatient. Suddenly she pushed the blind man forward; he stumbled out into the summer day. The others muttered protests; the guide called out – but she was running headlong into darkness, the last glint of sunlight broken by her tears like the sea beneath the tower, the river rushing by beneath. As the light vanished, she heard the first faint patter of the rain.

IN THE TUNNELS

Pauline E. Dungate

THE PLATFORM OF Birmingham's Moor Street Station was crowded. Late shoppers and office workers stood crushed together, waiting for the Leamington train. Bernie, who wanted the one that followed, stood out of the way near the mouth of the tunnel. It fascinated him, this dark cavern that ran under the city and disgorged trains at regular intervals. He had walked through it once, just before they had reopened the rail link between Moor Street and Snow Hill, the station at its far end. Again, there had been too many people on that special trek for him to be fully able to appreciate its echoing magnificence.

Just a minute or so before the train arrived, there was a disturbance. Shouting distracted Bernie from his contemplation of underground places. As he turned he saw a ripple of movement and a child-sized figure belting along the platform towards him, weaving and barging between commuters. Vaguely recognising the cries of "Stop thief!", Bernie prepared to make a grab for the boy. The child slowed, grinned at him and leapt onto the rails.

"Ilyas!" Bernie would have plunged after him if someone hadn't grabbed him from behind.

The figure disappeared into the tunnel moments before the lights of the train became visible round the curve in the track. He tensed, waiting for the impact. But the carriages drew quietly into the station. Doors banged open as passengers scrambled for seats, emptying the platform of all but those waiting for the Stratford train and a small knot of people halfway along.

"D'ya know the kid, sir?" the porter who had restrained him asked Bernie.

"Yes... no... it couldn't have been," he stuttered.

"But yer got a good look?"

"Yes, but..."

"An' yer'd know 'im agin."

"I think so."

"Could yer come an' 'ave a word with the station manager, then?"

Bernie glanced at the clock. The yellow numbers flicked over to show 17.39, one minute to his train. His mother would hardly notice if he was late for tea. She never did. "If you think I can help," he said.

There was a policeman in the Station Manager's office when they finally showed him in. A tearful woman was being led out as he entered.

"Now, young man, the constable would like you to answer a few questions if you don't mind."

Bernie nodded and gave his name and address.

"Do you know the bag-snatcher?" the policeman asked.

"No, sir. He just looked a bit like someone I knew at school."

"What was his name?"

"Ilyas. I can't remember his other name. He was in my class, that's all."

"This lad was about twelve," the manager said.

That's why it couldn't be him, Bernie thought. He wouldn't recognise most of the kids from school, just the few he saw sometimes down the market, like Javad who'd nick things off the stall if he wasn't watching, or Shazad who had a club foot. In six years, Ilyas was sure to have grown a bit, and changed.

The phone rang part-way through the interview. The manager listened, nodding his head from time to time. When he cradled the receiver, he spoke to the constable.

"He hasn't come out at Snow Hill yet. And none of the drivers have seen anyone on the track."

The policeman wrote it down in his notebook.

Finally, they let Bernie go just in time to catch the 18:40, the manager saying, "Thank you so much for your help, young man."

It was dark and raining when the train pulled out. Bernie sat staring at his reflection in the window, seeing the round, grinning face of Ilyas as he passed under the bridges that muted the sound of the wheels. Whoever the boy was, he couldn't have disappeared.

BERNIE FOUND HIMSELF searching crowds for familiar faces, especially those pushing their way through the market towards the subway leading to the station. He found it easy to superimpose features on his customers at the fruit stall. Once he was sure he caught sight of the small, dark-haired figure of Ilyas disappearing behind an unloading lorry. When the boy re-emerged, he could see clearly that it wasn't. But from the back...

"Stop day-dreaming, lad. We've got customers," his boss told him.

Bernie blinked and stared down at the change he was clasping tightly. He grinned nervously and handed it to the old lady, who counted the coins carefully before stowing them in her purse.

"Where's me oranges?" she said.

Bernie passed her the bag, thankful that no-one could see his blushes.

"I don't know what's got into you recently, lad," his boss said later when they were clearing away. "You've been a pretty good worker up till now. Don't spoil it."

Bernie gave himself a mental shake and resolved to concentrate.

At the station, Bernie took to standing as close to the tunnel entrance as he could. He remembered the station master's words about the boy not coming out at the other end. There were caverns under Birmingham, he had heard. Vast concrete hangers where they had stored supplies in the war. Perhaps there was a way in through the tunnel. He couldn't remember any side branches on the day he had walked through.

Bernie decided that he had to go through the tunnel again. Instead of heading for Moor Street as he usually did, he set off across town, deliberately choosing a roundabout route to take him through as many underpasses as possible. He liked the enclosed spaces and wished there were fewer people around. He wanted to hear his own footsteps rebound from the walls.

There was a busker in the one leading to the main line station, a bald, elderly violinist whose squeaky music followed him as he passed.

He walked through Old Square. They were just locking the

basement doors to Lewis's. He could see the security man of the department store through the heavy plate glass as he slid the bolts into place. Then down the ramp and past the toilets. He hadn't realised there were so many small men in the city centre. There was another of them leaning on a broom in the entrance to the gents'. He looked like a gnome.

Bernie glanced at his watch and began to hurry. He didn't want to miss the train.

The trip was a little disappointing. He managed to get a seat at the front so that he could see through the driver's cab and out onto the track, but it was difficult to watch both sides at once. There were lights strung all along the tunnel and although he could see the shadows of archways set into the walls, he missed any dark opening leading away.

Under Colmore Circus, he saw Ilyas again. Bernie had taken to staying later and later in the market area, taking the most circuitous route he could devise to the station and lingering in the empty subways. Some were shabby and rubbish-filled and stank of urine. Others had murals painted on them or incised in the tiles. He was surprised how little graffiti was added to those pictures, the street artists seeming to confine their efforts to the railway, scarring the walls along the lines with their spray-on paint.

Sometimes the subway would open out into an oasis of green. The walls of the Horsefair had a delicate mosaic depicting the old market, and plants grew unmolested in the centre. Bernie had almost forgotten his search for Ilyas in his growing delight with the variety of underground passages.

Then he saw him. The small figure had his back to him as he crossed the open space under the traffic island. Ilyas disappeared behind a supporting pillar. Bernie hurried after him.

"Ilyas!" he called.

The boy stopped and turned. Ilyas was exactly as he had been six years before, when they had both walked out of school for the last time. They had never been friends, and Bernie remembered him most for his broken front teeth and the fact that he only ever seemed to wear Wellies to school.

"It is Ilyas, isn't it?" Bernie said.

Ilyas grinned.

"It's me. Bernie Robinson. From school."

"Hi," Ilyas said.

"What are you doing these days?" It was an inane question, but Bernie couldn't think of anything else to say. He couldn't very well ask if he'd been stealing handbags.

Ilyas shrugged. "Working for my uncle."

"I've got a job in the market," Bernie said. "Selling fruit."

"That's nice. See you around." And Ilyas disappeared into the shadows so quickly that Bernie hardly saw him go. Bernie started after him, reluctant to lose him after all this time; but the doorway he thought he'd gone through was only a locked service duct. Bernie looked round, expecting to see Ilyas hurrying up one of the ramps. There was a movement to his left that quickly stilled when he turned that way, and an echo that might have been laughter or the tail-end of a whistled tune. The only other person in sight was an old tramp that Bernie was now used to seeing around town. He believed he slept on the steps outside the Nat West bank.

PEOPLE DIDN'T DISAPPEAR into walls. Only ghosts did that and Bernie didn't believe in ghosts. Ilyas was real. The more he thought about it, the more he was convinced that there was a way underground. Probably several ways.

He made up his mind and bought himself the most powerful torch he could find, and some spare batteries. He chose a Saturday night for his exploration, after the trains had ceased to run on the branch line, and caught the night service bus into town. If graffiti artists could get onto the railway line then so, Bernie reasoned, could he.

The subways, now totally deserted, resounded to the echoes of his feet. Bernie was torn between increasing the resonance of the sounds by stamping his feet and keeping quiet as he was about to break the law.

The station was locked up as expected, but next to the old part was a rutted car-parking lot surrounded by a high chain-link fence. He glanced around quickly before sauntering in through the gate. He had expected to have to climb the swaying fence but it lay in the dirt, trampled by other feet. He crossed boldly. To his left the old part of the station was secured from intruders, the fencing topped with vicious twists of barbed wire.

Bernie stepped over the rusting rails and walked round, past the sign that warned 'NO PASSENGERS BEYOND THIS POINT'.

Finally, he stood between the rails, looking into the maw of the tunnel. It was lightless. A solid wall of dark, facing him. Beckoning. His heart thudded with excitement, and fear. Bernie took two steps inside, then another two. The sound of the gravel beneath his feet was loud but muffled, as though the black air tried to erase his presence while the curved walls wanted to advertise it. He felt everything was being focused back on him.

He looked back and was reassured by the paler arch that marked the cavernous mouth, an orange-tinted grey fed by the lights of the city above. Bernie switched on his torch and began to walk slowly, swinging the beam from side to side, scanning the soot-coloured brickwork for doorways, anything that would suggest a way underground. A rat, startled by the light, scuttled along the wainscot and vanished into a recess. Bernie ran his hands over the brickwork, hunting for an opening. Nothing.

He went on.

At one point he switched off the torch and just stood. The darkness was total. Out of sight of either tunnel mouth, it enfolded him gently. Far above, he could hear the occasional rumble of passing cars. There was the odd tick of metal and mortar contracting. Bernie shivered. It was cooler than he had expected. It was supposed to get warmer the further you went underground.

He found it almost by accident. A streamer of paper had caught on the cable that was strung between the lamps. It stirred on an imaginary breeze as the torch beam flashed past it. Bernie looked upwards, expecting to see some shaft burrowing from the roof to the surface and creating an eddy. There was none. Neither was there a discernable wind through the tunnel itself. He stood still, wondering if his own movements had caused the fluttering. But no – the strip still jigged about in the torchlight.

Bernie crouched next to it, feeling for the air stream. He traced it to a crack at the base of the wall in another of the alcoves. He pushed tentatively. The brickwork seemed solid until he tapped it. It had a hollow ring. There was no catch that he could see. He pushed harder, in all the places and directions he could think of.

He grinned in the darkness as a panel slipped suddenly sideways. He shone the torch through the opening. It was a service passage running parallel with the tunnel and connected with it by a short linking corridor, five paces long. Cables and pipes stretched in both directions, but there was room for a small man to move carefully between them.

He jumped as the door slid and snicked back into place. He felt a momentary rise of panic as his beam caught the blank, closed wall. A quick check showed how easy it was to open again.

Bernie turned right towards Snow Hill. It was damp here, condensation forming and dripping from the ducts to form intermittent puddles. Some pipes gurgled with the passage of water through them.

There was a grill in the wall a little way along that concertinaed like the doors of old-fashioned lifts. Peering through, Bernie could see steps spiralling down. The passage was tiled with pale blue. It reminded him of the steps leading down to the lower levels of some of London's Underground stations. He'd spent a week's holiday there two years ago, haunting the network and wishing he could follow the trains that burrowed into the earth like giant worms.

The gate was held by a rusted padlock. Bernie stared longingly into the inviting gloom before searching for something to break it with. The penknife he always carried was too flimsy, the blade bending as he twisted it in the catch. He needed a more sturdy length of metal, like a screwdriver. He cast around for something suitable without much hope. The piece of wood he found snapped the moment he applied force.

Bernie tugged viciously at the padlock in his frustration. The loop snapped. It lay in the palm of his hand for a few moments before he realised what had happened. Then he carefully put it in his pocket. Passing through the gate he pulled it almost closed behind him, satisfied that he could get out easily.

His footsteps echoed, bouncing and reflecting from the curving walls, continuing after he stopped. It was almost as if there were someone before and behind him.

There was someone behind him. Another pair of shoes keeping

time with him. But not quite. The click of the heels was slightly different to the slap of his trainers.

"Who's there?" Bernie called. The cry stretched. Amplified by the stairs, it was returned to him altered: "Hoos sair".

Bernie dithered, knowing he was trespassing. As long as he remained still, so did the other. He tried tiptoeing down, then flashing the torch suddenly behind him, miscalculated and bashed it against the wall. The light flickered.

"You don't scare me," he whispered into the darkness.

"Scairee," it came back.

The torch went out.

"Scairee," the echo repeated.

Bernie froze. Being underground wasn't quite so much fun any more.

He started to creep back up the steps, fingers of one hand touching the tiles, the other holding the torch up as a club.

He encountered no-one.

He stumbled on the top step and sprawled across the floor, hitting his head on the gate. He hauled himself to his feet and pulled at the grid. It didn't move. He tugged again. And heard laughing.

He thought it was just the gurgle in the pipes above him, but it continued. Chuckling at first, then louder. A demented sound. Bernie shook and rattled the gate.

"Let me out," he shouted.

"Ow, ow, ow," came the reply from behind him.

He clasped his hands over his ears to shut out the sounds.

He could wait, he thought, wait until morning. Until someone came.

But perhaps no-one ever came.

He brushed a tickle from his cheek. It was wet. A tear. He wiped his face on his sleeve. Men didn't cry. And there must be another way. Besides, whoever it was had been behind him.

Without light, Bernie picked his way down the stairs again, feeling for every step with his toes before committing himself. It made his legs ache. But there were no echoes.

As he descended he became aware that he could see. Not clearly. Just the dim outline of his outstretched hand. There were lights below.

People.

Bernie stopped. People had locked him in. His throat was dry, his head sore and he could smell his own sweat. He edged round the last bend.

It wasn't much of a light. A pale glowing in the distance, its source blocked by a dark shadow. Bernie sank down, his back to the wall, shivering. He was in a cavern, he realised, the roof held up by massive columns.

The wartime caverns. Now empty. What was it he'd read in the newspaper? If the idea was to convert them into a huge bus depot, then there must be another way out. And the light must be a bonfire lit by vagrants. They would know.

Bernie bent his head to rest on his knees. To calm down. To still the fear. He would walk across to them. Warm himself, ask the way. It was nothing to get fretted about.

He was right up to them before he saw them. Grey figures stooping over a pile of burning sticks. One picked up a brand, straightened. He was no taller than a twelve-year-old boy. None of them were. Slowly they reached for the flaming torches. The flames illuminated just their faces. They were round and wrinkled and ugly. Like goblins.

One smiled. His teeth were small and sharp and pointed. Bernie spun round. They were behind him too. He panicked.

He screamed. He ran, heedless of the fact that he couldn't see.

He hit a pillar with his shoulder. He held his arms out before him and ran into another.

"BERNIE, BERNIE." SOMEONE was shaking his shoulder.

"The alarm's not gone off," he muttered, trying to pull the blankets over his head. There weren't any. He was cold.

"Bernie."

His head throbbed. His shoulder ached and there was pain in one of his wrists. He knew his eyes were open, but he couldn't see.

"It's Ilyas, Bernie. Do you remember me?"

"I can't see you," Bernie said.

"What are you doing here?" Ilyas asked again. There was a babble of unintelligible voices around him.

"Exploring," Bernie said.

One of the other people spoke to him. He couldn't understand. Ilyas answered in his own tongue, then in English. "I've told them we were at school together. That they cannot have you."

"What do you mean?" The feeling of panic was coming back, seeping through the pain of his hurts. He remembered the leering faces, the pointed, eager teeth.

"You must go," Ilyas said. "Can you stand?"

"I'm locked in. Someone locked the gate." He heard himself whining.

"I'll show you the way." Ilyas put his arm under Bernie's shoulder and helped him to his feet. Bernie swayed, disorientated. He felt invisible walls pressing in on him and the weight of Birmingham descending slowly to crush him. He whimpered.

The voice in the darkness spoke again, sharply, insistently. Ilyas again replied and began to lead Bernie forward.

Bernie felt hands pawing him, long nails touching his face. Ilyas spoke and they withdrew. Bernie could hear their feet shuffling after him, and somewhere the squeaky sound of a violin began to play. It was a dirge.

They splashed into water that became deeper, soaking his trainers and numbing his legs inside wet trousers. The sound changed as though they were entering a narrow, enclosed space.

"This is the river Rea," Ilyas said. "It runs underground here, down through Digbeth."

"What're you doing here?" Bernie asked, partly to drown the scuffles of their followers. He felt slightly safer now. The air around was slightly warmer, though it smelt a little of sewage.

"I live here. My people always have. We steal from above when we have to, and eat what comes down to us."

"But we were at school together."

"Times change. We have to adapt."

Progress was slow. Bernie staggered when he tried to walk unaided. He blundered into the tunnel wall. Pain shot up his arm from the damaged wrist.

He leant heavily on Ilyas, though it was uncomfortable due to the other's lack of stature. There were splashings and squealings from the water.

"Just rats," Ilyas said, 'squabbling over food."

Bernie shuddered. He would feel happier if he could see the animals. Something soft brushed by him. Far behind he thought he heard howling, the kind that could emanate from human throats.

Then Bernie could see. The end of the tunnel was a small orange-grey circle in the distance. It looked much too tiny for him to get through. The shaft they were traversing began to narrow. Old brick was replaced by smooth concrete. The water concentrated into the compressed space was deeper, swirled faster, tugging at his legs.

"You will have to crawl," Ilyas said. "There was no time to fetch the raft."

He tried, but his wrist gave way, throwing him into the water. He screamed with pain and swallowed foul-tasting liquid. He surfaced spluttering and sobbing.

"I can't," he said.

"You must. I can't keep them away for ever. There's a grid at the end but it lifts up easy. I used to come this way to school most days."

Bernie dragged himself through the tube. Cold and soaked, he kept watching the patch of light.

Ilyas started back the other way, whispering a hasty "Goodbye."

BERNIE PEERED THROUGH bars set about nine inches apart. Beyond them the river ran between steep banks, above which were silhouetted buildings outlined by sodium lights. The fringes of the water were studded with the debris of city life. He could hear the sound of an occasional car.

A piece of chicken wire stretched across the bottom of the bars, catching paper, twigs and gnawed bones as the river flowed out of the culvert. The gate itself was recently repaired and held in place by shiny new bolts. By stretching through, he could just reach them. He had drawn one when he heard a snuffling behind him, and a whispering. He stretched for the other. Refusing to glance behind, he stared out at freedom, and at the four men who were walking towards him.

A streetlamp created a brighter pool of light, illuminating the round wizened faces and the pointed teeth.

TOMB OF THE JANISSARIES

David Sutton

THE CAR SHUDDERED as it climbed the road, up the southern flank of Mount Ida. Old potholes and recent rock-falls were a constant hazard but not nearly as unnerving, Damon thought, as the thousand-foot drop that he could glimpse at every turn. Or, if he admitted it, Bill's driving was the more terrifying.

Damon had thought it a bloody miracle that they had reached the middle weekend of the holiday without writing off the hired car, and even more miraculous that there had been no arguments: until yesterday. He looked out of the side window dully, dust adhering to the glass as if it were sweating as much as he. In the distance, the green vista of the Messara Plain was hazed by the blinding sunlight.

With Zaros behind them, Damon thought he could relax and forget about the row. He hoped today's trip would herald a pleasant second week, with the argument forgotten; but now the details came flooding back.

Bill's driving was erratic, his swerving less to do with the omnipresent potholes than his speed. Damon reached across the rear seat and took Susan's hand in his, hoping it would help him relax. They exchanged a smile before Susan returned her attention to the view. His wife was still angry at the things that had been said yesterday, he could tell, but she was doing her best not to let them spoil her day.

The road curved, looping back on itself and back again, as it climbed higher. They'd had to keep the windows shut because of the dust, but now the air was clearer and Emily rolled down the front passenger seat window. Gusts of refreshing air blew in.

"Phew!" Emily removed her straw hat and held it out the window to dry off the sweat. Without turning, she shouted "What's this place?

Where we're going?"

Before Damon could reply, Bill interrupted. "Wherever it is, it'll suit you two I s'pose. I just hope there'll be somewhere to get a drink."

"At least we're starting to catch up with Dam's itinerary," Susan responded sharply. She may have had some sympathy for Emily and her condition, but when it came to Bill, she knew the philistine for what he was.

Nevertheless, Damon screwed up inside. The argument could flare up again, at any moment, if he didn't defuse the tension. As he wound down his window, the smell of wild thyme filled the car. Rocky outcrops blazed in sunlight. In the distant valley the green fields appeared to glow with artificial light, as if the whole landscape were sharing two realities, splitting the two couples up again.

If he admitted it, the row had been partly his fault. Long before the holiday, he'd worked out an elaborate itinerary. The fortnight had included days of sunbathing and shopping, interspersed with visits to archaeological and historical sites. Yet somehow the cultural part had been all but sidelined. Emily had complained at Gortys that the ground was too steep and it was too hot to wander around a 'load of old ruins'. She had invoked her MS as the excuse; yet there had been days in Agios Nikolaos when she and Susan had traipsed for hours around the shops, while he and Bill sat in a shady little bar. And at Iraklion's street market. Her multiple sclerosis had appeared to be still in remission then.

Damon had seethed as he'd watched the contents of his itinerary disappear with the days. Finally, he'd played his face. When an expected trip to Kato Zakros had evolved into a visit to a doomed banana plantation, he'd flared up, waving his neatly typed schedule at his friends as evidence of the exclusion of *his* bits.

The ensuing slanging match must have been heard halfway around Crete. With dying banana palms waving in the background, both couples had exclaimed the selfishness of the other, each screeching higher to drown out the other's expletives.

As the heat exhausted the quarrelling, Susan snatched the car keys from Damon – he'd been due to drive them back to town – and threw them at Bill. "Here, you take the fucking car, we'll find our own way back!"

That same evening at the apartment they'd patched things up. Damon had found it embarrassing; but bless her, Susan had taken the initiative. Afterwards the four of them had gone to the crappy taverna Emily liked and Susan had continued to act the diplomat over the grilled fish.

"I'm sure there'll be a bar somewhere up here," Damon said to the back of Bill's head. Actually, he wasn't so sure. The road was climbing steeper and rougher, glimpses of Mount Ida hazy in the heat and looking suspiciously uninhabited.

"You *still* haven't said where it is we're going!" Emily broke in petulantly.

"Vrontisi monastery." Saying that made Damon rack his brains about what it had said in the guidebook.

"At least it'll have a roof on. And four walls. And floors," Bill barked with laughter and Emily joined him. If this was a little joke at his expense, Damon felt he could rise to the bait quite easily. Susan squeezed his hand, sensing his thoughts.

"I suppose you have to use your imagination," she said unexpectedly, "when it comes to the palaces. Visualise how the buildings might have looked in their day." It didn't come out like a rebuke, but Damon felt secretly amused by her reply. What more *did* they expect to see of buildings three thousand years old?

"*Fuck!*"

The car swerved. The narrow road had swept up to an unbelievably steep incline, which then turned to the right at ninety degrees. Bill only just made it, and Damon had a few seconds of vertigo as he stared in horror at the vast open space below them.

"Fucking Greek fucking roads!" Bill was hunching himself in his seat, elbows sticking out like inflamed daggers, as his large hands spun the steering wheel and the car's momentum slowed. Gravel spurted from the wheels and a cloud of dust disappeared behind them over the abyss.

"I need a fucking beer."

Damon's whole body glistened with the sweat of fear and anger. The last thing he thought Bill should have was a beer.

"It's part of the charm of the place. It'd be pointless coming here if it looked like England." Susan's statement was delivered seemingly without malice, but her hand trembled in his. "We just have to drive more carefully."

"Bill couldn't be a more careful driver!" Emily scolded, flapping her straw hat. "He drives for the Social Services, remember."

All well and good, yet for the whole of the past week he'd tailgated other drivers and railed at their lack of courage. Damon willed Susan not to respond, but before she could the road wound past a roadside shrine and they were in the village of Voriza. Damon looked at the houses, their white-painted facades scummy with brown dirt. And sure enough, Bill found a bar: perched, it appeared, on the very edge of the Mountain. The four of them sat under a tattered sun umbrella in a walled-in garden, grateful to be in the shade. The garden's low wall gave a magnificent view south to the valley, and he wondered how he could do it justice with his camera while Bill ordered a round of drinks from an old Greek woman.

Shortly after ordering, a man arrived with the drinks and with dishes of cool tomatoes and cucumber, and a bowl of olives. Damon ploughed into the olives while the man unexpectedly drew up a chair, sat down, and produced a thick wad of dog-eared photographs.

Bill and Emily had snorted with derision as he began to pass them around. Susan, however, showed enough eagerness to encourage him. Not that he needed encouragement: the pictures had been touted to tourists many times and were obviously his pride and joy.

Although the sun had bleached many of the pictures, their constant theme was tediously obvious. All the photos were of couples or groups, sitting at this taverna.

"Dimitris." He pointed to himself posing in one of the photos. "You like to take picture?" he added.

"I'll do it," Damon said and swept his camera from the table. Dimitris dragged his chair next to Susan and ushered Bill and Emily closer together. After the film spooled a couple of frames, Damon wondered whether he would actually make the effort to post or take the photos back to the taverna. Many people obviously had done.

At the table, Dimitris' photos were becoming monotonous when Damon noticed a familiar face on one of them.

"That's, oh, whatsisname... from *The Holiday Programme*. Years ago." Damon stared at the creased, white-framed square, its colours faded out. "That's it. Frank – 'I love Winscale' – Bough. They must have done a programme here."

"Uh?" Bill mumbled through his beer glass.

"Winscale, Seascale, Sellafield. They change the name every few years, hoping people will forget 1957. I seem to remember Frank Bough being very pro-nuclear power in the seventies. So I always thought of him that way. He used to do *The Holiday Programme*."

"You said that," Emily piped up. Damon could tell she was struggling with the significance of the year, but didn't like to show her ignorance.

"Fuck him," Bill said.

It took Damon a second to realise Bill wasn't talking about him.

When Dimitris left, his snapshots exhausted, they sat in silence – and the quiet was, Damon thought, wonderful. No-one stirred in the village and the absence of traffic noise or radios was wonderfully calming.

"It's so peaceful here." Emily had noticed the atmosphere almost as soon as Damon. He saw that she was gazing at several clay planters perched on the wall, bright with blossoms. That could make the photo, he thought, standing to take a picture.

"How far now to Bronte monastery?" Bill asked.

The SLR's shutter clicked and the film wound on with a wheeze. "Vrontisi." Damon clenched his teeth as he returned to the shade. "Not far. A few miles."

"I think we'll stay here a bit and have a rest," Emily chirped in.

"It is a wonderful spot." Susan stretched back in her seat and drew in a lungful of the breezy Mountain air. Damon began to relax too. After a second beer he thought it safe to mention the monastery, just in case either Emily or Bill suggested they'd gone far enough up Mount Ida and they should call it a day.

"The monastery dates from the fifteenth century, so it should be interesting." Damon hoped rather than spoke from sure knowledge. He began to recall other facts in case he needed them.

"Didn't you say that some famous Greek painter had something to do with Vrontisi?" Susan asked, keeping the subject going.

35

"Yes, Mikhail Damaskinos painted six famous icons, but they were moved to Iraklion in the nineteenth century to escape the Turkish invasion. The Turks destroyed everything else, including the library that was once there."

"There won't be much left to see, then." Damon ignored Emily. These oft-repeated words were becoming her mantra.

"At least there'll be walls and a roof. And floors!"

Tired of their sniping, Damon chose to ignore both of them. Bees buzzed near the blossoms, and their drone merged with the drone of the muted conversation between Susan and the others. He began to feel utterly relaxed, for the first time that day.

As he snoozes, Damon observes Zeus in the Diktean cave. Minos, one of his three sons, carving the tablets of the law while Damon secretly watches. When Minos sleeps, Damon throws the tablets into an underground well and chisels them anew with his own version of the laws.

The scraping of his chisel becomes the drone of bees and light invades his darkness.

"The sleeper awakes." As he opens his eyes, Bill shoves another glass of beer towards him.

"Dreaming?" Susan asks.

"He always is," Emily countered, as if imagination were a crime.

"For a moment I was with Zeus and Minos."

"Fuck miners, let's drink up and get to old greasy monastery."

"Vrontisi."

THERE WERE NO other tourists at Vrontisi and for that, Damon was grateful. Bill had a habit of displaying his ignorance in a raucous, condescending voice, one that made Damon cringe with embarrassment.

Bill had parked the car right next to the entrance, blocking a good photograph of the Venetian fountain.

Once through a gateway guarded by two massive plane trees, Vrontisi's simple bell tower rose before them in a courtyard of plain grey concrete.

"Is this it?" The tone of Emily's voice was at once derogatory and exasperated. As if Vrontisi's unsophisticated architecture symbolised the whole holiday. The holiday that Damon had urged they take.

Bill was about to add his tuppence worth when the monk–Vrontisi only had the one, Damon recalled from the guidebook–emerged from a more modern building to the left.

"Deutsche? English, yes. I will tell you about Vrontisi. Then I will show you Vrontisi monastery." The monk ushered them to a long table with benches, shaded by palm trees. He was about their age, Damon guessed, heavy, with a thick, dark beard wreathing his chin. He was wearing a black cap and a black tunic that skirted dusty calf-length boots.

"First coffee." Damon was pleased that the monk had managed to silence Emily and Bill for once. They sat sipping Greek coffee as the monk raised an index finger to gain the visitors' undivided attention.

"Today is an anniversary. So I tell you a special story of Vrontisi. It is a story of *blood*."

Damon was intrigued. He could tell that Susan was, too. "In sisten sisty-nine to eighteen ninety-seven, Crete ruled by Turks. By, how to say, Turkish Cretans." The monk smoothed coffee out of his bristling moustache with a thumb and forefinger and he pondered. "Turks who were Cretans."

Bill started to look glazed, uninterested.

"In that time, these Janissaries did not recognise Ottoman rule and there were many massacres."

"What are –"

The monk held up his hand to silence Emily. "The Janissaries – soldiers of the Ottoman Empire – recruited from Christians. The *Ambadiot* Janissaries lived by blood and terror. This is a story of Vrontisi and the Ambadiots, who lived in the villages around Mount Psiloritis." Mount Ida, as it's now known, Damon reminded himself. "In those days there were many monks at Vrontisi and when the Janissaries came on their horses, we were forced to feed and shelter them. If it was after their raiding, they would bring Christian girls to the monastery and . . ."

A cloud slid across the sun and the whole courtyard was coated in shadow. The monk rose from the bench and began walking up and down, scowling and wringing his hands.

"I tell you, we monks took so much and no more!"

A breeze rustled the fronds of the palm trees, as if trying to shake off the shade into which they had been plunged. Damon watched the wind ever so gently swing the two bells in the open bell tower. They might want to ring out, it seemed, but the monk's growing agitation gave them pause.

"The next time they came, the Ambadiots were alone. We fed their horses. We said to them to join our festival and offered much food and wine. The Janissaries ate a rich meal and drank our wine."

Bill clattered his cup into its saucer to indicate his growing boredom. If he deliberately wanted to break the spell the monk was weaving, he would fail, Damon thought.

"They drank wine and fell into deep sleep. In this courtyard, they were." He spread his arms to indicate. "We waited. We rose up from hiding, with axes and daggers. We – men of God – *butchered* the Janissaries in their sleep. *Their blood ran in rivers*."

"God," Susan said. "I mean – how awful."

Damon glanced at her and smiled. He was enjoying the story, enjoying the way the monk spoke of the events as if he had been there to witness them.

Both Bill and Emily squirmed in their seats. The monk might have interpreted their discomfort as a sign that his story had affected them too. Damon knew otherwise.

"The horses? We set them free in the Mountains. The mutilated corpses? The corpses we took to a cave now called the Tomb of Chalepa. And we threw them into the cave. We left Vrontisi. We took the icons and left the monastery, because there would be, how to say . . . reprisals."

Bill feigned a yawn. "Yeah. I saw the film."

Bill's facetiousness would be lost on the monk, Damon hoped. "What a fascinating story," he said.

"And a terrible one," Susan added.

"Can we see this here tomb?" Emily was hoping to catch sight of a few dead bodies to make up for missing her Saturday night horror videos.

"Today is the anniversary." The monk sat beside them again and the intensity of his gaze unnerved Damon. "It was justified, what was done." Then: "Today you will see the monastery *and* the cave. Which first?"

"The cave!" Bill and Emily chorused.

No contest then, Damon thought dismally.

"And then the monastery," Susan sliced in. Good for her.

"One kilometre to walk," the monk said as he stood and began the journey. Damon looked at the landscape, the slopes and rocky outcrops. Easy for Emily, since she wants to do it, he told himself waspishly. In fact, even Damon found the walk strenuous.

The heat bore down relentlessly as they plodded in a single line following the monk. The landscape was of cracked and jagged rocks interspersed with withered olive trees. Damon imagined it was a landscape blighted by its history.

The ground began to dip into a small valley and unceremoniously, the cave was before them.

"The tomb of the Janissaries," announced the monk.

Twenty feet below where they stood, bare, jagged horizontal slabs of rock bordered a fissure in the ground. At one time olive trees and scrub had hidden the hole from view, but now desiccated branches clambered only thinly over the exposed rock. The cave was not how Damon had assumed it would be. This appeared more like a small cleft than a cave.

"Can't we get inside?" Bill's growl sounded disappointed. Damon felt the same. It might be no more than a hole in the ground, but it looked like it might need Mountaineering equipment to conquer.

"Is it deep?" Emily asked, no doubt thinking of her health and whether it was worth invoking it now they were here.

"I'm sure it'll be too difficult," Susan concurred. "There's still the monastery."

"No, no, no." The monk began to scramble down the slope, disturbing scree, which tumbled into the cave with a hollow rattle. "Here, you come, my friends? Yes." The monk was clearing away some pieces of twisted timber before Damon realised it was a makeshift ladder, which the monk began to slide into the cave. "We go inside!" From the knapsack he carried with him, he produced a handful of church candles and a disposable lighter. "Who first? I pass the candle."

Awkwardly, Bill was helping Emily down the rough ground, and Damon was amazed that she actually wanted to explore the cave. When Susan began her descent he raised his eyes heavenward and thought, go with the flow.

"Coming, are we?" Bill bawled up at him, and there was a faint echo as his words descended into the fissure.

Damon felt uneasy. There was no sight of the monastery from here. All he could see was the ravine through which they had passed, choked with gnarled trees and gorse. There was an emptiness and silence that in other circumstances Damon would have appreciated. Now the isolation, the distant Mountain peaks and the cloying air of the ravine sent a shiver up his neck.

If they had an accident up here, no-one would come looking for them.

"Maybe one of us should stay above ground." Damon's words sounded insipid.

Below, Bill had already disappeared into the cave and Damon thought he could see the glimmer of a candle flame. A hand reached up to help Emily, who had begun to negotiate the ladder, her weight making it creak alarmingly.

"Many tourists come. The cave is safe." Damon wanted to believe the monk, but somehow he did not think that there were that many visitors, not with the walk here and the lack of facilities.

When Susan began to climb the ladder, Damon quickly tried to forget his misgivings and scrambled down to the opening.

With candle in hand, Damon felt oddly like he was about to enter a hallowed place, the candle an offering to ancient gods. "You go. I follow." The monk's booming voice allowed for no dissent. "You wait at bottom. All wait," he shouted down.

When Damon reached the floor of the cave, wondering how Emily had managed the ladder, three disembodied heads greeted him. The flickering candles threw the background behind them into greater darkness. As the ladder rattled behind him, he suddenly feared that the monk was about to withdraw it and leave them stranded in the cave.

"Welcome to the cave of the Janissaries," the monk intoned. "You follow."

40

The monk's candle strode ahead, the skirt of his tunic flapping like a bat's wing in faint light.

The others trotted after him, their candles stumbling to keep up. Damon followed last, lighting up the floor, which was worn smooth as if by the march of many feet. As they descended, it grew wet with the constant drip of water from above. The vaulted ceiling was never far above, and did not widen. The slick rock was white or occasionally rusty orange, and was coated with stalactites imitating organ pipes. To either side, mounds of stalagmites stood like blighted grey fungi as Damon's candle flame threw them into relief.

The monk was silent as they made their way down the slippery incline. With every carefully placed step, Damon became uneasier. This tour was not turning out the way he had expected. Places of interest, even caves, felt safe. They had electric lighting. Handrails. Things like that.

Ahead of him, Susan had slowed her pace. She turned her head briefly, and Damon's candle revealed her creased brow and a nervous gleam in her eye. He put his hand on her shoulder as if to reassure her, but she jumped and nearly lost her footing, sliding three or four feet on the marble-smooth floor before regaining her balance.

"*Shit!*"

"Sorry..."

The sweat on Damon's face cooled as the temperature in the cave began to drop. They had religiously followed the monk, but for all he knew, there might be innumerable passages connected to this one. If the monk had a heart attack, would they be able to find their way out? None of the others was airing such questions and he contemplated doing so himself, even though Bill would undoubtedly find some wisecrack to flick back at him.

"I... I don't think... I can go..." Emily's voice faltered, coagulating in the slime from her lungs. She had turned around and was looking towards Bill, her round face mooned by the flame.

Damon had wondered when she would remember her illness. But now he didn't mind, because they could retreat without losing face.

"Oi! Mr. Monk. Wait a tick!" Bill's shout echoed around them.

The monk seemed oblivious and was a good way ahead of them,

his flame dimming. Then he stopped and turned.

"My friends." He whispered. At first, Damon thought he was speaking to them, until he saw what the monk's light was illuminating.

"Blimey!"

"Look, Dam!" Susan said.

The monk had arrived at a semi-circular chamber, its walls wreathed in folds of stone like curtains. On the floor were the scattered bones of many human skeletons.

"The Jansary's?" Emily asked, forgetting she was exhausted for a moment.

Without thinking, the four of them had slithered down to where the monk stood. Damon had no doubt that these bones were the remains of the murdered Janissaries. The monk had been as good as his word. He relaxed a little, expecting the cleric to add further detail to his gruesome story.

But the monk was busy fixing his candle onto a natural shelf, using melted wax to hold it in place. On the shelf were three *kataifi* cakes – what Bill had insisted (until it was no longer funny) on calling 'shredded wheaties'. They looked fresh, and oddly, each had a small candle on top, like little birthday cakes.

Damon was half expecting Bill to regurgitate his quip when he realised what the cakes reminded him of: an offering. It was as if, he thought, the monk were making an offering. And this was, indeed, a sacred place.

By now the monk was lighting the cake candles and whispering a prayer that echoed around them. Perhaps the monastery had the tradition, because Vrontisi's monks had committed murder, of praying for the dead Janissaries – and for the souls of the brethren. It made a kind of sense, though why hadn't the monk mentioned it?

The smell of burning wax began to fill the air, smoke wreathing about in streamers with nowhere to go. Skulls and limb bones surrounded them, bony fingers clawed against wet rock, as if struggling for purchase. Damon shrank from empty eye sockets, shadows shifting across racks of teeth. His gaze moved to where the bones lay in greatest abundance, piled up against the twisted hewn trunk of an olive tree.

"Dam?"

Damon was trying to figure what a piece of timber was doing down here, and moved forward to get a better view.

"Dam. I think we ought to be getting back." The nervousness was apparent in Susan's voice, but Damon was not listening. His flame had revealed elaborate carvings in the tree-trunk. Three female human faces, like masks, each pointing in a different direction. The style of the carvings was classical Cretan, far older than the Greek Orthodox, or for that matter the time of the Turkish occupation.

Damon felt a tug at the back of his tee-shirt. "Damon. *Let's get out.*" Susan pulled him farther away from the others, who had become mesmerised by the tableaux. At last, Damon was aware of Susan's terror, though it took him longer to realise his own. He was still wrestling with the meaning of the cakes and the carvings. What did they represent? Damon tried to remember his Greek myths.

Pulled again, he allowed Susan to steer him back up the cave. The monk was knelt in prayer before the little altar, the role of tour guide forgotten.

"What about Bill and Em?" he whispered in Susan's ear.

"I'm more worried about us," she replied. "Can't you feel it? This place?"

As one they turned and began to stumble as quietly as they could towards the cave's entrance. Damon's blood surged in his brain, adrenaline driving it now they were escaping, not merely returning. He turned once to look back, thinking that Bill and Emily deserved his help, even if he'd come to hate both of them. Then he saw what were escorting his former friends deeper into the cave.

"The little cakes are an offering, Damon." Susan's grasp of mythology was much stronger than his. "They are known as Hecate's Suppers. She is often represented as a statue with three faces, or *three wooden masks on a pole.*"

Behind them, Emily was screaming something unintelligible. Bill could be heard hooting, like a dog howling. Later Damon thought that it probably hadn't been either of them making those sounds.

"Hecate is associated with the underworld and with the ghosts of suicides and those who suffer untimely deaths." Susan hissed fiercely. "Let's not be included in her ritual."

Her words drifted across his mind as his gaze tried to penetrate the growing smoke haze below. Bill and Emily each had two escorts, grey and slender, strings of mummified muscle wrapped around bones. Bulbous heads nodded atop pipe-thin necks, nodding to the rhythm of the monk's chanted prayer. Damon would always remember with a shudder the featureless backs of those grey skulls. Better that, though, than to have seen to whom those Janissaries were taking Bill and Emily.

THE EMPTY ROOM
Tim Lebbon

I KNEW NATHAN would believe me when I told him that there were ghosts down there. What I didn't know was just how keen he'd be to meet them.

Max had told us about the place. He was a wheezing old git but sometimes he came up trumps. Between passing out from drinking cheap cider, smoking fags made from scavenged butts and scratching his crotch, Max spent his time telling us kids stories of the Old Town. He called it that because the whole place had now been built up, factories razed and new estates constructed to cover the bruises left on the land. This time, Max's story had contained a whiff of truth that we'd wanted to follow up.

An old manor house, he'd said, out in Tempton Woods. He reckoned its owners had once owned the woods as their private estate, but as the family died out and the manor fell to ruin the wilds grew in to possess it. Angry at their years of subservience, he said. Whatever that meant. He'd farted and closed his eyes, and the bottle he'd been drinking from tipped to mix cider with the puddle of piss around his legs. Disgusting old sod, but as I said he sometimes came up trumps.

"Old Max was right!" Nathan gushed. "But it isn't really haunted, is it?" His eyes held the excited glint of a scared kid who doesn't quite know how scared he should be.

I nodded. "Sure. Ghosts of the woods come here now that the place isn't lived in any more. They spend their nights here because it's so dark. Not touched by moonlight, or anything."

The manor was no longer there. Its roof and walls had long since fallen and been subsumed beneath trees and plants, leaving nothing but a rubble-strewn mound to indicate where grandness had once

45

stood. But there was a hole, like the open mouth of a sleeping giant, sheer sides leading down into what appeared to be a basement. Though this was one deep bugger. If I shone my torch down there I could not see a floor, only the jet black of a deeper hole. Deeper than my light could travel. *How far does light travel,* I thought, *before it stops? Why doesn't it go on forever? Maybe it just gets eaten.*

Nathan glanced over at me to make sure I wasn't kidding. I was, but he couldn't see that. "All down there?"

I nodded. "That's why it's so dark. The ghosts eat the light."

"I never heard that one."

"Well what the hell else do you think they'd eat, it'd just fall out of their stomachs!"

Nathan was quiet for a while as he mulled this over; I could see his jaw tensing and stretching as his brain worked. That's what I'd always loved about Nathan, he was so transparent. And dull. Susceptible. I liked to tell him stories.

What I didn't like was what he did next.

"Come on then!" he shouted, and fell to his knees. Before I could grab at him he'd shimmied backwards until his feet were hanging over the edge of the hole.

"The ghosts–" I shouted.

"I want to meet them! Maybe…" He didn't finish, but I knew what he was thinking. He'd always been intrigued by the unseen. *Maybe I'll be able to talk to them.*

He went over the edge. I heard him scampering down the walls of the hole, so confident because he expected to strike the floor within a few seconds. More shuffling, and a gasp. Then silence for a couple of seconds … a seemingly endless couple of seconds … before the dull thud of his body impacting far below.

I stepped back and held my breath. For a crazy minute none of this had happened, and I looked around to see where I was. The woods were watching. Roots hunched out of the ground like the ridged backs of petrified swine. Trees stood high and proud, older than me, my house, my parents, swaying contentedly in the breeze as time hurried by around them.

Then Nathan cried out, a faint plaintive plea for help.

My life would never be the same again.

"HELP ME!"

"Nathan?"

"Help me..."

"What? What can I do?" I giggled. The sound scared me but it also felt good, as being scared from a distance so often does. "Any ghosts, Nath?"

Silence, like a held breath. Perhaps he was looking around, trying to see into the dark in case there was anything darker.

"Nath? You all right?"

"Get me out of here!"

Even from the depths his scream made me tremble, a disembodied cocktail of terror and rage. I giggled again and this time it felt even better. My imagination leapt several hours into the future: questions; panic; concern; arms holding me; people crying because I was there, crying also because Nathan was not.

Attention.

"It's dark, I can't see, my leg hurts, I can't even see the sky, the hole bends, it's wet and there's something ... there's something moving." I heard a sob and a sniff. "You can have all my Willard Price books if you get me out. All of them!" The promise came from the dark like a whisper from a forgotten genie.

I pondered his offer. All his Willard Price books. I'd never read any of them – my parents thought reading was for pansies, and Nathan never lent his books out – but I knew how much he adored those volumes, how much he took care to keep them in the right order, spines facing out, never bending the covers back too far. He'd read them all at least three times.

I tried to imagine the books on a shelf in my empty room. I'd have to build the shelf myself, of course. I doubted my dad would do it for me. He did very little for me by then.

I also considered what else Nathan would offer if he were down there just a few hours more. His signed Han Solo baseball cap (signed by the actor who played him, of course, not Solo himself)? His pirated copy of *Resident Evil IV*? His ... surely not, but maybe his signed Oasis album? Maybe.

I turned and walked away through the woods. Nathan's cries were soon drowned by nature coming to life around me, as if it had held its breath pending my decision. I smiled as a rook took flight and cawed its way across the sky. For want of anything better to do I decided to follow it, and soon I was running along a faint path between the trees, straining my neck with the effort of trying to keep tabs on the bird.

I lost it almost straight away. But as I exited the woods and slumped down in a field, I pretended the bird was still watching me, awaiting my next decision.

I ONLY WENT home for a drink. I don't think Nathan even crossed my mind all the way there. It was a ten-minute walk buzzing with plans of where to put the Willard Price books, how to build the shelf, whether to bother asking Dad if he'd help me. There was also a niggling doubt, too, a fear that once the books were in my possession they would be taken away again just as quickly. Taken by my parents and given to poor dead Danny.

Mum and Dad were out when I arrived home, so I went straight up to my bedroom and slumped on the unmade bed. There was nothing there for me. The wallpaper was a ghastly splash of motorbikes on one wall, steam trains on another, the remaining two woodchipped and painted a bright yellow. I'd wanted blue, but Dad had yellow paint left over from doing Danny's room. What was good enough for Danny, he said, was good enough for me. He didn't mean it. He had no intention of hurting me, making me feel inadequate, unloved, transparent. He just said what came naturally, because he was too wrapped up in the past to let the present concern him too much.

My ceiling was a cracked maze of crumbling Artex, years old now and providing home to creepies and crawlies in its myriad splits. The carpet was threadbare, the bed functional... and that was all. Nothing else. No furnishings; no cupboards or shelves; no Airfix models hanging from the ceiling with bubbled glue congealed around the cockpits; no comics splayed across the floor, open at a dozen different worlds.

Nothing. Zilch. Squat.

It was all in Danny's room.

It was an act of worship more than anything else. I see that now, but when I was a kid all I could understand was that my parents stripped my room to furnish my dead brother's. I'd loved Danny, yeah, and I mourned him, but I grew to hate him in a short space of time. Or rather, I grew to hate his memory. Because it was his memory that was stealing my parents away from me.

I lay on the bed for ten minutes that day, considering where the books would look best. Then I thought I got up to go and help Nathan from his hole.

Waking two hours later still on the bed, I realised that I'd only dreamed of doing it.

I ran through Tempton Woods. For a horrible few minutes I could not find the ruined manor, but then it loomed out of the shadows like a hibernating beast smothered with rampant shrubs.

I stood at the edge of the hole. And I heard nothing.

"NATHAN!" THERE WAS no echo. The hole was a deep wound in the woodland floor, fringed by inquisitive shrubs. The sun found its way into the first few feet and lit up the sides, old brickwork pocked by frost and time, mortar powdered and bleeding down the walls like black tears. Further in the darkness was impenetrable. No light from above, and certainly none from below. No sound either, no hint that down there, somewhere, my friend may be injured or…

"Nathan! Nath! You there?"

It was as if the hole spoke to me. Nathan's voice was lower, grittier, maybe because he was thirsty. That's what I thought at the time.

"There's something down here with me," he said. He was trying to whisper, but the old brick basement was an echo chamber. "Something alive, but… It touches me. It reaches out of the dark and touches me."

"Nath, it may be one of the ghosts." At the time I wasn't quite sure why I said it. It was cruel and unkind and Nathan was a friend of mine, but perhaps those Price books just didn't hold the allure any more. Perhaps the Han Solo cap was calling to me, causing vibrations in the Force: *Own me, own me.*

"It's not," he said, whimpering. "You have to get me out. It says it's the king of the dark. It says it'll stud its crown with my eyeballs and make a ladder from my bones and escape." His voice hitched, a fog-horn gasp in the basement's throat. "It says it only likes dead flesh. It'll wait until ... until..."

"Nath, ghosts don't eat people," I said. "I told you, they only eat light." I sat down and looked around at the trees: those close in young and still shimmering with their ground-taking victory, those further away older, probably already here when the manor was in its prime. I tried to recall the late-night horror films I'd watched with Danny when he was still alive, the ones Mum and Dad thought weren't too bad for us because they were so old. How do you tell your parents that blood in black and white is somehow more frightening?

"No, not ghosts," I said. "What you've got there is a zombie."

"I can hear it, it's coming, it's–"

"Well, maybe a ghostly zombie. If there is such a thing." I twirled some grass stalks around my fingers and wondered just what was down there with Nathan. A cat or a fox or a rabbit, I guessed. Not a zombie. Surely not a ghost. Surely not.

"It's coming, get me out, you can have all my comic books, all of them, just get me out!"

"And the Willard Price books?"

"Yes!"

"And the–"

He screamed. It was as if the ground itself were crying out in fear. Birds took flight in agitated abundance, other things scurried around the trees. I stood quickly and backed away from the hole, expecting Nathan's bloodied hands to appear at any minute, his eyes wide and full of rage. Or maybe there would be something else there ... something with Nathan's blood running down its chin ... something using splintered bones to haul itself up out of the earth...

The screaming ceased. Then his voice again, throatier than before, clotted with fear. "Get me out. Get me out. Get me out."

Nathan had a full set of *2000 AD*s, from Issue One onwards. His father had given him the early few hundred and Nathan had collected the rest, going to comic conventions and fairs, spending hard-saved pocket money. I'd never been too keen … but I thought how cool they'd look scattered on my floor and arranged across my unmade bed. It would bring my empty room to life.

Nathan had everything. I'd once had something until Danny had died.

How much more would Nathan give me to save him?

I turned and walked away. He must have screamed for hours, because I was sure I still heard him when I arrived home.

"HAVE YOU SEEN Nathan?"

I shook my head.

"His mother was asking after him. You went out with him this morning, didn't you?"

I nodded. "He went off this afternoon. Said he was going home."

My Mum glanced at me, then back at the ceiling. "You sure?"

I nodded. "Course."

She glanced down again and smiled a paltry smile. She could never look me in the eye for more than a few seconds at a time. When I was younger and Danny was still alive, she'd always said we had the same striking eyes.

I went upstairs and found that Mum had made my bed. The room looked even emptier now, maybe because I'd been imagining it scattered with comics, the walls lined with books. I sat on my bed for a few seconds, looking around, wondering just what I was going to do. Darkness nudged at the window. I thought of the king of the dark down there with Nathan, sitting patiently, waiting for him to die so he could eat his dead flesh and use his bones for a ladder. I tried to clothe the idea of the king with flesh and bones himself, but I could conjure nothing in my mind's eye. I decided Nathan read too much.

Closing my eyes brought Danny. I remembered all the good times but they were soured, not by his death so much as what had occurred since then. If he were still alive I'd have games to play, models to make, things to do. As it was I had my bed and the darkness behind my eyelids.

I started to hum a song. Whatever I was going to do about Nathan, it would have to wait until tomorrow.

LATER I TURNED out the light and sat staring out towards Tempton Woods. I concentrated on the shadows spilling from between the trees, trying to see Nathan's screams and taste his fear. Musing upon what such a recipe would drive him to offer me in the morning.

I heard my mother and father go to bed. They followed their nightly ritual of opening Danny's door and going into his room, breathing in deeply as if memories could invoke lost aromas, whispering to each other but, in reality, talking to Danny. They must have run their hands over Danny's old toys, and my new ones turned old by their removal and placing in a dead brother's room.

At the time it all seemed natural to me. I felt something I could not understand – now I realise it was a youthful form of distaste – but their ritual was also my own. I would gaze at the empty walls of my room as my parents creaked floorboards next door, whispered goodnight to Danny and then went to bed. I used to hear them moving in the night, but that had not happened since Danny had died.

I did not go to sleep for a long time. There was a three-quarter moon, by which I tried to make out where I could put the Price books and the comics Nathan had promised me. I realised quite quickly that they would do little to fill my empty room. Rather, their presence would do more to draw attention to the vacuum my life had become.

Perhaps Nathan would need another day or two to decide.

THE NEXT MORNING was a Sunday. The day of rest. My mum and dad had been sitting up all night with Nathan's parents, trying to soothe them, trying to reassure them, but only making matters worse. The police had spread out through the town to look for him. I said I was going to help them search, and nobody tried to stop me.

Walking into the woods I thought something had changed. It was as if someone had taken something away, but I could not work out what; I only knew that it had gone. If Nathan was out of the hole I'd have known by now, but as I neared I knew he was still there. He was screaming. And the woods were silent – that's what was missing. The woods were totally silent. No birds calling, no bushes rustling…

The police had obviously not yet come this far.

"He – elp me. He – elp me." They were gasps more than screams, exhortations pushed past a throat swollen by crying or dried out from thirst. They drifted from the open mouth of the hole like puffs of darkness seeking impossible escape. He screamed between his cries for help, a high, ululating call invoking memories of old Hammer films, virgins fleeing black-clad monsters, camp mummies stumbling blindly at their prey.

I sat at the edge of the hole and listened. His voice was quieter than it had been the day before, as if he were moving away down some subterranean tunnel. Or being moved.

The surrounding trees swung to their own rhythm, undergrowth hiding all manner of unknowns on the forest floor. If I stared up through the canopy at the blue sky I could have been anywhere, not just here in the woods, listening to my friend screaming for help that might never come.

"Nathan," I said.

The screaming stopped. He must have heard me, must have sensed my presence from down in the pit. "Get me out!" he hissed.

"Well –"

"There's something here. It touched me. It … touched me, you know? I can see it even though it's dark. It wants out. It touched me, and it wants out. It's the king. It'll use my eyes to stud its crown, my fingers to pick its teeth. It'll use me, climb my bones, build a ladder from my bones."

"Nath, don't be so dramatic," I said, honestly believing he was going way over the top. Sure, I'd left him for a day, but it wasn't as if he was out in the open where he could get wet, where things could find him. And really, I never believed there was anything down there with him. "Don't believe everything I tell you about ghosts and zombies. It's probably a vampire!"

I giggled and frowned at the same time. Perhaps even then I wondered just what the hell I was doing.

"My leg's broken. I can't move. I'm thirsty. I want my … I want my mum." He began to cry then, useless tears shed in the dark where no-one could see them. "And it *is* a zombie."

He cried for a long while, sobs and sighs rising out of the ground and taking flight into the trees. Perhaps, I thought, they sat there watching me, the products of his anger and fear marking and remembering me. I whistled softly. Dampness from the ground soaked through the butt of my jeans. I wondered how wet Nathan was.

"It wet down there?"

Nathan did not answer. The tears continued, but his voice had been stolen by the dark.

I stood and edged closer to the hole, and for a few minutes I was going to rescue him. I tried to spot protruding bricks and other handholds to see if I could make it down into the basement myself, or whether I could guide Nathan up. But then I remembered he'd broken his leg. I remembered my empty room, his books, his comics, mine, and I wondered once again what more he could possibly offer me.

"Nathan, you know your Han Solo cap? And your Playstation?"

"What are you on about? Why's it so dark? It's sitting beside me, it's breathing on me, I can smell its breath. It's waiting… it's waiting for me to die."

"Your stuff, Nath? You'll give it to me? You'll give it all to me?"

"Just help me! I don't want to stay down– No! Don't touch me! Don't, no, no…"

There was no more.

I left Tempton Woods again, strolling through the pine-scented shadows, listening to the sounds of the forest increasing around me as I moved further away from the hole in the ground. I thought at the time it was because Nathan could no longer be heard screaming.

Now, I think maybe it was something different. Maybe there was something down there with him, and the woods could sense it, and around the hole they were silent. They did not want to attract attention to themselves.

WHEN I ARRIVED home my parents were waiting on the doorstep.

The most complicated part was explaining what I'd been doing that morning. I kept it simple. I said I'd gone to look for Nathan in the park, but when I couldn't find him I went for a walk on my own. Along the canal, I said. That lie became my unintentional saviour because I was not allowed by the canal, and my parents' anger changed tack slightly until they were berating me for wandering off on my own. *There might be someone out there,* they said. *Someone nasty.*

I was quizzed by other people, of course, when Nathan didn't show. The police (they went gentle – I was a traumatised friend and they had no reason to ride slipshod all over me); his mum and dad (who reminded me so much of my own parents when Danny had died that for a time, I felt like a child shared between four); friends at school. My reactions were always as expected and no suspicion was aroused.

I never went back to Tempton Woods. I was afraid I'd lead them to him, and consequently to the truth of my crime. Nathan faded in my memory probably at the same time his life was fading from him, down there in the dark.

Nathan's parents did not handle their bereavement like Mum and Dad. His room was stripped and decorated within months, and they handed me many of his things: his collection of books; his comics; his Han Solo cap. They also gave me his signed Oasis album. They said he'd have wanted it that way.

After searching the countryside and the town, the police went into Tempton Woods, scoured the old manor estate, sent their dogs in to sniff out what they were now expecting to be a corpse.

They never found Nathan.

I WENT BACK to the town quite recently on a business trip, but I only stayed for a couple of hours. Max, the filthy old tramp, was still alive, still there, still swimming in piss. I don't think he recognised me, but when I posed a tentative question about Tempton Woods he told me of the haunted manor that lay ruined there.

"Haunted by what?" I asked.

"Take your pick," he said. "Ghosts, memories, guilt. Whatever takes your fancy."

I live in a small flat on my own in London. One room is jam-packed full of belongings, from books to toys to clothes, packed floor to ceiling so that there is barely space for me to crawl in and sit in the armchair squeezed into the centre. The other room – my bedroom – is minimalist to the extreme. All except for a row of books on the wall, a hat on my bed and a splash of comics across the floor. I still have nothing.

I think about the woods. I remember Nathan's screams. I wonder if a thing ever did come out of that hole, hauling itself up on a ladder made of bones, its ambiguous shape impossible in the sunlight.

And I wonder where that thing is now.

'WHERE ONCE I DID MY LOVE BEGUILE'

John Howard

WITHOUT KNOWING IT, Stephen Langley was about to undergo an experience that would change his life forever.

He was five years old. Stephen was at school, walking around the playing field on a warm spring day. He ambled along, next to the wire fence that separated the field from the back gardens of the houses of Chapel Street. He was running his hand along the rusting diamond-shaped links, looking every now and then at the brown stains growing on his small fingers.

Suddenly he stopped, his self-absorption ended by seeing something glinting in the corner of an eye. He looked through the fence, gripping it now with both hands. Flakes of rust fell away, through his fingers into the grass.

On the other side of the fence, sitting on a battered chair in his garden, was an old man. He took his cap off and wiped his forehead. He had been weeding, and was hot. He unfastened another button on his collarless shirt and fanned his leathery face with his other hand. And in his waistcoat there hung a bright watch-chain that caught the sun and glittered into the eye of the small boy now gazing through the fence.

Stephen was still gripping the fence with both hands. It rattled slightly. The man in his garden looked up and saw him. "Hello," he said, smiling.

"Hello," said Stephen. Then he released the fence and pointed at the man's waistcoat. "What's that?" he asked.

"This? It's my watch-chain. Now look."

He took the watch itself out, slowly, and popped it open. He got up and walked over to the fence, showing the boy the watch.

Stephen looked at it intently. His eyes narrowed into slits as he gazed at it. "That's not the time," he said after a while, as if the man was trying to trick him.

The man laughed. "No, you're right there, boy," he said. "Watch's busted. Too old. A bit like me. You like it?"

The gold caught the sun again, glinting in the boy's face. Stephen's eyes lit up with more than the yellow light, and he tried to put his hand through the links of the fence. Perhaps he thought that the old man would give him the shining watch, with its pent-up time.

The boy still looked happy, even though he must have realised that he wasn't going to get the watch. He looked at the man. "*You're not busted,*" he said. "You do all that in your garden. Can I hold it?"

"It won't fit through the fence," the man replied. For a moment he thought the boy was going to cry. "Tell you what, boy," he said. "If your Mum doesn't mind, you can come round here after school tomorrow and see it. You can hold it if you like. How's that?"

Just then a teacher started ringing the hand bell to indicate that the lunchtime break was over. Stephen turned and began to run back to school. But he was grinning, and shouted "Thank you! Thank you!" as he ran away.

THE NEXT AFTERNOON, Stan was working in his front garden. It was tiny, almost too small to turn round in, but it faced Chapel Street, and the children had to pass it on their way home after school.

Stan was often lonely these days. His wife Edith had died two years before. He'd retired from his job at Collier's, the furniture factory at the top of the street, and spent most of his time gardening or sitting in his front room drinking tea and looking at the photos on his mantelpiece. Now seventy, he looked forward to the change of a visit, though the thought of closeness to a child awoke in him an expectant uncertainty. He and his wife had had no children of their own.

Stan took a rest, and sat on the low front wall of his garden. Now children walked and ran past, shouting and screaming. Mothers pushed prams and walked in small groups down the street.

"Hello!"

Stan turned round as he heard the small voice and felt a tapping low down on his back. The boy was standing there in the street, a shy grin on his face as before.

"Hello, boy," Stan said.

"Can I see it? Can I?" Stephen held out his hand.

"Hold on, hold on!" Stan said, laughing. After a hesitation, he put his hand on the wall next to him. "Sit up here."

Stephen scrambled up. "Please?" he said.

"Does your mother know you're here? Where do you live?"

Stephen looked serious for a moment. He nodded. "I live at 95 Willoughby Way," he recited.

"That's one of the new houses," Stan said. "Well, and what's your name, boy?"

"Stephen Langley."

"That's a good Littleworth Green name," Stan said.

He found out later that Stephen was related to the Langleys who ran the hardware shop in the High Street, and that he had moved to Littleworth Green after his father had died in an accident.

Stephen said, "You're Mr Lacey." As if he was daring Stan to deny it. "Miss Stretton said."

"Did she say what my first name is?"

He thought for a moment. "No."

"Shall I tell you?"

"Yes please!"

"Well, it begins with S, then a T..."

"Stephen!"

"No, it's Stanley. You can call me Stan. Everyone does."

"Can I see that watch now?" Stephen said.

Stan laughed. His face creased up. "That's what you're here for, isn't it, boy?"

He took the watch out of his waistcoat pocket and dangled it in front of Stephen's eyes. Then he opened it.

Stephen reached out and touched the glass gently. "It's still all wrong," he said.

"It's busted," Stan said. "Look how old it is." He showed the boy the engraving on the inside of the lid. *Reginald Lacey from His Father 26 February 1887.* "Nearly eighty years ago," Stan said. "That was *my* dad. Given to him by his father. That watch was old then, as well. I got it from my father when I joined Kitchener's lot.

Surprised it lasted as long as it did. Hasn't told the time since the Silver Jubilee. But I like to wear it."

Stephen touched the watch again as Stan held it in front of him. It turned slowly on its chain. It appeared to be hypnotising the boy. Then he gazed at Stan, who knew what Stephen wanted. He lowered the watch into Stephen's outstretched hands. The boy cupped them around the watch, as if it was going to escape him.

"Wow," Stephen said under his breath. Then he looked up at Stan again. "Maybe if I hold it long enough tomorrow won't come and school won't come and I can stay home and play or come and help you." His words tumbled out in a rush.

Stan laughed. "But then it'll never be Christmas or holidays or your birthday!"

Stephen's forehead screwed up. "Oh. Yeah. Don't like birthdays much, anyway."

He held the watch out to Stan, who snapped it shut and slipped it away, back in his waistcoat pocket. "Gone," he said. "But you can see it again, if you like."

"Stan, if the watch went backwards I could get to before when things went bad until it stopped again."

"You're a deep one," Stan said. For a moment he wondered if he might be getting into something. "You'll have to ask your mother or teacher about that. Anyway, you'd better get on home, boy. Look at the clock when you get in. See what time it is."

"I can tell the time," Stephen said proudly.

"I know you can!"

"Thank you for letting me see the watch. See you tomorrow!" He jumped off the wall and ran on down Chapel Street, and round the corner past the pub.

Stan shook his head to himself, and went indoors. He fingered the watch in its pocket.

The next afternoon he was sitting in his front room, reading the paper. He heard the children coming out of school, running and shouting. Then there was a knock on the front door.

Answering it, Stan saw Stephen standing there, together with a woman he assumed to be his mother. "Afternoon," he said. He looked down at Stephen. "Hello, young man."

Mrs Langley smiled back, looking a bit harrassed. "I hope you don't mind me coming round with Stephen," she said. "He told me he'd seen you yesterday, and I just wanted to make sure that he wasn't being a nuisance."

Stan rubbed his jaw. He hadn't bothered to shave that morning. Since his wife had died he didn't always bother.

"He wasn't a nuisance. He just wanted to look at my old watch. He's a fine lad, I reckon."

She smiled awkwardly. "Yes, last night I couldn't stop him going on about it. I think he wants to be a time traveller when he grows up!" She laughed. "But as long as you don't mind..."

Stephen started to pull on his mother's hand. "Ask him, ask him," he said.

"Mr Lacey," she said, "would you mind if he came to see you some more, sometimes? His father died last year, and I have my hands so full sometimes. He'd really like to help your garden. I don't have the time at home... And he really liked looking at your watch. It fascinated him."

Stephen looked up at Stan while he held onto his mother's hand. "Just after school, sometimes Stan," he said.

"Stephen!"

"He said I could call him that. It's his name."

Stan nodded. "It's all right."

"Can I come? Can I? You said I could!"

Stan thought for a moment. Years of habit and emptiness churned in his mind. "Of course you can, boy. You can help me in the garden, and I might have a few other things you'd be interested in."

"Thank you, Mr Lacey," Mrs Langley said. "I'm really grateful. He won't be any problem. He's a good boy. He should have an older man to look up to."

Stephen pointed at Stan's waistcoat, where the watch-chain hung. He smiled up at his mother, pulling her hand. Stan took the watch out and opened it, lowering it to the level of Stephen's eyes. Stephen touched the glass reverently, and gazed at the frozen hands for a long and inscrutable moment.

OVER THE NEXT two or three years Stephen visited Stan at least once a week, usually after school. He helped out in the garden, and nearly always asked to look at the watch.

Once Stephen's class did a project on the forthcoming centenary of the school, and Stephen asked Stan if he could see any old photos. Stan showed him his photographs, papers and medals from the First World War. Stephen gazed at them intently, shuffling them and holding them gently. As if they were his vital windows into another time.

One warm afternoon, Stephen knocked on Stan's front door after school. "Stan, Stan," he said. "On Sunday we went to West Wycombe and we went up the Golden Ball and had some ice cream, and then we went into some caves. It was great!"

"You went to the Hellfire Caves? Let's see, I haven't been there since they were opened up again, oh, ten years ago, maybe a bit more..."

Stan had always known about the Caves. As a child, he and other Littleworth Green boys had walked over to West Wycombe for church outings and fights with the West Wycombe boys.

The ruined and boarded-up entrance had always fascinated Stan as a lad. Once he had talked about getting into the Caves, and even made friends with some West Wycombe boys who were going to break in and explore. But the lads changed their minds, and Lord Desborough had the boards strengthened and padlocked.

Stan had first met his wife at a social in West Wycombe, when she was in service at the House. Edith had never talked about the Caves. Apart from a few of the local boys, no-one in the village ever mentioned them, and certainly not to outsiders. The villagers didn't hate the Caves. They just ignored them, and preferred it that way. As if West Wycombe Hill's interior darkness was boarded up and kept at bay by a wall of silence and forgetfulness. Over the years, Stan had all but forgotten about the Caves as well.

In the early 1950s, the new Lord Desborough had woken up to the commercial potential of the Hellfire Caves. He had a proper door fitted to the entrance, and parties of visitors went down with candles and miners' helmets.

Stan had never thought about his one secret trip down the Caves until now. He remembered the Caves as being chilly and damp, with nothing to see except for the flickering of candles on the rough chalk walls.

"It was really brilliant Stan," Stephen was saying. "It was like a place where there are ghosts and things. I got chalk all over my arm. It was all wet and cold. I ran away from Mum but I didn't get lost!"

"It was just dark and dirty when I went there. Did you have proper lamps?"

"There's 'lectric lights. And they've got talking statues all lit up and dressed like in the olden days. And Lord Desborough–"

"Hmmm. Sounds like you had an interesting time. Maybe I'll get back down there one day."

Stephen said, still excited, "I'm going back there lots!"

They went into the back garden and began work.

WHEN HE WAS eleven, Stephen went to Faulkner Road Secondary School. He was no longer able to walk past Stan's house on his way to and from school, or to talk to him through the fence. But he still visited Stan and helped him, talked and listened.

One afternoon Stephen came round after school and showed Stan a pamphlet about the Hellfire Caves. He said he'd been there with some friends from school. His mother had given him ten new pence to spend, and he'd bought the booklet.

Stephen talked on about the Caves, like he was a little boy again. He was enthralled by the map of the Caves in the back of the booklet. It was as if he'd been given a secret plan, a map to a genuine treasure trove, an exclusive document, in order to discover great secrets that no-one else had ever been able to. He traced the passages with his finger. "We walked all the way down there – to the River Styx and back," he said. "We ran around the Catacombs. I got out first. I remembered it all."

Stan looked at the map. It was one long black line with several curves and corners, dead-end passages and returns, thick pillars and circular rooms carved out of the solid chalk. The cover of the pamphlet showed one of the model groups in the Caves – the first Lord Desborough showing his old crony Benjamin Franklin around.

Stan was a bit bewildered by Stephen's sudden interest in what he remembered as a long dark filthy hole in the ground. But he saw

Stephen as the excited little boy after his first visit to an unusual place, and he shook his head and smiled.

"They're great," Stephen said. "I really like going down the Caves. I can't wait to go again. I can go there every Sunday if I use my pocket money."

OVER THE NEXT Couple of years, Stan's arthritis slowly got worse. Stephen did more and more of the actual work in the garden, while Stan sat down and told him what to do, or listened to Stephen talking about school, his friends, life at home.

When he was fourteen, and now taller than Stan, Stephen announced that he wanted to be known as Steve. Stan told him that he only became known as Stan when he began work at Collier's, and that his parents had always called him Stanley.

ONE DAY THE following year, Steve was sitting in Stan's front room drinking tea when he got out his Hellfire Caves booklet. By then it was getting well worn, tattered and taped on the edges. He had read it over and over again.

He held the booklet out to Stan. "I've been looking at this," he said. "Have you ever heard of it? Do you remember it?" Steve pointed at the open page. "The rhyme, there."

> Take twenty steps and rest awhile;
> Then take a pick and find the stile
> Where once I did my love beguile.
>
> 'Twas twenty-two in Desboro's time,
> Perhaps to hide this cell divine
> Where lay my love in peace sublime.

Stan read the rhyme through. He couldn't make anything of it. "Never heard of it, boy," he said. "I don't understand it."

Steve looked disappointed. "I thought you might know about it," he said. "What with you knowing about lots of old local things, and your wife coming from West Wycombe."

Stan thought. Edith had never mentioned or repeated the rhyme to him, any more than anyone else from West Wycombe ever had, even though the booklet said it was an ancient village rhyme.

Steve pointed at the open page again. "There," he said. "How can you have a stile in a cave, anyway?"

"I don't know. I told you I couldn't make it out."

"It must be the key to a secret passage or something. Look at this bit, on the next page. It's another poem. About a secret room in the Caves. It says 'Under the Temple', so that must be the church, I suppose. There must be a secret room down there. It'd be brilliant to find it!"

He showed Stan the other poem. "I don't know," he said. "It still doesn't make much sense to me."

Steve closed the booklet. For a moment he looked like the little boy that Stan had first showed his watch to. Like he had a bright future, something to fill his life, give it purpose.

"Stan, I'm going to find that secret room."

Perhaps Stan didn't seem to take Steve seriously enough. "The best of luck to you, boy," he said.

Steve spoke fiercely. "I *will* find it. I'm going to learn all I can about the Caves. Start again now, get interested again, like when I was a kid. Except better!"

The next afternoon Steve and Stan were sitting in the cool front room, resting after working at laying turf.

Steve said, "I asked my English teacher about the rhyme. I showed it to him. He said that a stile can also mean part of a door. So it's not like a stile you have to get over on a path. There *must* be a secret door down there. In the booklet it mentioned workmen feeling breezes when they were restoring the Caves. I'm going down there on Saturday. And Sunday."

Stan nodded. By now he wasn't sure that he understood Steve at all, if he ever really had. He remembered that when he'd been Steve's age he'd already started work. He poured more tea and changed the subject. "What are you going to do when you leave school, then?" he asked.

Steve shrugged his shoulders. "You have to be sixteen now. I've got all my exams yet. I don't know. Anything, I suppose... There's Mum as well."

Stan recalled that he hadn't seen Mrs Langley around the High Street recently. "How is she?" he asked.

Steve shrugged again. "I don't know. Oh, she's fine. Really great. There's this new bloke around. It's serious this time. He's called Brian. She goes out with him most evenings. Last night she was talking about moving away from Littleworth Green. I don't want to move away. I like it here."

"Maybe she won't want to move far," Stan said. "Just to somewhere else round Wycombe."

"Stan, I don't know at all," Steve said. "Brian's OK, and I'm pleased Mum's got someone, but I don't want it to change things. I can hardly remember my Dad, now. And I want to stay around here."

Stan was at a loss for words. He didn't want to sound insincere. "Things will turn out all right," he said eventually. "They have a way of doing that."

Stan decided to change the subject yet again. "So, boy," he said. "When are you going to get yourself a young lady? When I was your age–"

Steve blushed. Then he looked rather pleased, as if he'd been affirmed or been asked to join a special club. Stan realised that Steve had been looking smarter recently. And today he was wearing new trousers.

"Don't know," he replied.

"Got your eye on anyone then?"

"Not sure. Maybe." Then he got up. "Better be going now, Stan," he said. "I'll help you finish on Monday. I'm going down the Caves Saturday and Sunday."

Steve came round after school on Monday as he'd promised. As they drank their tea, Steve produced a book from his jacket pocket. "Look what I got on Saturday," he said.

He handed Stan the book. He looked at the cover. It was bright, like a horror poster, and showed a large skull with some ruins.

"It's all about the history of the Hellfire Club," Steve said. "It's superb. I've been up late reading it. It's got all about the Caves and what went on. It's got the rhymes as well. Look."

He showed Stan the pages. Stan didn't think there was much

more explanation than in the booklet. But Steve was as taken with it all as ever.

"It'll keep you busy," Stan said as he gave the book back. "It looks odd to me. I bet most of it's made up."

"The secret passage stuff can't be," Steve said earnestly. "I'm sure I felt a breeze down there yesterday. Near the carving, the XXII the rhyme says about. You can't miss that. There must be a secret room or something, where the Club members did all their really special, you know, things. And I'm going to find it!"

"Hmm. You sure you're not courting?" Stan said.

Suddenly Steve grinned. "Well, OK, there's this girl in my class..."

"What's her name?"

"Karen."

"Is she fair or dark?"

"She's got dark hair."

Stan smiled. "Well, just you watch it, boy. And all this Caves lark."

He didn't want to get Steve worked up too much. But it made Stan realise how quickly time was going. It seemed to him only yesterday that a little boy had stood at the school fence, looking at his old watch as if all his world depended on it. Now he was growing up fast.

OVER THE NEXT few weeks, Steve visited Stan once a week. But instead of working he just sat drinking tea, talking. He sat in his usual armchair opposite Stan and talked, sometimes in such an intense monotone that Stan thought he was in a trance. Or he got excited and began to talk fast, as if he had the need to convince Stan that his experiences and impressions of the Caves were wholly true, but yet open to doubt or needing confirmation by a certain time.

"I go down there as often as I can," he would say. "I take the map and check it all out. I pace the distances and stand still so I can feel any air-currents from secret openings. I have to make sure no-one can see me.

"It's like being inside something alive. The passages are all cool and glistening, and the rooms are like stomachs and things. Spending lots of time down there makes me think of being inside a sort of living body, like in blood vessels or intestines or something. I have to make sure I don't slip over on the slopes or trip over if I'm looking at something.

"I wish they'd get rid of the models and Lord Desborough's commentary. I'd really like to see the Caves all dark and silent, like you used to be able to. Maybe I could ask Lord Desborough, show him all my work. Maybe Mr Lloyd from school would help... Or I could hide down there at closing time...

"Right at the bottom of the Caves I can almost feel the weight of the Hill, as if it could all crash in at any minute. But I know it won't. Not on me. The Caves are like sort of holding their breath when I'm there. Like they know me, like I know every bit of them they've shown me so far."

Stan sometimes felt worried about Steve's obsession with the Caves, especially now. But Steve also said that things were going well with Karen as well, so Stan thought she must be keeping Steve in balance.

One afternoon, Stan and Steve were raking up grass in the back garden. Steve said, "Stan, when did you first, well, you know, do..."

Stan was shocked. This was a different Steve. "Mind your own business," he snapped. He muttered under his breath as he watched Steve raking up the cut grass.

"I can't wait," Steve said as he continued working. It didn't seem to matter to him whether or not Stan was listening. "All my mates reckon they're up to it," he carried on. "But I know it's what the Caves are all *really* about. It's all in the map. I never took any notice until I started going out with Karen. It says in the Hellfire Club book. The Caves are shaped like a woman, you know, like a woman's—"

"Why are you going on like this?" Stan said. "You lads should watch it."

"The map showed me. How to make everything good again and OK in the future. Like having it off with a girl."

Stan thought he shouldn't really be shocked at Steve. Stan had never been a prude. He hadn't only gone out to work when he'd been Steve's age. But his father would've belted him for talking like that at home, wage-earner though he'd been. But Steve just went on talking.

"They're all doing it," he said. "It's right, me going down the Caves. It'll make things great."

Stan said, "I don't understand what you're going on about. If you want to stay here, then clean your mouth out!"

Steve threw the rake down and went out through the house. Stan heard the front door being slammed.

A week or so later, Stan was coming out of the Mason's Arms after a lunchtime pint. He went over to the High Street Stores to buy some bread. On his way out he met Steve. He had a girl with him.

"Hello Stan," Steve said.

"Afternoon, young man."

"Are you OK?"

"I'm all right. Come round if you like. You know where I live. Nothing's changed."

The girl said, "Steve...?"

"Oh, this is Mr Lacey, er, Stan. I've told you about him." He looked at Stan. "Meet Karen."

Stan thought that she was certainly very pretty, like Edith had been when they'd first met. "Pleased to meet you," he said, putting out his hand.

They laughed and carried on walking towards the Common. "See you around," Steve said, over his shoulder.

The next week, Steve started coming round again.

IT WAS LATE on a Saturday night in the autumn. Stan was sitting in his front room, thinking about switching his TV off. Suddenly there was a banging on the front door. When he opened it, Steve was standing there. He was looking in a state. He had been smartly dressed, but now his trousers were torn, and his elbows and hands were cut and dirty, as if he'd fallen over and been crawling. He had clearly been crying as well.

Stan let him in and sat him down in his usual place.

"It's no good Stan," Steve wailed. "It's Karen. She's chucked me. We went to this party and she told me that she wanted to be just friends now, and she went off. There were lots of tins of lager and some wine so I had some. And before I went out Mum said that

Brian's asked her to marry him and she's going to say yes. I was happy until she said we'd all move from Littleworth Green and I don't want to..."

He really started to cry then, wrenching sobs that shook his entire body.

Stan went and got Steve a damp towel, so he could clean himself up. "There, there," he said, over and over again. Eventually Steve calmed down.

"What can I do, Stan? You must've had girlfriends before you got married and all that."

In spite of the situation, Stan smiled. "Well, yes, I did. And they sometimes gave me the push as well, and I played the field a bit. You're young. You've plenty of time yet."

That seemed to galvanize Steve. Then he said, "But I loved her."

"You'll get over it, boy."

"I'm going back down the Caves again. I've got to. I can do it this time. I can think right this time down there. Things'll start to be OK. Everything. I know they will."

"What do you mean now?"

"It's all in my Hellfire Club book. The one I showed you. Like I said. And the map. It explains it all. The Inner Temple is the end, where it all begins, like in a womb." He pulled a torn piece of paper out of his pocket. "I always have it," Steve said.

Stan took the map reluctantly. He remembered the one from the Caves booklet. The passage curved under West Wycombe Hill, inwards and downwards. The triangular passages before the River Styx and Inner Temple were obvious in their symbolism. Stan thought, not for the first time, that the first Lord Desborough and his Hellfire Club had certainly been a strange bunch of characters.

"It mightn't mean anything," Stan said.

"It does! It must! I've marked it all!" Steve insisted. "Everything'll be OK for me if I get down there again. It'll be good with Mum and Brian and I can stay where I want to be. Things'll be like when I was a kid and you showed me your watch and you talked about your medals and things. I know I can find the stile and secret stuff, and get to the heart..."

A few minutes later Steve left, having apologised for causing a fuss. Stan went to bed. He noticed that his watch wasn't on the mantelpiece, but thought he must have left it somewhere else. He didn't think about it again until he was forced to.

ON SUNDAY, MRS Langley came round and asked Stan if he'd seen Steve. He said that he hadn't. After she'd gone back home to phone the police, Stan sat down in his front room. He felt for his watch-chain, and then remembered that he hadn't seen the watch since the previous day. He searched, but couldn't find it anywhere in the small house.

On Monday afternoon, Stan walked to the phone box by the Post Office in the High Street and, for the first time in his life, called a taxi. The driver took him by the circling road to the graveyard at the top of West Wycombe Hill. "Collect me from the entrance to the Caves in an hour," Stan told the driver.

Stan had never been to look at his wife's grave, but now it seemed right to. He hadn't been to the Hill since the funeral. He found the grave and stood in front of it, apparently praying in the warm October sun. Then he turned away to walk down the Hill: down the long clear slope in front of the Desborough Mausoleum, where he'd played football during the reign of King Edward VII, when the Caves had been boarded up, secure and ignored.

Walking slowly, Stan arrived at the entrance to the Caves. It had been rebuilt, the ruined Gothic arches completed again. There was a café and shop just outside the entrance itself, which was still like a dark wound, slit into the hillside.

Stan sat down in the café and ordered a cup of tea.

"Are you going down the Caves?" the assistant asked.

"No, I don't think so," Stan replied. "I'm a bit shaky on the pins..." He laughed.

The assistant started to tidy the counter. Before he turned away, Stan said, "Did you get many visitors yesterday?"

"Oh yes, lots. When it gets like that, you've always got to be so careful about not locking anyone in. The little kids are the worst. They think it's fun to try and hide down there."

"No-one tried it on, then?"

"No. But there was some lost property. We found this, down in the Inner Temple. You know, right as far in as you can go."

She reached under the counter and pulled out an old-fashioned watch on a chain. "This must be valuable," she said. "I suppose I'd better let Lord Desborough know." It swung, hypnotically, in the sunlight streaming in through the window. "It's very old, but it's still working."

GOING UNDERGROUND

Mike McKeown

EVERY EVENING, JORDAN Reichert was delivered into the bowels of the Earth: not once, but twice.

At least, that was how it felt as he maintained his rigid stance on the ancient wooden escalators that transported him from the heart of the City of London down to the Tube platform that would receive the train to take him home. As the adverts drifted by in repetitive sequence and he bore resentfully the buffets of those whose impatience led them to skip lightly down the clanking steps, knocking his shoulders with a regularity as monotonous as the reappearance of the flyer for Lloyd-Webber's latest travesty of a 'musical', he would brood and wish impotently that he had the belligerent temperament to slide a little to the left and provide an obstinate obstacle to the queue-jumpers, the boy-racers of Hatton Garden. Instead, he invariably settled for a subvocalised "harrumph" and a glare.

Reichert hated the fact that the Tube lines were so far below the surface: the oppressive weight of dozens of metres of solid matter suspended above his head terrified him. The tightly-packed carriages, the press of humanity offended his sensibilities: the touch, the odour, the invasion of his space, the whole experience was a dreadful ordeal that he had to put up with to get his pay packet at the end of each month. Every day he bore the journey with fortitude, breathing a glorious sigh of relief on being released into the sweet evening air, the uncluttered avenues of Ruislip.

Today was no different; after the first escalator, sandwiched between others who, like him, stood still and awaited their descent with dignity, passed at two-second intervals by the rush-hour rushers, he stepped off into the ruck of the central concourse, forcing his way through the flowing masses to the second escalator. After the next downward flight, he streamed toward his platform amid a seething mass of fellow commuters. At every step he was forced into contact with other people, carried along in the crush by sheer momentum.

AHEAD HE COULD see a breach forming, a pocket or bubble in the crowd. As he could hear no music, he realised immediately that there must be a beggar – not a busker, just someone dunning for coins – up in front of him. As usual, he attempted to push his way to the side of the corridor so as to place others between him and the beggar. Avoid all confrontation. At that moment, he realised he needed to sneeze, and reached into his jacket pocket for one of the mini-tissues he always kept about his person. Somehow, in between blowing his nose forcibly and trying to regain his orientation, he found himself directly in the beggar's path.

A reek of unwashed flesh, a vision of bedraggled black beard and hair atop a threadbare tweed jacket and blue jeans with the knees out, draped over a pale and emaciated frame, loomed before Reichert. A hand with long, pointed fingernails and coarse, matted black hair on its back was thrust before his eyes.

"Help an old trader," came a rasping croak from within the bird's-nest beard. Penetrating eyes, silvery and somehow threatening, impaled him with their fierce, maddened gaze. Reichert didn't know where to turn. He stammered out "I don't know if … I never give…" but the stare wouldn't let him go. Panicked, he thrust the freshly-used snotty tissue he still held in his left hand into the eager grasp of his accoster. He turned to try and squeeze his way back into the flow of his fellow workers, but no gap presented itself.

"Aaaah." The voice behind him seemed almost satisfied. "Don't go." Now the rasp seemed to vanish, and the beggar's voice grew smoother. "I must repay this … generous gift." A touch of menace seemed to creep into the words. Puzzled and a little alarmed, Reichert turned again and faced the freeloader. A clawlike fist reached deep into the pockets of the disreputable jacket, then lifted to the beggar's mouth.

"What…" Reichert began, when a fit of coughing overtook him as the tramp blew a palmful of dust, or fluff, directly into his face.

An arm bashed into him and, with his eyes streaming and his throat burning, he was carried back into the flow of commuters. Seconds later he regained his self-control, but when he looked back he could see no trace of the beggar. The crowd had closed in over the space the reprobate had occupied, like ripples over a sinking stone.

Within moments the memory faded, and the urgent need to get home, out of here, regained control of Reichert's thoughts. He resumed his familiar fight to get along the corridor and down the short fixed flight of steps that would lead to his platform, his escape from this hideous, overbearing bustle. His watering eyes, though, seemed to be causing an extraordinary illusion.

Overhead, the curved beige roof of the corridor grew pinker and damper, glistening with not-quite-defined moisture. To Reichert's left and right, the walls appeared to draw closer together. The people around him didn't notice, even whilst being pressed tighter into one another and pushing tightly against him. Their speed seemed to increase, like water being pushed through a narrow passage: the noise levels rose noticeably, and as the undifferentiated hubbub grew louder Reichert became more uncomfortable.

HE WAS STANDING on the platform at last, but things got no better. As a sweaty flush overtook him, Reichert began to wonder if somehow the beggar had managed to drug him. The noise of the people on the crushingly-crowded platform faded away into the background, and as he stared upwards the letters on the destination board blurred maddeningly out of definition, refusing to take shape. On the other side of the rails, the colours of the billboard posters smeared into one another. To Reichert's eyes the far wall looked like it was coated with a slick, oily film, patches of impure colour sliding by one another in an eye-wrenching liquid dance, unpleasantly like a lava lamp.

With startling clarity, the PA system burst into life over the muted murmur of the crowd. "LRT apologises, but the next train will not be stopping at this station." Reichert grimaced. *Why?* The platform was already packed. His gaze flicked from one end of the platform to the other. No-one's face seemed clear; his nearest neighbours had smoky blurs where their eyes should be, and noses and mouths that seemed hastily drawn on by a small child. The further away he looked, the less definition he saw, till at the far end the commuters' faces were nothing but featureless pink and brown ovals. *Drugged,* he thought. *I've definitely been drugged. Bastard tramp must have been carrying something in his coat pocket.*

A warm breath of wind from the maw of the Tube tunnel blew past Reichert's face, and the familiar rumble of an approaching train could be heard dimly. The train emerged into the station, but Reichert's eyesight seemed to be getting worse. He saw the train pull up with a flickering action almost like poor stop-motion animation. For a few moments he seemed almost to black out, then the train was pulling away again. *That's right,* he rationalised, *it isn't supposed to stop.* Then he realised how empty the platform was. The crowds had vanished, leaving no more than half a dozen people waiting, all the others being faceless ones from the far end of the platform. No-one else seemed to be coming onto the platform. *Bomb scare?* thought Reichert. *But where has everyone else gone?*

The tannoy crackled into action again. It repeated the same message as before, and Reichert grew uneasier. What if he was trapped down here, dozens of metres below ground, with no trains stopping and a bomb between him and the surface? Gradually he realised that the other passengers were moving slowly towards him. As they approached, the warm breeze of the next incoming train stroked past his cheek again, and the lights flickered and dimmed. At the same time he noticed that the faces of the people ambling towards him were not forming features. Each face was as smooth and undifferentiated as an egg.

Something rolled out of the tunnel. As the faceless travellers shuffled closer to Reichert, their arms lifted toward him in mute supplication, what had at first appeared to be the front carriage of a train rippled and split from roof to chassis. Where the access door should have been, a vertical mouth opened and began snapping rhythmically. Reichert caught a glimpse of steeled saw-teeth, a chestnut-red leathery tongue, before spinning away in disbelief and smacking his face firmly into the ceramic tiles of the platform wall. A whirring clatter rushed by him, a rank scent filling his nostrils. He cowered by the wall, not daring to look at whatever was going on around him. As the echoing rumble died away, he opened his eyes and turned back.

The platform was utterly empty and silent.

The station lights flickered and dimmed again, the light barely reaching the far wall across the rails. The platform seemed to narrow, and the tunnel entrance and exit shrank slightly and began to pulse faintly. A chill overcame Reichert as the air in the station cooled suddenly and, without warning, the display boards darkened and died. He licked his dry lips and gave a nervous laugh to confirm that the silence could still be broken. The laugh sounded flat, faded. It didn't reverberate off the walls of the platform as he thought it should.

The lines of grouting between the tiles on the walls blurred into broad smears and sank without trace, leaving a smooth, unblemished surface wherever there were no signs or posters. A wind that wasn't a wind, a hot moist breath, wafted across the platform from the tunnel mouth, together with a menacing rumble that carried subsonic undertones and felt like it was rattling at the ground under Reichert's feet. He stumbled backwards. This time as the train emerged, the razor-edged steel lips were already opening, the carriage twisting like a demented snake. The cavernous vertical mouth was snapping across the whole width of the platform, writhing towards Reichert…

…who screamed and tripped backwards, moving as fast as he dared without taking his eyes off the approaching apparition. He managed to back off into the stairway, and as he did so the edge of the archway to the platform rippled and collapsed in on itself, cutting off the nightmare image of the living train. Reichert shook his head, trying to shake off the effects of the drug. He rested his hand against the passage wall. In a second he was screaming again, because his hand and wrist were sinking into the wall as though it were made of porridge, not concrete. He pulled it out again as if stung; the impression of his hand stayed on the wall. He probed it cautiously with one finger. Solid. No fluidity at all.

The way to the platform was gone, sealed off as though it had never existed. Reichert was alone at the foot of a staircase that led back up to the corridors of the station proper. The walls and ceiling all around him were looking damper again, and with a tinge of red creeping through. He touched a wall again, but only for an instant.

The stone was warm, with some elastic give in it. The word 'fleshy' ran through his mind. All surfaces, including the steps under his feet, were taking on the same texture and qualities.

And starting to shiver ominously.

Reichert started to run, taking the steps two and then three at a time. By the time he reached the level ground of the next passageway, he could feel his feet sinking slightly at every step and the suction of the ground as it tried weakly to prevent him moving on. The walls and ceiling were contracting slowly, narrowing the passage in front of him. He ran faster. A ripple ran along the corridor, like peristaltic action. As Reichert ran, he could sense the walls trying to grab and squeeze at him. Soon he was scrabbling along in a crouch, using his hands and knees as well as his feet to move forwards … the channel ahead was narrow and low.

And blocked.

In front of him now, some ten metres away, was the tramp. The miserable derelict who had initiated this fugue. The tramp's mouth was set in a snarl; his strange silver-steel eyes seemed to taunt Reichert with their insolence. There was no way past the old busker, whose hairy flesh made him look almost lupine and whose hands now reached out to Reichert like grasping claws. Behind, the passage was achieving closure … there was no way back. Reichert's rage built and he charged forward, heedless. At full pelt, he made solid contact in only a few seconds. But the beggar, too, seemed less than substantial, and Reichert felt their two bodies meld, merging into a single form that was more than real. He felt ill, loathing the idea of even touching this creature who had ruined his mind in minutes…

WITHOUT WARNING, EVERYTHING changed. He stood once more on a normal, crowded Tube platform, waiting for the next train and deafened by the noise of the so-welcome crowd pressing in on him from all sides. Smugly he noticed that he was right at the front, and correctly placed for the third carriage of the next train to stop with its doors directly in front of him. With a massive internal sigh of relief, he realised that the insane drug episode was over.

There was a soiled paper tissue crumpled up, held in his left hand. What? He threw it dismissively down to the tracks. As he congratulated himself on throwing off the effects of what must have been some form of hallucinogen, a train stopped. For the merest fraction of a second, it appeared translucent; but as the doors opened, Reichert was simply very self-satisfied – in spite of the strange hallucination, he had indeed positioned himself perfectly to be the first to board.

By a lucky chance it also seemed that no-one on the train wanted to leave, at least through these doors. Reichert stepped aboard contentedly. He had just a moment to register the disreputable, ragged sleeves of his jacket and the emaciated, hairy hands at the ends of them.

A COUPLE OF metres away, a young girl watched the old tramp in utter disbelief. *He's stepping out, off the platform! He's not jumping or diving, it's like he actually thinks there's a train there!* The hot wind and trundle reached her thoughts as she watched the stranger tumble headlong onto the tracks. There was a scream of brakes, and a scarlet spray of bright blood onto the front of the stopping train.

AT THE ENTRANCE to the tube station, just before leaving, a smart young man stopped and checked himself over. *Nice suit,* he thought. He pinched the flesh of one arm lightly with the fingers of the other hand, to get a feel for the fat and protein content of the body. Enough material there for a couple of weeks, before he would need to return. He checked the wallet he had just retrieved from an inner pocket. After extracting the cash and pocketing it, he examined and stroked each credit card in turn. Every time, the embossed name J REICHERT flowed into the card surface, then reformed as ADAM SMITH. On the back of the cards, the signature writhed and knotted itself into an unreadable squiggle. The young man then discarded the wallet and its remaining contents in the nearest litterbin. Adam Smith gave a feral grin and, with his silver-steel eyes aglow, stepped out into the evening city.

LOST AND FOUND

Simon Avery

1971. BY TEN P.M. Daniel had peaked. His producer sent him home to Haverstock Hill in a taxi. Clutching his guitar case between those spindly legs of his, Danny saw London through a dope haze. He'd scored some powerful skunk-weed called Black Pearl from a hippy commune in Wiltshire some months ago, before his problems began. He was catching glimpses of what he was becoming, he wrote in that first letter; and through the wrong end of a telescope, what he used to be.

That night he'd dreamt he was tethered to a string, like a roaming kite. The sky pulled him up into itself and he had no choice but to acquiesce. "There aren't any choices any more," he wrote. "I go where the river flows."

The day was dawning; a brittle light was falling through London's cracks and hollows – Danny saw it all with a rare, piercing insight. People were leaving their homes, making their way to unspecified jobs; trains had started to rattle towards destinations, feeding bodies like blood into and out of the heart of the city. He flew unseen above it all – the streets still cool before the sunlight had burnt through the haze – and woke on the Underground in his shirt and cords and socks, hair uncombed, heading south on the Northern Line, just leaving Camden Town. It was quiet by this time on the train: the mid-morning lull of housewives and toddlers or pensioners, exchanging hospital tales. Danny stood for a while, trying to determine where to alight, then seated himself again, confused, a little bit scared. It wasn't the first time that he'd woken to find himself beneath London; he believed that his body was luring him towards something his mind couldn't yet admit to.

He considered transferring and paying a visit to Sarah at her flat in Battersea, but thought better of it. His sister's face in his mind made him feel as if there was a hard stone in his chest, crushing his emotions. He had no idea how long he stayed on the train. It felt quiet inside him, he wrote, like being left alone in a church. When he did finally propel himself up and out onto a platform, he was in Leicester Square.

There was a cluster of ostentatious American tourists around the Underground map nearby. Their voices made his mind barren; the way he felt after taking the medication his doctor had prescribed. They stared at him in his grubby socks, and one of the younger ones laughed behind his hand. Daniel felt a spark of naked embarrassment, and stumbled out to the escalators, mouthing the words on the frayed bill-posters like a mantra that might set him free from himself.

The brilliant light of a summer's day in Leicester Square paralysed him. People were chasing their shadows down the street, eyeing him with cautious sideways glances. The traffic was at a suffocating standstill; a radio was drifting music down from an open office window, playing something American that he imagined Sarah or I might know.

The glimpse of someone nearby making gestures with his empty hands, as if he was folding air into boxes or origami shapes, made Danny doubly nervous. Perhaps he was a street magician, Danny mused, or a mime. But he swore he could hear his name being repeated out of gritted teeth, through the street noise: "DannyDannyDannyDanny..."

He felt a terrible sense of apprehension as he retraced his steps and pushed his way back down the escalator, reciting the poster mantra in reverse. It hadn't served him well forwards, and his seemed like a paltry ritual compared to the magician's at-the station entrance. When he reached the platform, his shirt clung to the small of his back, and the inside of his skull felt itchy with expectation – like waiting for MDMA to kick in, or too much coffee in the system. The heat and noise of the sticky dinner-hour throng, their proximity, made him stumble closer to the edge of the platform. He could see tiny mice scurrying beneath the rails.

There was a rush of warm, summery air and Daniel stumbled clumsily out onto the tracks. He suddenly felt terribly embarrassed and afraid. Out of the corner of his narrowed vision, he saw a huge dark shape, and faces behind him with mouths that had become dark Os. He felt no regret, he wrote, no sense of loss. In the slow, soporific lull before the blackness and the terrible pain, Danny imagined that the train might stop in time, and cheat him.

SARAH'S ACTIONS AND words seemed slower now, more deliberate. She spoke in clipped, contemplated sentences. But it was nothing more than age. It had been almost thirty years. Even prize-fighters grew more measured and circumspect in the later rounds. Had I changed too? I still felt clumsy beside her, a bit reckless; befuddled by the clamour of my feelings. I discovered what I was saying when I said it. I always had.

When our emotions finally got in the way of what we were saying, our hands took over quite involuntarily, and we found ourselves at the end of an initially civilised evening on the edge of my bed, flustered and coy, refastening buttons and turning the lights back on.

"We don't have to do anything, sweet."

"No, I know."

"There's plenty of time. All the time in the world."

"Yes. Yes of course."

After that we went downstairs, lit some candles that I found beneath the sink, opened some wine, and talked into the night. Sarah was still very proper and polite; quite upper-middle class, but coming to nursing in her mid-thirties seemed to have worn much of the reserve right out of her. She'd ended up in Birmingham during the eighties, a little bit lost after a divorce that had felt too clean and too easy a break from so many years of love. "Too much equanimity," she said. "I felt obliged to be civilised. He remarried a couple of months later, of course. He'd been seeing this woman for two years, while we were still married. Although she wasn't a woman. She was seventeen. *Seventeen*."

She ended up working in a children's hospital, and I could imagine her as the lines deepened in her face, strands of grey creeping out of her curls; walking down some pale corridor, speaking softly to youngsters, sat unblinking in front of the telly, wrapped up in dressing-gowns, wearing silly slippers: "Just sit up, love, while I fluff your pillow."

As Sarah spoke in my living-room, I saw her falling asleep on the bus home, carrying a basket around Sainsbury's (she never needed a trolley), talking to her cat as it curled around her ankles when she opened the door to her flat in Stirchley, the radio on for noise, keys in the ashtray, a warm bath, drawing the curtains, reading in bed until she dozed off with a finger marking her place... It was romantic alchemy. We held hands as our shadows grew around the room, the wine making us drowsy. Her eyes kept glancing to the window, as if she was expecting someone; it kept jarring me awake. I kept forgetting to ask why she'd really come back. I thought I could hear dogs scrapping outside, but when I looked there were only the streetlamps, stooping in from the corner of the street; and after a while, I was too exhausted to care. Sarah eventually closed the curtains and we went to bed.

In the morning I stood outside in the back yard in last night's clothes, watching my coffee go cold. Something had already changed in me. I could feel a warmth beneath my skin that had nothing to do with the July morning, unveiling itself as neighbours opened curtains, let dogs out to piss, turned on their radios. It was like vertigo.

Sarah came out with her coat over her arm. For a moment I glimpsed the girl from 1971, hiding between the lines of Danny's second letter. It had been waiting on the doormat in a plain envelope when I brought the milk in. I kept catching glimpses of us all then, when Sarah was not the only one to have hair past her shoulders; our history, like a shorthand of the years.

But my mind couldn't be trusted. I'd made Sarah extraordinary in her absence, given her too much life, too many happy years; used too many colours, and instead, here we were, waiting for the rug to be pulled from beneath us, still moving in the same diminished circles at fifty; lost and found, lost and found.

She kissed me and left her new phone number, written on my palm, like we were still teenagers, and left through the back gate.

DANIEL RETURNED TO the Underground almost every day, as if he were courting a lover, or mourning a departed one. It was 1972 by this time, but the train continued to lead him out of sleep every morning: tons of steel emerging from the tunnel, and beyond that the same tableaux of memories in different arrangements.

Waking up in intensive care, with a clipboard at the end of his bed listing a league table of injuries. Days of morphine. A mélange of faces: Sarah, myself, his producer and sound engineer, someone from the record company, various musicians from Hampstead Heath, where most of us had digs back then. After a week or so he finally discovered that his left arm was gone from below the elbow. Sarah held him stiffly during the tears, talked to him as much as was possible, cut his hair, mothered him a bit. She was just glad he was alive. Months of physiotherapy; feeling the pull of gravity after three months on his back due to an additional spinal injury. Days of silence, which led Sarah to me, to cry helplessly on my shoulder. They transferred him eventually to a psychiatric ward, where every face that stared back at him seemed impenetrable with medication. No progress, only pills. Danny had been here once before. He recognised the girl with the sickly smile who sat in the waiting room all day, pissing herself rather than move. Interminable hours spent staring out of the wire-reinforced windows of the day room, which smelt of cigarettes and farts; thinking about his guitar and the stump of his left arm; it felt like a joke waiting for a punchline. A couple of music journalists turned up, but he wilfully baffled them with esoterica about black American blues guitarists from the forties and fifties.

By the turn of the year, Danny had slipped through the net. He still had his flat in a large, somewhat decrepit Victorian house near Chalk Farm tube station, where an executive from his record company had his weekly stipend of £15 posted, despite the fact that there would clearly be no more recordings from Danny. He still had friends in high places who were deeply concerned for his welfare.

But he was rarely at the house. By this time he was fixated on the Underground. "I don't know why exactly," he wrote at that point, "but I dare say I shall find out. I just feel *drawn*."

In that second letter there were moments of startling clarity, then childish aimlessness. I remember him at that time: if he had been a book of poetry, then he was steadily dwindling to a verse, a word, a blank page. I envisioned him outside Victoria Station, hunched in the rain, with his jacket collar pulled up beneath his ears, staring at people's faces, looking for *something*: eyes as vacant or haunted as his own, perhaps; or the street magician, folding air with his hands.

Daniel took shelter inside eventually. He hadn't realised how loud the rain sounded, he wrote, until he was in the cavernous calm of the station. He caught voices like stray radio bands. A young lad was slumped in front of a coat littered with change, strumming Bob Dylan songs. But it was background noise; there was another reason that Danny was here, something that was altogether touching to someone who had known him – his shyness, his sense of cultural reserve.

"She was reading *Catch-22*..." he wrote, and my heart ached for him. Danny had been watching her all through spring, working up the nerve to make his approach. He'd bought the book himself, and couldn't quite understand why. It was all alien territory to him. He was a lovestruck adolescent. Ridiculously, he went over, fumbled some loose change from his long unwashed cords, and bought a mixed bunch from her as the sound of station announcements sang in his ears. He didn't say anything initially, of course; chronic shyness would take his voice from him at crucial moments such as these. But he had made the vital first connection.

"She was probably no more than twenty," he wrote, "perhaps younger. Thin. Very pale skin. She kept pulling the hem of her skirt down over her thighs, and then looking around nervously."

She was waiting for someone to coax her out of her chrysalis. She said to him: "Are you Daniel Faulkner? I have your record, you know. It's really very good."

Danny confused her by smiling nervously, nodding mutely, then folding the stump of his arm into his coat.

"Oh..." she said, as if she'd only just realised the connotations of his lost hand. He was suddenly painfully aware not only of that, but of his unwashed clothes and hair. He couldn't control his gaze; it was all he could do to ignore the soft swell of her breasts above the V-neck of her sweater, the nervous movement of her slender hands, the hair that she pulled back behind her ears. Danny felt at a loss. He didn't recognise this vulgar, sweaty man with his dirty thoughts.

The girl hesitated, possibly confused by his reticence, and went back to the stall to serve someone. Danny walked away into the station, then returned, hovered: chess in Victoria Station. She watched him from behind *Catch-22*, bemused, no longer reading. Danny felt as if everyone in the station could read his sad cloying mind. The heat inside him made his shirt cling to his back. He smelt of rain and sweat.

In the end, the girl re-approached him, said her name was Molly, and invited him back to her flat in Bethnal Green. Her forwardness took him aback. It felt, he wrote, like something that happened to other people. He'd heard all the stories from acquaintances who played the local circuit. If you were a muso, then you were virtually guaranteed at least a knee-trembler around the back of the venue. But this wasn't that, he felt. He couldn't say why.

While she emptied the stall, he stood, hypnotised at first by her pale ankles and then by the loose leaves and bright petals floating in the buckets of water around her. She brought some of the flowers with her when he offered to pay for a taxi to ferry them across London. He hated being on the streets at any time, but particularly at dusk; a cab would deliver them straight to her door.

The skies had turned a deep purple. In the concrete car parks of pubs, locals lounged around their cars, the doors open, pints balanced on the bonnets. Their voices carried through the taxi's open windows. Danny was intoxicated by the smell of flowers between Molly's legs, and the way she'd slid her shoes off until they were hanging from her toes. But he couldn't look at her face or talk. His mind was a blank.

"It was one of those anonymous East End terraced streets," he wrote. "Concrete gardens. Children playing in the road. A chip shop at one end, an off-licence at the other. It was the kind of place you'd never find twice."

Her bedsit, lit with a dim yellow bulb, was already crowded with flowers in vases and cracked tumblers. "I can't just chuck them out," she said in her defence, as if they were lodgers.

They both sat for a while in a kind of dazed silence. Danny felt as if they'd arrived for parts in a play for which they had no lines, but then Danny *always* felt that way. Molly made tea for them, which passed some time. Then, hesitantly, over the kettle, she said, "Would you like to smoke a joint?"

The way that she said it made him laugh, and it seemed to break the ice somewhat. Delighted by the smile on his face, she took him back outside: up the road to the off-licence for twenty Embassy, a pack of Rizla papers, and a bottle of cheap wine that would sit in her fridge long after she was dead. Danny's softened demeanour drew Molly out of herself somehow. He felt her hand brushing his fingers as she spoke breathlessly about the little village in Yorkshire where she'd been born, and her sisters who'd spread out through England, eager to be away. Danny didn't discover why, for as they left the shop, Molly's smile stiffened suddenly on her face, and he caught sight of a figure across the street, hovering outside the light of a streetlamp beside a rusted Anglia. He unclasped his hands and then regarded them solemnly. It was a movement that Danny felt he'd just missed the extent of, and the sudden furtive movement further into the darkness confirmed it. The memory of the street magician in Leicester Square, folding air, compartmentalising it, rose in Danny's mind. He registered dully that Molly had taken hold of his hand and was dragging him back up the street. She looked as apprehensive as he felt. But when Danny peered back into the dusk between the pools of streetlamp light, he could only see a shape easing itself into the car, nestling into its darkness, starting the engine, then letting it tick over. Danny couldn't decide what had just happened, but the stump of his arm was aching. He saw the train emerging from the tunnel of his mind as Molly fumbled with her keys.

He tried inadequately to draw her out afterwards; but as she sat cross-legged on the bed, rolling the joints, her hair tumbling over her eyes, the stiff expression of concentration on her face seemed impenetrable. The bright bloom of her earlier exuberance seemed to have vanished entirely.

They smoked for a while in silence, black hash – eight quid an ounce, she told him – but the sense of closeness that had threatened to grow between them had diminished. Molly's eyes looked barren, he wrote; resolved. "Like a little girl whose party kept being spoiled." Danny had no idea what to do or say. But after an hour or so, a little bit stoned, she made her first tentative inroads towards him. He resisted initially, of course, as if he were some upper-class twit being propositioned by a socialist: it was in his breeding. Shyly she slid her sweater off. Her body, moving through the fabric, stirred something within him that seemed beyond resisting. "I can protect you," she said, covering his sallow neck in breath and kisses. Slow, drowsy circles with her hands. "If you want me to."

The words made no sense. Danny only felt childishly giddy. She opened a window to air the room a little from the smoke; and as the breeze made goose-pimples on her skin, they both smiled to each other again. In the languid summer silence, he felt an exhilarating vertiginous delight in the way it progressed; their bodies releasing him in a way that words could not.

When she pulled him down beside her, every moment he'd ever had seemed to coalesce. He heard a sudden rain shower begin beyond the window, and when he looked, the sky had suddenly gone black. Starless and black. Danny felt watched by it as it swelled in the frame. But there was something else: the room seemed heavy with electric light and heat. In that moment, he wrote, Molly was transformed the way dust or rain is when sunlight catches it. He could suddenly feel every detail of her, combined and beatific, and he was drunk on it – the *realness* of her: the flush in her cheeks and breasts; the painted red fingernails, chipped and bitten to the quick; the way her patent leather shoes had rubbed the skin on her ankles red; the wet heat that she fumbled his shaking fingers into. Briefly he saw a glimpse of her life: the gap-toothed girl she'd surely once been in school photographs; the child with a bucket and spade on the beach in Blackpool; the dead-eyed teenager beside a hospital bed, clutching her mother's hand; her body entwined with another girl's in a field by a grey church...

Danny thought it was over, but then suddenly there was more, more than Molly could have lived: he saw her old and weathered, but unmistakeably *her*, in a nondescript backyard, with two small children on either side of her (he could hear them saying "Cheese!" brightly, then scampering away); he saw her, ten years from that moment, loading Safeway carrier bags into the back of her Metro; putting on glasses to tend to crocuses; laughing at the TV, her body nestled into a young man's, both of them no more than fifteen; queuing for lottery tickets, wearing a headscarf and overcoat...

The moment was too much. Danny couldn't decide if she was more or less than human. Clearly, nothing leading up to this point had been accidental. Molly was unfolding her hands, crying out to the darkness: "You can fuck off! Leave us alone!" And then, urgently, to Danny: "Do it now. *Fuck* me. Do it now. *Go on.*"

She led him clumsily inside her. Danny could hardly move. He looked away from her eyes; her gaze seemed to see into him, and he was suddenly scared that this exposed how little there was to find in him. Her face was drained of joy. He pressed his into her neck, feeling surplus to requirements suddenly. He felt sick and alone when he came, and withdrew immediately, thinking the act over. The breeze from the open window dried the film of sweat off his body while he removed his trousers, which were tangled around his ankles. When he turned back to Molly, she was reaching out for him, pushing her fingers through his hair, and the look on her face hovered between sadness and fondness. The light had gone from the room, the swelling darkness from the window.

"Protect *me* now," she said, closing her wrists together and raising her clasped hands to her chest. The gesture was unselfconscious, pure sudden need. Her resolve had gone, he realised. But as much as he wanted to, it was a final gulf that Danny could not cross, despite what she might have given him. "I simply hadn't the strength for two," he wrote.

DANNY WOKE TO the sound of buses lumbering up Bethnal Green Road; birds singing; the milkman making his rounds. When he reached out expectantly, he found the bed empty, but the sheets were drenched with blood.

There was a dreadful resolve to his initial movements, though his ears were ringing with fear. The trail of blood led down off the far side of the bed, and around the room, like manic dance steps. The open window couldn't quell the smell of it sufficiently. The flowers, he wrote, had all died in a kind of crazed poetic inevitability. The pale shape at the corner of his vision seemed to swarm, beckon his gaze. Danny said her name, and his voice sounded like an intrusion on the stillness of the room. The absolute quiet suddenly seemed to have infected the streets outside, as if all of its elements – the buses, the birds, the milkman – were waiting for his next move.

When he finally crossed the room and forced himself to face Molly, he felt his throat tighten, tears sting his eyes. The edges of his mind were beginning to fray dangerously. Now he had set eyes on her, he couldn't remove his gaze. I imagined him, an obscure folk singer without his trousers, standing over the teenager's body curled in a corner. It was as if she had turned to porcelain. Her skin looked pale and unblemished against the carpet of blood beneath her. He wanted to gather her up into his skinny arms; but in an act of wanton perversity, they had removed her head and placed it between her legs, put a hand in her hair. Clearly, her tryst with Danny had antagonised them beyond measure. He was shaking with rage, his fists clenched in fury. *They.* He was seeing them, folding air, moving lightly up the stairs, through the window, silent as ballerinas; opening her up with their bare hands, *never once touching her,* then removing her from the bed, letting the blood spill around her.

Suddenly, Danny felt terribly abandoned. Molly was in the room, he wrote, yet she was not. There was only a body and some belongings: clothes, paperbacks, some dusty vinyl, towels on a chair near the fire, a box of tampons on the sink, the ashtrays filled with curled joints. The memory of all of her lives kept flashing in front of him. He couldn't decide on the truth of things. All he knew for sure was that she had been killed because of him. It was too much for his mind.

He retrieved his clothes and fled downstairs, stared at the payphone in the hall for a moment, then picked it up with the intention of calling the police. But the dead sound that he pressed to his ear made him feel transparent; and the voice, when it came, sounded like something huge and made of blackness, reaching up, out of the depths.

I WATCHED SARAH watching Andrew from the touchlines as the light faded and the little floodlamps in the park came on. In the still evening air, they cast long, lazy shadows from the players – thin-legged schoolboys with skinned knees and muddy faces. A smattering of parents hollered and whistled from the sidelines, clutching bottles of Evian or cappucinos from the Starbucks across the street. I saw my ex-wife, and waved.

By the time we'd sold the house and the divorce was finalised, Deborah had found a little place in Sevenoaks for herself and our son, Andrew. We'd had him quite late in life (I was thirty-eight at the time, Deborah thirty-six), and the changed circumstance of that, combined with other less specific things, pushed us away from one another. I never found the perspective that children were supposed to give you. Like Sarah's divorce, it turned out to be a little too amicable, a little too clean. Like pulling at one thread that unravels everything. In panic, I'd imagined that the weight of our past, all the assorted ups and downs and photo albums full of our lives together, might solve our problems – look at what we've done! How much we've gone through! But it hadn't been that way at all. For Deborah, it seemed only to be a relief.

She came over after the game to give Sarah a cursory inspection, and then took Andrew off home in her new husband's Rover. Waving, I watched the rear lights vanish; saw the remainder of the evening light exhaust itself entirely. Sarah had barely managed to acknowledge Deborah or Andrew. She'd been initially disturbed, then quietly preoccupied by Daniel's letters. I had no intention of keeping them from her; we were together too often in any case: she had underwear in my drawers by this time, a toothbrush in the bathroom, make-up, tights on the radiator. I was determined to be as open as possible, even though I knew the letters would upset her. She was already lost, somewhere in 1972.

On the way home she eventually said, "He phoned me from a station. Monument or Bank – I can't recall. He could hardly speak. I mean it was bloody ridiculous, but I knew it was Danny. I managed to discover where he was and said I'd be there as soon as possible. I was his breakdown service. *Ridiculous.* When I found him, he was in one of the pedestrian tunnels, sitting on his coat with his guitar in his hand. He looked bewildered."

Sarah stopped in the street, hesitated with the words that she wanted to say. I remained silent; heard the clatter of plates carry from an open kitchen window; watched as lights came on in houses and a high-rise nearby; watched as light flared from the cigarette that Sarah lit while she looked inside herself and then finally back to me.

"I felt awful," she said. "Like there was something I could have done for him before it had got to that point."

I took her hands. "You couldn't reach him," I said. "We all tried at some time or other. But people have to want to be helped, and I don't think he did."

She nodded. "But that was the illness in him. How could he know what he wanted? I've read all those articles people have written about him in the music press and Sunday supplements; they seem to think he was born wearing black and listening to Leonard Cohen. We had a *lovely* childhood, you know. We had a dog, family holidays abroad; our parents were well off, put us through public school, University; plenty of friends. We were *fine*. And then we were all so terribly pleased when he got that recording contract.

"But it was London. Somehow, once it got hold of him, it was corrosive. And those last few years, he got away from me. I let him. Sometimes it's only distance that saves us. He always managed to make people feel somehow accountable for all of his feelings, but he nurtured that in me the most, you know – look what you let me do! Why didn't you look after me?

"But anyway, seeing him there with his guitar, I *did* feel ashamed. I had to help him into a gent's loo, where he retched into a urinal. He had no weight on him. My hands just closed around his arms. I could feel his ribs through his pullover. And then I found the cigarette burns on the stump of his arm. I went through the roof. 'Look at this,' I said. 'What the *bloody hell* do you call this, Daniel?' But he didn't care. I don't think he was listening.

"We ended up on a platform and when he *did* start talking, he sounded so confused, I just thought it was the medication. He was insistent that we shouldn't go out of the Underground, so I bought him a sandwich and he ate a bit of it on a bench with all these people running past. 'They killed her,' he kept saying, but he wouldn't specify who. 'Just a girl. Just a girl.' He was terrified that he'd be accused – that someone might have witnessed him speaking to this girl, or that the taxi driver who took him to her place in Bethnal Green would remember him. I bought some newspapers and couldn't find anything. Perhaps she hadn't been found, but it didn't pacify him really. He kept telling me things about her, or about other women. He couldn't decide if it was the same person. But he seemed to know very specific details. It was like he couldn't keep them in.

There was too much.

"Eventually he was so tired that I managed to get him on a train and back to my flat. I slept on the sofa. He didn't ask why everything was in boxes, why I was packing my bags. I suppose he'd realised it would happen eventually. I knew he was going to be terribly lonely in London without me there, but I had to leave. After you and I split up, I felt weepy and depressed all the time, and I realised that I had to be stronger than that. Otherwise you just make a vicious circle for yourself.

"But I woke up in the middle of the night, and Danny was knelt beside me, stroking my hair. He stared at me until I had to look away. That was such a *huge* thing for Danny to do. I think perhaps he was scared for me after what had happened to this girl. I was so touched that I tried to put my arms around him, but that seemed to break the spell. He retreated back into himself and he didn't speak to me after that; not even in the morning when I told him I was moving away. 'How can I bloody well help you when you never talk to me?' That was the last thing I ever said to him."

Sarah didn't offer anything else the rest of the way home. She'd talked herself into some regretful place. I tried to draw her out, change the subject, but she'd retreated just as Danny had. She seemed more contented by my arms around her in bed than by anything I could say.

During the night, I woke to find her gone. After all we'd spoken about, I felt a panic rise in me. Halfway down the staircase, I heard her voice: she was speaking quietly to someone in the kitchen. When she said Danny's name, panic made me stumble downwards, two, three steps at a time. Until that point I had seen the letters and my life as separate entities. Perhaps I had been ignorant.

When I reached the kitchen, however, I found Sarah asleep at the breakfast table. I touched her hair, and the panic subsided to something softer, warmer. I felt ridiculous, easily alarmed; a bit old. Perhaps she had been talking in her sleep. But as I considered waking her, I heard a sudden frenzied scrabbling outside, and then a panting, like breathless dogs fighting. The back door was ajar, I realised.

Without thinking, I crossed the kitchen quickly and stepped outside in my bare feet. But without my glasses, the back yard could have had my son's football team in it and I wouldn't have seen them. All I could hear by that time was the washing flapping stiffly in the soft breeze, the sound of taxis idling streets away. My mind kept leading me back to folding hands and young girls with multiple lives. I locked the door, checked the windows, and then woke Sarah, who was only disorientated to find herself downstairs. Then we went back to bed.

Perhaps I should have made more sense of things there and then, made some correlation, however ridiculous. But I didn't.

AFTER LEAVING SARAH'S flat in Battersea, Danny rode the Underground, criss-crossing lines throughout central London. There was a pull inside him by now that was distorting his thoughts. His memory failed him. He felt bereaved and couldn't recall why. But he knew somehow that he was stumbling around the precipice of the truth.

Somehow he made it back to his place in Haverstock Hill, which was across the road from the entrance to Chalk Farm tube station. I remember his flat purely by the paucity of his belongings. He lived like a squatter. It was a back room away from the street, huge French windows overlooking the gardens. The sun rose through them in the morning. As it crept along the bare wooden floorboards that morning, Danny destroyed everything systematically: the record player next to a stack of vinyl; his small-bodied Guild guitar; his reel to reel for demos; the print of the cover of his debut album, framed on the wall; the faded Penguin paperbacks, mouldering beneath the window. "I hated it all," he wrote. "None of it had anything to do with what remained of my life."

Afterwards, breathless and sated, he swallowed some of his prescription drugs with tap water, drew the curtains and lay down on his mattress amongst the detritus, imagining that Molly was beside him.

He woke on another crowded tube train. For a brief moment he was as disorientated as ever: he always left sleep with the confusion of a homeless man. The compartment was so full that he couldn't rise from the seat he found himself in. When he tried to catch the eyes of other passengers, their faces were all somehow turned away. Danny felt a sudden surge of paranoia and panic rise in him, like too much breath in his lungs, just as the train slowed, sighed to a halt. The doors hissed open. No-one moved. Danny struggled to get out of his seat again, but the bodies around him were as rigid as statues. He was too polite, too reserved to raise his voice to the unyielding throng, so he acquiesced. He craned his neck in order to see which station they'd stopped at, but the platform was unlit, deserted. He could smell earth through the open doors, he wrote: the rich scent of freshly dug soil; and he knew then, as the doors closed and the train lurched forward, that he was finally being led to whatever it was that had plagued him all this time.

The conclusion gave him strength. Suddenly he was out of his seat and fumbling through the cluster of passengers. He felt no air of anticipation in the crowd, no fear; nothing at all. When he came face to face with one of them, it was like looking at a mask. The eyes were vacant, unlocatable. It was the very least that a face could be. "I wondered," Danny wrote, "if it saw the same in me. But how could it? The rest of them seemed to share a complicity in their inactivity, their silence." They might as well have been sneering at him.

When the train began to slow again, Danny unthreaded himself from the throng of bodies, and then stepped out onto the platform. When he turned to look back at the open doors, the cluster of figures, seated, standing, stared blankly back at him. He recognised details finally: raincoats, shopping bags, umbrellas, a child with perfect round eyes, still in its pyjamas.

Danny fell back onto a hard plastic bench and curled up, his hand closed over his face. He couldn't think clearly. His head felt leaden, as if he had taken a double dose of his medication. His limbs were heavy with lethargy.

But still. The smell of fresh earth. "Like after a rain shower," he wrote. He was thinking of the heat of a summer's day, somewhere above him, and the vacated rooms and roads where all of these people should have been, if their bodies had not been lured away. That pull. They'd felt it too.

The sense of activity nearby made Danny rise and watch as the passengers began to disembark jerkily, jumping down onto the tracks between the train and the platform. *Mind the gap,* Danny thought.

Was this their destination? A point of no return? He wanted to run, but he knew that simply wasn't possible, despite his apparent distinction from the rest of the passengers. And he had to know. This was, I suppose, his treeful of angels.

The passengers were drifting into the next tunnel: a huge, silent procession from the carriages, slowly being enveloped by the dark. Danny hesitated until the train had been emptied in its entirety. He was reluctant to be in close proximity to the rest of them for fear of losing his autonomy somehow. Pulling his coat tightly around him, he jumped down between the tracks and followed the tail-end of the line into the tunnel, where they became a grey mass, swarming before his eyes. He stretched his undamaged arm out in front of himself, and stumbled blindly forward for some time until the gloom began to glow; gradually the tunnel was opening out into an immense cavern. The temperature had dropped palpably. It took Danny's breath away momentarily; and then, once he'd grasped the sheer size of the cave, astonishment did the same. He couldn't see the ceiling. The slightest sound of movement rose and lingered in the air, echoing for long moments. "It was like a cathedral," he wrote. Amongst the stalagmite basins and the stalactite pillars, he could hear the sound of something like prayer. He was terrified and in awe.

The crowd were disrobing, casting off their clothes with cold, mechanical efficiency. Danny hovered on their periphery. He could feel an itching in his head to do the same, become part of the mass. The sight of the handfolders, moving amongst the crowd, gesticulating silently, only made him more fearful. Although it was a magic still beyond his comprehension, he had first-hand knowledge of their capabilities. The air was growing restless around them; there were strange phosphorescent seeds, drifting from their hands and through the air, like fireflies. Suddenly they were everywhere, multiplying in the gloom before Danny's eyes.

When he heard the dull rumble of trains around him, he looked back at the mouth of the tunnel; but then he realised that the sound belonged to something else, something vast, waiting in the darkness: a huge invisible presence, suddenly invoked. For a brief, devastating moment, softened by the enveloping brown atmosphere, hypnotised by the seeds and the sound, Danny and the crowd were delivered to a clear, untouched beach. There were no lights inland, no-one at sea; no other signs of life. But in the deafening silence, Danny found himself staring up at a sky that seemed too full of stars, and at a darkness that was swiftly eclipsing them: vast shapes like broken satellites, plummeting at astonishing speed, out of the night and into the ocean. The crowd's ensuing murmurs sounded to Danny like massed prayer. At the explosion and the colossal tidal wave that rose back up, seemingly into the stars, they were delivered back into the gloom of the cave to cower before the giant, impassive presence that had somehow found its way beneath the world, in exile, licking its wounds through the millennia.

Danny felt humbled and terrified all at once, rooted to the moist earth beneath his feet. The crowd had begun to move, he realised. The seeds floating in the air seemed to multiply again, until their glow made his vision blur. The people began to merge and unpeel, to soften. They left pale trails in the air, like after-images on his eyes, as if he'd stared at a light-bulb for too long. "The afterbirth of ghosts," Danny wrote. They were coming undone. He could smell the scent of grass after rainfall, or semen on skin perhaps; then the sweet, heady smell of wild flowers on a summer evening. Molly's face came unbidden to his mind, like a light to follow. Danny realised then that he could *feel* the shapes that the crowd had metamorphosed into: they were like turbulent portraits of lives, to be offered to and consumed by the darkness. They were all participants in its resurrection. At Danny's sudden realisation, the presence heaved and he felt a rush of vertigo as the soil beneath his feet shied away from him. There were seeds in his mouth; they tasted of salt and raw eggs as they slid to the back of his throat. His mind loosened until he was screaming against the diminishing crowd's prayer. Then he was floundering away from it all, stumbling through the cast-off clothes, somehow spared.

As Danny bolted back into the tunnel, he could only think of Molly and her memories: all those lives. Somehow with every step, they were unpeeling from him: the school photos; the teenager by the bed; the couple in the field; the old woman in the backyard; loading bags into her car; tending crocuses; a multitude more, until all that remained was the shell of her memory. It was the sacrifice that let him leave, he believed; but somewhere between the dark and the light, Danny came essentially to the end of his life. He wrote that without a trace of loss.

When he woke in the familiar surroundings of the psychiatric hospital that he'd left only a few months previously, he cursed Molly for sparing him. Everything was the same: the blanket of medication; the sad, vapid stares; the moments of sheer claustrophobia and panic; even the girl with the smile in the waiting room, still pissing herself after all this time. I visited him once, and he spent most of the time asking me about Sarah; but when she had left London, we had simply lost touch in those intervening years.

It was 1973 when he was released. Winter edging tentatively into spring. He loathed the diminished winter days. Dark by four p.m. He went down to the nearest tube station, but something had changed. "I no longer felt the pull," he wrote. Something was gone, or had never been there at all. Sometimes he looked for Molly, sensing that she was no longer a corpse in a Bethnal Green bedsit, but was probably back selling flowers somewhere. He couldn't find her either. Deep in his damaged mind, he felt a sense of loss; like finding that someone no longer loved you enough to keep you.

It was as if there were no more pertinent years in Danny's life. He popped up from time to time, of course. Various people would say that they'd spotted him in hostels, homeless shelters, subways at night; or hanging around his old studio in Chelsea. Apocryphal tales of his playing some notes of piano on someone's record; singing in a club with a young man purported to be his lover, playing guitar. Eventually his record company released an album of the songs he'd been working on before his suicide attempt, and bookended it with demos and live recordings. That and his debut record have stayed on catalogue ever since. There was enough residual affection and respect for him to become a myth to journalists and photographers in the music press; a cult. But there were no more letters.

AFTER MUCH DELIBERATION, Sarah and I moved in together. Our money stretched to buying a two-bedroom terrace in Primrose Hill, despite the fact that I had wanted to move from London altogether. Sarah decorated it in pastel shades, and we bought new furniture to fill it with. She found a nursing job in a psychiatric unit, just three miles down the road. Andrew stayed every other weekend, and helped us pick a sad-eyed mongrel from the Battersea pound; we called her Sash. I wrapped the letters from Danny in an elastic band, hid them in a drawer upstairs, and pretended to forget about them. We were cautiously happy.

Then one day, six months after Danny's last missive, I arrived home to find Sarah gone. I waited half the evening, then phoned the hospital. The sister in charge said that she hadn't been in work for the past week. When I woke the following morning alone, I alerted the police, and stayed in for the first few days, expecting a call, waiting for Sarah to return. Then, instinctively, I went out and down to the Underground, and travelled most of the lines for much of that day and the next. Half of me expected to find her, looking perplexed and dishevelled on a platform bench, but I didn't. I re-read Danny's letters eventually, trying to find something, some path he had taken that I could retread some thirty years on. Read without the comfort of scepticism, they terrified me all the more. And I realised too that perhaps he had known that whatever was down there was exerting its influence again, *calling* somehow.

I remembered Sarah telling me how she had woken that last night with Danny to find him stroking her hair protectively, and I realised then that the letters had never really been intended for me. They had been written at the time as a warning, but Sarah had left London and saved herself. I imagined Danny on the periphery of our lives, trying to protect us; somehow he'd known that his sister had returned, had felt that pull. Perhaps he'd thought that those old letters might still stave off the dark as Molly's lives had. But whatever their purpose, Sarah and I had failed to see them for what they were. How could we?

I often went down to the Underground in the subsequent weeks, each time with my hope a little more diminished. Nothing redeemed me, not even Andrew. I travelled aimlessly beneath London, often finding myself there at ten or eleven at night poring over the tube map, trying to plot my way back onto the Northern Line, then sitting on platforms, staring vacantly. Once I had accepted that she was gone, I wanted to feel a similar pull in me, feel my body luring me away. I started looking into the shadows for indistinct figures with their hands folding air, or a flower seller with lives to give away. It was like waiting to be loved by a stranger.

Instead I would reach our home, exhausted and empty, feed the dog, turn lights on and off, push Sarah's clothes to my face and inhale, and then dream of her all night. Sometimes I'd wake up bewildered in the small hours and find her side of the bed empty, stumble downstairs and expect to find her asleep at the kitchen table with the door ajar. But it was the wrong house, and I realised eventually that it was too late in life to continue feeling that way: waiting for the rug to be pulled, moving in circles; lost and found, lost and found.

With Deborah's assistance, I put the house back on the market and decided to move away from London. I spent several weeks in despair, indecision. Too much paperwork and too many details to finalise. I hated the nights most. I hated telling Andrew that I'd not see him as often. I had to reassure myself that I was not simply *fleeing*. Deborah never said as much, but I think she assumed I was making a drama out of it all: that Sarah had simply wised up to me and buggered off back to Birmingham. Still, who knew the truth? A mad, washed-up folk singer in his fifties, living rough? Perhaps, but I kept hearing Sarah saying *Sometimes it's only distance that saves us.* So I sold everything that she and I had bought, put the rest of it in the car, and Sash too, with her sad, wet eyes, and drove away one morning. I held Sarah in my mind for a while. Then at some point, many miles beyond London, I realised what I was doing, and let distance and time take her away from me forever.

GRENDEL'S LAIR

Paul Finch

Heorot came to symbolise all that was fine in Hrothgar's kingdom. There was music and laughter there, and a vast display of wealth and craftsmanship. Hrothgar intended it to be his legacy to the world, but there is no physical trace of it in this modern age...

THE PRISON INTERVIEW-ROOM was Spartan, its floor and walls stark grey cement, its only window a two-by-two mesh square in the high north corner. There was one table in there and two chairs, all made from plastic … though a hard, durable sort of plastic, as drab and colourless as the walls. Each item was, of course, bolted down.

At present, there were only two men in the room. They observed each other from either side of the table. One of them was in his mid-forties, lean and shaven-headed. His stained T-shirt revealed ash-pale arms which, though long and rangy, had a look of hidden strength about them. His face was ridged and bony, though it might once have been handsome … even pretty. Judging by its various pits and scars, multiple beatings had gradually disfigured it over a period of years, though the man didn't seem unduly concerned. He smoked idly, and leaned forward on his elbows. The other man was markedly different, being older and heavier, but smartly suited, with a head of preened, snow-white hair and a clipped moustache.

This older man, who was a visitor to the prison and a detective chief-superintendent by trade, began proceedings. He straightened his tie-knot, then leaned forward. "Isn't DNA wonderful?" he said.

The other man gave him a blank look. "Is it?"

The detective grinned. "It is for us. Not for you, unfortunately."

The other man gave a wry smile, as if this didn't surprise him.

"What do you think it is we've found, Grimwood?"

The man called Grimwood blew out a stream of smoke. "Another calling in life."

The chief-super chuckled. "Very good. Don't worry… I'll give you a clue. Do these three words mean anything to you? Kirsty… Ann… McGregor?"

Grimwood considered, then sniffed. "Yeah. Little girl, wasn't she? Disappeared a few years back?"

"In 1979, to be precise. Course, you know all about her."

Grimwood made a vague gesture. "Only what I've read. Sad tale."

"Very sad," the detective agreed. "Especially for her parents, who still don't know exactly what happened to her … who haven't been able to give her the decent burial she deserved."

Again Grimwood shrugged, continued to smoke.

"You don't feel anything for them at all?" the detective asked.

"Me? Why should I?"

"Because you murdered their daughter, you bastard!"

Grimwood's eyebrows lifted. "You're out of order, Laycock. I've never been convicted of murder."

"Sue me then! Let me make my case in court!"

The convict sat back in his chair. He seemed genuinely offended by the accusation.

"You see, this is where the DNA comes in, Gordon," the chief-super added. "Don't know if they let you watch TV in here, but you might've heard about new developments in technology and how we've started re-analysing old murder cases, putting together detailed biological profiles of suspects and all that." He grinned again. "Though as far as you're concerned, we didn't exactly need a profile – we've already got half a ton of your muck in test-tubes in police labs all over the country."

Grimwood stubbed his cigarette out on the table. His brutalised face was impassive, but he was clearly listening.

"It was a simple matter of compare and contrast," the policeman added. "And guess what? Guess whose DNA sample married up identically with the tiny specks of blood found on the teeth of Kirsty Ann's poor little dead poodle?"

Still the convict said nothing.

Laycock stood up. "The judge recommended you serve thirty years minimum, didn't he? After this, he'll be recommending you never come out at all."

THEY DROVE QUIETLY through the darkened town.

There were four of them in the first car, a sleek grey Jaguar, unmarked but registered to Halliwell CID. Detective Sergeant Brunton was driving. He was young, blond and bullish, and crammed tightly into a smart rugby club blazer and tie. Next to him sat Laycock. In the back, fastened into a plastic overcoat, his hands cuffed in his lap, Grimwood was experiencing his first trip beyond prison walls for fifteen years. Close beside him was the final member of the team, a firearms-response inspector called Craegan; he was currently in jeans and sweater, but of tall, military appearance. He looked more than capable of kicking all their butts put together; but just in case he couldn't, a black steel Glock SLP was holstered at his armpit.

Another vehicle travelled behind them, an unmarked Sierra, this one packed with plain-clothes HMPs. They'd insisted on coming along, but Laycock had advised them to keep a reasonable distance if they didn't want dragging to Crown Court to give evidence in a new murder trial. That had not been his real reason, of course … in truth, this was a potentially tricky case where rules might need to get bent, and he didn't want amateurs clogging up the works. But the story he'd given them had done the trick nicely; whatever happened, it was unlikely they'd interfere.

"If it's any consolation, Gordon," the chief-super said, "you've made the right decision. If we find her, it'll stand in your favour."

Grimwood glanced out at the passing houses and gardens. "Much good it'll do me."

"Maybe it'll help you sleep at night?"

"I sleep all right," the prisoner replied.

"Sure about that?" DS Brunton wondered. "Prison bunks not a tad too clean for you?"

"You can get used to anything, if you put up with it long enough," said Grimwood.

Laycock snorted. "Well, you're the living proof of that."

Grendel is described variously as a fiend, an ogre, a tormented spirit of Hell – but above all, as an outcast. He listened to the rejoicing of the Danes from his dank underground lair, and went mad with bitterness and jealousy...

THE GORDON GRIMWOOD case belonged exclusively to the 'sensational and bizarre' file. It occupied a similar position in the annals of British crime to the Yorkshire Ripper, the Black Panther and the Moors Murderers in that, horrible and revolting as its details might be, the general public couldn't get enough of it. Years after the prison door was finally slammed on Grimwood – "a disgrace to humanity", in the words of the trial judge – books were still being written on the subject, television documentaries recorded. Temperatures still rose at the mention of his name: there was lingering criticism of the police, who at the time were alleged to have bungled the investigation; while certain misguided, though some would also say 'attention-seeking', politicians, were constantly airing their view that the criminal was mad rather than bad, and should not therefore have been sent to jail at all, but to the more humane environs of a mental hospital.

The entire affair had started inauspiciously in 1972, in the industrial town of Halliwell, South Lancashire. A young woman disturbed a burglar in her flat. He was wearing an old Parka coat and a scarf over his nose and mouth. Instead of running, however, the burglar punched the girl in the face and then kicked her unconscious as she lay on the floor. Three nights later, he struck again in Tulip Drive, a neighbouring street. This incident was even more serious: a mother of two, whose husband was away on the night-shift, awoke around one-thirty in the morning to find a man in her bedroom. Again, he was dressed in an old Parka coat and had a scarf around his face. An unprovoked attack then followed, the intruder raping the woman and badly beating her. Throughout her ordeal, he also insulted her in the filthiest language … calling her "a whore" and "a slattern", and saying that this was what she deserved.

Despite later frustration, the initial police response was swift and efficient. Detectives deduced that the assailant was a local man, as he'd clearly had prior knowledge about his victim's husband. This line of enquiry was given credence when the woman aired a suspicion that she recognised his voice. With some persuasion, she finally named Gordon Grimwood, a young workmate of her husband's, who lived with his elderly mother only five doors away. Checks with the factory where Grimwood was employed confirmed that the suspect had been absent on sick-leave on both nights when the offences took place.

When officers arrived at Grimwood's home address, however, there was no trace of him. His mother, who as well as being elderly was also an invalid, reported that she hadn't seen him for several days. The house was searched, but no clue was found as to Grimwood's whereabouts. From that moment on, a constant watch was maintained on the property, but the suspect did not return. By the end of that year, the conclusion was reluctantly drawn that he'd gone abroad.

There was something of a development in 1975, when a schoolgirl was accosted on nearby spoil-land, indecently assaulted and savagely beaten, though on this occasion the description of the assailant in no way matched the youthful labourer detectives had wanted to question three years earlier. This latest victim described her attacker as being dirty and ragged, with long hair and a straggling beard. As a result, no immediate association was made between the cases, though this new and even more frightening figure was to reappear again and again over the next few years. In fact, nobody knew it then, but a reign of terror had begun.

By 1980, the maniac had struck at least twenty times – not just in Halliwell, but in neighbouring towns and even beyond the county borders in Merseyside and Greater Manchester. With each sighting, he grew more ghoulish to look at … being ever hairier, dirtier and more bestial; on one occasion, he was described as "resembling an animal rather than a man". The ferocity of his crimes also intensified; rape seemed to be his prime motive, usually accompanied by a ferocious bare-handed battery, though by this stage he had also graduated to humiliation and robbery, stripping his victims of their clothes and valuables, and leaving them bound and naked. It was through no effort of his that none of the women died, though several were mauled to the very brink of death. Suspicion was also growing that the disappearance of six-year-old Kirsty Ann McGregor, who went to infant school in Halliwell, might have something to do with this 'Beast of Lancashire', as the newspapers were now calling him.

A major police response was by this time in progress, a special squad drawn from various forces having been assigned to catch the psychopath; but stunningly little ground was made. This was still the pre-computerised age, and the filing and assessment of such a colossal mass of evidence caused more problems than it solved, while the capture of other 'real murderers' was still the prime concern for CID departments across the North of England. Ironically, when the culprit was finally arrested, it had nothing to do with any CID officer, either divisional or 'task-force'. It was the spring of 1984, and a student, having arrived home from university for her Easter break, was walking through a Halliwell park when a stinking and heavily-bearded man jumped out at her. The girl was prepared for this, however. She pulled a flick-knife from her coat pocket and stabbed the molester twice. He staggered away in silence, but left a very visible trail of blood, which twenty minutes later a police dog was pursuing. Incredibly, the trail led back to a house that detectives had already visited several times during the course of the enquiry ... 41 Tulip Drive, the home of Mary Grimwood, mother of the long-missing sex-offender Gordon Grimwood.

From this point on, sensation followed sensation. While officers turned the little house upside-down, the elderly lady who lived there suddenly became foul-mouthed and struck at one of them with a knitting-needle, an incident that led to her being arrested herself and later sectioned in a secure ward. After this, the search went on with even greater thoroughness; and though it uncovered bloodstains in the kitchen, where an injured person had clearly tried to tend himself, there was little else. Only when an officer made a casual remark to a colleague that "they'll have to bring in the bulldozers next", did the case finally break. To everyone's astonishment, the carpet in the lounge suddenly lifted, and from under the floorboards emerged a ghastly vision. It was Gordon Grimwood ... not that he was recognisable as such at the time. He stank to high Heaven, and his clothes, which were little more than dirt-blackened tatters, were infested with lice – as were his hair and beard, both of which hung in dense, oily masses. What was more, he was badly hurt: two knife-wounds, which he'd been unable to staunch, had leaked a copious amount of blood; and fearing death more than incarceration, the rapist had finally opted to give himself up.

The horror didn't end there, however. A search of the crawlspace under the house revealed a cave-like den where the fugitive had dwelt for the past twelve years, hidden from the world and only emerging to gratify his violent and perverted lusts. It was a squalid, filthy hole, strewn with a foul detritus of half-eaten food, drinks cartons and scattered cigarette butts. Several reeking slop-buckets swam with human waste and crawled with vermin. There was also a large supply of dog-eared reading matter – old newspapers and paperback books, not to mention a hefty supply of hardcore pornography.

The revelation that Grimwood had been living in the very midst of the community he'd terrorised for so long not only led to scandal and recrimination among investigating police teams, who were accused of everything from criminal negligence to rampant misogyny, but caused nationwide revulsion … the physical state of the man, the conditions he'd been found inhabiting, the apparent compliance of his outwardly decent parent, all combined to create an astonishing news story that sent shock-waves across the country…

For twelve years Heorot was subjected to a non-stop assault by Grendel, whose only solace was to create as much horror and despair as he could. So evil would their memory be of his depredations that for ever afterwards, night would be a thing of terror to Hrothgar's people…

EVERY NEWSPAPER LED on the Grimwood case for weeks; one particularly enterprising Fleet Street journal even managed to get hold of a police photograph of the criminal's subterranean refuge, and plastered it across the front page. The paper headlined its scoop: THE BEAST'S LAIR.

Not that the place looked especially scary or even mysterious on the night Laycock's Jag pulled quietly up at the front of it. To all intents and purposes, it was another red-brick house in a typical terraced street ... a street now largely derelict, in fact. The only movement was the fluttering of litter in the rubble-strewn gutters. Few lights were visible.

Grimwood, closely accompanied by his escorts, climbed from the car. He gazed at his surroundings as if bewildered.

"What's the matter?" Brunton wondered. "Surprised there's no crowd here to meet you? Lucky for you – they'd have brought tar and feathers. We've had to keep it well quiet."

"I'm more surprised about the mill," Grimwood replied.

Brunton looked nonplussed. "What mill?"

The rapist nodded to the skyline, now empty and black. In his youth, the towering Victorian structure of Myrtle & Son had dominated the neighbourhood like a fortress. It seemed impossible that something so huge and cruel could have been demolished in as short a time as fifteen years.

"Hardly matters to you, does it?" said Brunton irritably. "Come on, we haven't got all night."

Grimwood turned. "Any chance of a cig first?"

The DS snorted in contempt. "Your lungs must be like ash-pits."

"Yeah, well they're *my* lungs. Come on, you promised."

The criminal had had a nicotine dependency since boyhood, which now provided a nice carrot for them to dangle. Needless to say, they weren't trusting him with matches, cigarettes or anything else at present ... not while he was on the outside. Brunton was carrying all the necessaries. Grudgingly, he reached into his jacket, but Laycock stopped him.

"We did promise you, Gordon, you're right," the chief-super said. "But you promised us too." He nodded towards the nearest house. "We'll see Kirsty Ann before we get the smokes out."

Grimwood gazed at the place that had once been his home. Its brick frontage was sorely dilapidated: the long-broken window had been nailed across with planks; the door was old and scabby, the paint coming off it in long strips, though the number 41 was still visible in tarnished brass.

"I take it no-one's lived here since?" the prisoner said.

"Not likely," Laycock replied. He produced a key. "Hardly an investment, is it?"

"People have a thing about houses where nutters used to hang out," Brunton added.

"That's right," said the chief-super. "Worried they'll end up like those poor sods who moved into Christie's place. Where was it, Baz?"

Brunton shrugged.

"Rillington Place," put in Craegan.

It was the first time the firearms man had spoken, and they all looked at him. He didn't appear to be sharing the two detectives' dark humour, but Grimwood suspected this had nothing to do with sympathy for their prisoner. Creagan had a long, thin face, with a mouth like a steel trap and eyes as big and cold as ice cubes. He was gazing at the convict intensely, as if he fancied a spot of target-practice right at that moment.

"That's it," said Laycock. "Ten, Rillington Place. You remember, Gordon? They'd been in half a day and there were bodies flopping out the cupboards. That how you see yourself? Christie and his like?"

"I was never convicted of murder," the rapist replied quietly.

The chief-super unlocked the front door and pushed it open. Stale odours wafted out. "No – but you're not worried by it either, are you? I mean, why else agree to bring us here?" He stepped inside. "It's all part of the fun for blokes like you, isn't it … the darkness, the spookiness?" He flicked his torch on; it showed bare floorboards, peeling wallpaper. "Course, it's just an act," he added. "You know what the girls used to call Christie behind his back? Reggie No-Dick. Fred West, he was another. He used to advertise for studs to come and fuck his wife, because he couldn't keep up with her himself."

"And what about you, Laycock?" Grimwood suddenly asked. "What kind of legend do you want to be?"

The detective looked sharply round. For a moment he seemed surprised that someone had dared challenge him. It was certainly the first time their prisoner had spoken his mind. And he didn't stop there.

"I bet there was no holding you back when this one came up,

was there?" he added. "Fancied crowning your career, did you? Or maybe making your career? Maybe your career's been so shit, you needed something like this!"

A hand took the nape of his neck ... it was Craegan's. "You mouthy bastard!" he snarled, shoving Grimwood into the house.

"Thought you'd be the man who broke the Lancashire Beast, eh?" the convict sniggered. He was thrown backwards against a wall. "Even though you had nothing to do with catching him…"

A rock-hard punch slammed into his guts and drove the wind from him. He doubled over with a gasp, but someone snatched his collar and yanked him upright again. Then a cold and circular object pressed into his temple. Grimwood didn't need to see the torchlight gleam on the slick steel barrel to know it was the muzzle of the Glock firm in Craegan's grip. The torch now appeared beside it, glaring into his eyes. Behind it, Laycock's head was suddenly a featureless mass.

"Your mates from Durham are sitting in their car about two hundred yards down the road, playing cards and taking the piss," the chief-super said in a low but tremulous monotone. "You know what that means, Grimwood? It means we've got free rein. It means they don't give a fuck about you. Nobody does. Whatever the prison shrinks say, bastards like you are fucking scum and beyond the law." He clamped the convict's throat in a fat, hairy hand. "Do you get me, son?"

"Some hero you are," Grimwood choked.

Laycock squeezed his throat even harder. "There's no such thing as heroes. Only people like us … me and you. So let's cut the bullshit and understand one another. You are going to take us to the body of Kirsty Ann McGregor. And afterwards, you are going to confess in detail to how you murdered and probably – you disgusting pig – raped her! Now this is not lynch-law or backstreet justice, or whatever else you and your do-gooding politician friends like to call it. I *know* you killed that child, and you *know* I *know*."

A second passed, and the chief-super released his grip. "If it makes you feel any better, though, Gordon … yeah you're right, I just want a fucking result. But if you know anything about coppers at all, you'll know that's all the more reason not to fucking disappoint me!"

Hrothgar is referred to as a 'ring-giver'; in other words, he amply rewarded loyal service. It is impossible to disassociate Beowulf from this. In the Viking tradition, courage in battle was a self-fulfilling prophecy, but gifts and glory were always expected...

THE MEN STOOD back as Brunton produced a pry-bar, fitted it under the first floorboard and, with some effort, cracked it loose. Several more followed, until a gaping hole yawned before them. Strong torchlight revealed that it wasn't the chasm it appeared to be, however. It was perhaps four feet deep and ran the length of the room; its floor was beaten dirt, and now alive with cockroaches scurrying to escape the powerful beam. A dank earthy smell, which was actually no worse than the stench pervading the rest of the abandoned house, drifted slowly upwards.

Laycock snorted. "The Beast's Lair... I ask you." He glowered at Grimwood. "If only those hacks knew the truth about blokes like you. Worst thing we ever did in this country was abolish public executions. At least in those days people got to see what snivelling wretches you lot are. Locking you up in solitary just adds to the mystique, doesn't it?"

Grimwood said nothing. He stared down into the crawlspace, as if trying to remember something.

"I hope you haven't forgotten where you put her," the chief-super added, suddenly suspicious. "Not after bringing us all this way."

The rapist glanced at him. "I'll need to get down and look."

Laycock stepped aside. "Be our guest."

Grimwood was about to jump when the muzzle of the revolver jammed into his spine. "Don't think about trying anything," Craegan advised. "I'll blow you in fucking half."

The convict nodded, then leaped into the hole and crouched down to shuffle out of sight under the remaining floorboards. Laycock handed Brunton the torch. "Go with him, Baz."

The burly DS did as he was told. A few moments later, he was hunkered down beside Grimwood, his flashlight reflecting off loose and aged brickwork.

Grimwood patted it, then sat back and raised his foot. "This isn't part of the foundation wall," he said. "It looks like it, but it isn't. I discovered this when I was a lad."

And he rammed his foot forward... once, twice, three times. At first the bricks resisted, only dust trickling down, though with the third blow their positions visibly altered. Encouraged, Grimwood tried again, this time harder ... until at last, one by one, the bricks dislodged and fell through into darkness. Their mortar had long ago crumbled to powder, and a jagged cavity was now visible that was large enough for a man to climb through.

"What's going on?" Laycock asked from above.

"There's more space down here than we thought, Boss," Brunton replied. He turned to Grimwood. "What's through there?"

"I'll show you."

The rapist made to clamber forwards, but the sergeant stopped him. "Just a minute. Boss! You'd best get down and have a look at this!"

With some grunting, and no little sweating in the confined and dusty space, Laycock and Craegan joined them.

"It's the old air-raid shelters," Grimwood explained. "From Myrtle & Son. They were derelict even when I was a kid ... hadn't been used for ten years. But this is how I used to get in and out of our house without anyone seeing."

Laycock stared through the hole. The torchlight illuminated a passage beyond it, with a facing wall of bare concrete. "Are you telling me the original investigation team didn't find this?"

Grimwood shook his head.

"Fucking woodentops," Brunton muttered.

The rapist glanced at him, amused. "You wouldn't have found it, if I hadn't shown you."

"Shut the fuck up!"

"See if you can get through, Barry," Laycock put in.

Nodding but still scowling at Grimwood, the big sergeant bent forwards and, inch by inch, squeezed his bulk through the aperture. He swore aloud as something snagged and ripped his jacket; but a minute or so later, he was standing up on the other side. "It seems all right," he said, his voice now hollow and echoing. "Bloody cold, though. And watch the step – it's about a foot and a half down."

Craegan prodded Grimwood in the back. "You next."

The rapist complied, followed by the firearms expert and then the chief-superintendent.

The air-raid shelter had a more 'underground' feel to it than the crawlspace: dank and cool, with the sounds of dripping water in its farthest depths. It was comprised mainly of identical passages, each one made from concrete and wide enough only for two men to walk abreast. In that classic 1930s style, the ceilings were all smoothly arched, though many were also riddled with fractures or had actually fallen in, strewing the floorway with rubble and masonry. None of this seemed to put Grimwood off ... boldly, he started walking. The cops shuffled warily in pursuit, dense blackness hemming them in from both front and rear. Even the strong torch shone for only twenty or thirty yards ahead.

"You know our radios won't work down here, don't you?" Craegan said quietly.

Laycock grimaced. Immediately, he fished his PR from his pocket and tried to call Halliwell Comms. Only dead airwaves came back, however. He also tried his mobile phone, punching out the direct line to the CID office. Again, there was no response.

He shrugged. "Don't need it anyway, do we? Not like we're a bunch of birds who this arsehole can beat up and stick his dick in."

They pressed on through what, it was rapidly becoming clear, was a labyrinth. There were numerous turn-offs – some that they took, others that they ignored – and several complex junctions. One open space even had a table and a couple of very old school-chairs in it; in faded red letters, on a high portion of wall, the wording 'ASSEMBLY AREA TWO' was stencilled. The group waited there for a moment, while Grimwood tried to get his bearings.

"Used to know this place like the back of my hand," he said quietly. "Newspapers thought I spent twelve years under my mum's lounge." He snorted, as if in derision. "No chance ... not when I had all this to explore."

"How far does it go?" Laycock asked, trying to modulate his voice.

The chief-super didn't want to admit it, but he suddenly felt as if he'd lost the initiative. They'd only been walking two or three minutes, and he was already unsure about the way back. The atmosphere was also getting to him … the chill, the damp, the enclosed nature of the place. Laycock didn't suffer from claustrophobia; but it wasn't pleasant to contemplate the many layers of rock and soil above, largely – from what he could see – without any form of support.

Grimwood moved on, taking the second of two right-hand passages. "Quite a distance," he replied. "There used to be ways up to the surface, but they all got blocked with cement to stop kids getting in."

"Where the fuck are you taking us to?" Brunton asked. He was still coming the heavy, but the eyes were now darting about rabbit-like in his red, pudgy face.

"We're almost there," the convict answered, a curious half-smile twisting his mouth.

A few minutes later they entered an area of tunnel more heaped with debris than anything they'd so far seen; huge sections of its roof and walls had long ago collapsed. In consequence, this space was the tightest and dingiest yet. A black fungus coated the damp and rotted fragments of wall that were still visible… It seemed to leach away what minuscule light there was, and fuelled the sensation that the party had now burrowed down to the very deepest point of the air-raid shelters. In that respect, the fact that Grimwood suddenly stopped to think, then chuckled and hunkered down, and with his cuffed hands began to scoop bricks and dirt away from the piled rubble, filled the three cops with something like revulsion.

"Can you imagine," Craegan said slowly, "this slimy little toe-rag brought a child down here!" His gun was trained firmly on the rapist's back; sweat gleamed on his pallid face.

Laycock glanced warily at the firearms man. "That's behind him now though, isn't it? Eh… Gordon?"

Grimwood made no reply.

"Confession's good for the soul," Laycock added.

"So's prison," Craegan said, his voice steadily rising. "Too good. He should've been strung up for what he did!"

Grimwood ignored him and continued to dig.

"Easy, Craegan," Laycock advised.

"Easy?" For the first time, the firearms man looked round at the chief-super. "Easy? *He's* had it easy … for way too long!"

They didn't notice the convict suddenly stand up, or see him brush a few crumbs of dirt from the long, heavy screwdriver with the sharpened tip that he'd just extricated from the heap of rubble. Even when Grimwood turned stiffly to face them, the weapon clasped horizontal but handle-first against his stomach, they were too nonplussed to register the imminent threat.

"What are you playing a–" Brunton was in the process of saying when the criminal suddenly thrust the spike forwards and up, plunging it hard into Craegan's left eye, driving it virtually to the hilt.

There was a millisecond of stunned silence before the firearms man tottered backwards against the passage wall. The other two officers reacted explosively. Laycock gave a wild shout, Brunton threw a massive punch. Grimwood had been expecting this, however, and ducked to the ground, the sergeant's heavy fist thus impacting on his own chief superintendent's nose, smashing it and hurling him off his feet.

"You shit-arse!" Brunton screamed.

Craegan had begun to shoot. Not because he was acting professionally and following his detailed training. But because he was already dead from acute brain damage, and his finger was locked on the Glock's trigger. As his legs buckled and he slid lifelessly down the wall, the revolver went off repeatedly in his hand. Shots started to ricochet, screaming left and right – and punching three neat holes in Detective Sergeant Brunton's barrel chest. The policeman dropped like a stone, the flashlight falling from his grasp.

The deafening echoes of the fusillade took several seconds to die away. When they finally did, Laycock was still on the ground, half-dazed. Only when he looked weakly up again did it suddenly strike him where he was and what peril he was in. Grimwood was crouching a matter of five or six yards away, watching in predatory silence, his battered face written with jack-o-lantern glee. Laycock's blood ran cold … especially when he spotted the Glock. It was lying right beside the psychopath; in fact, Grimwood was reaching down for it at that very moment. The chief-super froze, went bug-eyed…

Then he moved, as fast as he could, diving for the dropped flashlight and switching it off, plunging them both into Stygian blackness.

There was a moment of complete quiet … not a scrape of a shoe, not even a breath. Laycock was still on his hands and knees. His clothes clung like a second skin to his sweat-sodden body. His nose stung abominably – clearly it was broken, but he knew he couldn't risk even a whimper. Grimwood needed only to pick up the gun and start firing. He had a few shots left, and then he might possess sense enough to rifle Craegan's pockets for spare clips.

Then there was a sound … a rasping chuckle. And a voice. It was Grimwood's, soft and spooky and taunting: "I told you fifty times, Laycock, that I wasn't a murderer … well, now you've made me one. Congratulations."

The detective tried to shift backwards. He was way too close to the madman for comfort.

"Where do you think you're going?" Grimwood asked. "There's about two miles of interconnecting tunnels down here. Even with your torch, you won't find your way out."

Laycock bit his lip, but the pain and fear were overwhelming and suddenly he couldn't resist replying. "You won't get away with this, you bastard!"

Grimwood's chuckle rose into a throaty laugh. "Laycock… I never get away with anything. In fact, I've spent most of my life getting leathered. I've had it off you sons of bitches, off the screws at Durham, I've even had it off my fellow inmates. Not that I can't handle it… I mean before all this started, I was getting it off my Mum, who regretted the day I was born and cursed the sin that brought me to her." The laugh faded again, into something darker, more bitter. "I couldn't even look at a girl, never mind bring one home, without the stick coming out, or the belt, or the fucking fire-poker. Course, it was when she used to press my hand against the scalding kettle that it really got unpleasant…"

"But what do you think you're going to achieve with this?" the cop asked, using the conversation to mask the crunch of bricks as he rose cautiously to his feet.

Grimwood mused. "Oh… a moment's pleasant distraction. That's all I've ever wanted, really."

Panic-stricken thoughts rushed through the detective's head. If he turned and legged it, would the maniac give immediate chase or did he still need to find the weapon? Laycock hadn't actually seen the bastard pick it up, which meant he might have to scrabble about in the dark for a minute or two. That could create a sufficient time-differential in which to reach the outside world. It was risky, to say the least, but what other option was there?

The killer seemed to be reading his mind, however. "Just remember," he sneered, "when you run. Apart from where we came in, all the other exits and entrances have been sealed off. Run blindly, and you could easily end up at some dead end. Which will be quite appropriate."

"Fuck you!" the cop hissed.

"Defiant to the end. Or just pig-ignorant?" Grimwood began to titter. "Get it? *Pig*-ignorant?"

Laycock backed away, then turned and began to stumble along the passage. Immediately, rubble got in the way of his feet, cobwebs trailed in his face ... but he was determined not to switch on the flashlight, not yet. He would steer by the walls, both of which he could touch with his outstretched hands.

"I'll give you a count of five," Grimwood called after him. "One, two..."

"Help!" Laycock shouted. "Someone ... help me please!"

"Don't waste your breath!" the rapist laughed. "You're ten feet under and about fifty yards from the nearest road. Even those lazy-arsed HMPs can't hear you. Three, four..."

The detective reached a corner and staggered around it. His heart was now banging against his ribs; sweat streamed off him. He wasn't even vaguely fit, he realised; he hadn't done a spot of real exercise for twenty years or more ... wouldn't be able to play hide 'n' seek with his grand-kids, let alone manage something like this. Maybe the same rule applied to Grimwood, but Laycock didn't believe it. The guy looked thin but not wasted; perhaps he'd been working out in jail. Even if he hadn't, he was the one who'd once spent twelve years down here. He'd know it blindfolded.

"Coming!" came a cheerful shout from somewhere behind.

The cop stopped in his tracks, panting hard, thoughts racing. Did he switch the light on yet? No ... it would be a total give-away.

He blundered desperately on, turning another corner, realising he was already taking passages at random rather than trying to remember the way out, but keeping going all the same because at present, only putting distance between himself and Grimwood would save his life.

Then he smashed into a concrete wall.

The pain of it was shocking. The chief-super's already shattered nose was flattened against his face; there was a hammer-blow to his forehead, a searing flash behind his eyes. Worse than any of this, however, his torch took the brunt of the collision and virtually exploded in his hand. Laycock slumped to the ground, stunned, fresh hot fluid trickling over his lips, but thinking only of the flashlight. When he was suitably *compos mentis*, he groped around for it, finally laying his fingers on a hunk of crumpled metal and broken glass.

He wanted to yowl out in despair, but didn't ... because now he heard someone approaching. Footfalls, definitely footfalls, coming steadily nearer; and not in a tentative, fumbling fashion the way his had been, but strong, sure. Laycock crouched in the blackness, holding his breath. The footsteps were almost upon him. The cop closed his eyes tightly, even though it was already impossible to see anything. The wild thought occurred to him to snatch up some half-brick or lump of masonry, and go immediately onto the attack. But with the convict armed, that would surely be suicide. Best just to hunker down and wait for the inevitable.

Though the inevitable didn't come straight away.

The approaching feet, which were making no apparent effort to conceal themselves, tramped heavily past the end of the passage; and though they might have faltered there for a moment – as if their owner had suddenly halted to listen – they were soon fading away again into the distance.

Laycock opened his eyes warily. Obsidian darkness still cloaked everything, but now he felt a vague hope. Over-confidence might be the psychopath's undoing. And why not? The detective didn't have a sportsman's physique any more, but he had thirty years' police experience under his belt, and had dealt effectively with a wide range of dangerous criminals. If Grimwood thought he was dealing with

Mickey Mouse, he'd be in for a shock.

The chief-super strained his ears again for a moment to ensure the killer had moved on, then dug out his phone and radio, trying to make contact on them one more time. Both devices were still dead. He returned them to his pocket, grim but not too distressed. He'd expected as much.

Grendel's death was significant in more ways than one. When Beowulf tore off his arm, he fled into the night wailing, and was therefore deemed, at heart, to be a coward. There was a double-bluff in the poet's words, however; when the monster's arm was nailed to the overhead beam, it was still so large and hideous that the King's hearth-men could only shudder with fear when they gazed at it...

IT WAS DIFFICULT enough walking, but walking quietly was a virtual impossibility. Within two or three minutes, Laycock had all but given up and was stumping his way along, slapping his hands on the walls, scattering rubble with his feet. He could only pray that he found the exit to the empty house soon. As far as he could remember, when they'd first come in they'd made a left, then a right, then a left, then a right, then another right ... something like that at least. He swallowed dust as he progressed. It also coated his body, adhering thickly to his seeping sweat. Of course ... all those directions would now need to be reversed. In which case, did that mean it was a left, then a left, then a right? His thoughts tailed off maddeningly. What if he'd missed a turn? Had they ignored certain passages?

The voice of rising panic was telling him that this was a lost cause, that he would never be able to find his way out of such a maze even in broad daylight. Instinctively he took a sharp left, but a second later was slogging through ankle-deep water. He backtracked and took a right. This way seemed clearer, but now there were openings to both left and right. Laycock ventured into some, others he bypassed ... there was no reason or logic behind any of it. He knew the position was hopeless. He wanted to shout again, to scream even, but now there was another problem.

He couldn't be sure, but just for a second then he'd fancied he heard something. He stopped in his tracks and listened intently. Almost certainly this place was crawling with rats, and that might explain what had just sounded distinctly like the soft patter of footsteps. It *might*.

The detective's spine began to prickle. Hurriedly he pushed on, darting down any corridor he came across. He was almost running, but continued to trip and slide on the endless heaps of debris. Eventually, the agonising thump of his heart and the near-total exhaustion that wracked his untrained body brought him to another halt. He was sobbing for breath, the echoes of his flight still dying away in the adjoining passages. Nevertheless, he heard it again. This time there was no mistake … footfalls were encroaching from somewhere behind.

With a strangled gasp, Laycock set off as quickly as he could; but now he was hobbling and grunting with effort. At one point he fell full-length, ripping the knees of his trousers and the skin beneath. Even as he clambered up and staggered on, the feet sounded closer … *much* closer and far less cautious, as though concealing the sound of their approach was no longer a priority. Blood pounded in the policeman's ears, sweat dribbled stingingly into his eyes. He rounded corner after corner, for several minutes enjoying phenomenal luck in that he didn't actually collide with anything. Inevitably, a moment later … that luck ran out.

Laycock went head over heels on some heavy but yielding object that lay across his path. His chin struck concrete, and for several moments he was too dizzy to realise what it was he'd fallen over. At length, he came back to himself … and tensed sharply, sitting wildly up, his ears straining for the slightest sound. Weirdly, however, there was now only silence. A second passed, then another, finally several. Still there was nothing. Had he eluded his pursuer? Thrown him off track with his wild zig-zagging through the corridors? Laycock hardly dared believe it, but eventually a minute had passed and still there was no noise.

Warily, he reached out and felt around him. As he suspected, the thing he'd tripped over was a dead body … either Brunton or Craegan. The chief-super groped further. It was slumped against the side of the passage, as if seated, which meant it was Craegan. He was the one who had died in that posture. Then something struck Laycock. The *spike* or *screwdriver*, or whatever it was that had killed the poor bastard! It might still be there. He knelt up, suddenly enthused. It would be a crude and brutal sort of weapon; but he'd seen for himself how effective it could be, and anything was better than nothing.

As hurriedly as he dared, but also rather gingerly, he felt at the pulverised mask that had once been the firearms expert's face. It was icy to the touch, and damp and lifeless as clay. It was also covered in crusty streaks. Laycock wanted to yank his hand back immediately, but managed to swallow his revulsion and continued to probe; and a second later, to his relief, he felt his fingers alight on the heavy, jutting handle of the screwdriver. It remained exactly where Grimwood had embedded it.

Initially, however, the thing wouldn't even budge. Laycock first tried to work it loose, but it was much too secure. Then he hauled at it, only succeeding in pulling Craegan forwards, the cold body slumping down onto its front. With some effort, the chief-super heaved it back. Even now, after so many years in the job, it never ceased to amaze him how heavy a dead man could be. A second passed as he regained his breath, then he stood up and tried a different tack. He placed a foot on Craegan's left shoulder, took the screwdriver in both hands and tugged as hard as he could, leaning backwards to add his own weight to the effort. For a moment or two, the wretched thing remained wedged in place; then, unexpectedly, it moved an inch. Laycock tottered and almost fell, but quickly repositioned himself; and bracing his foot against the corpse again – this on time its face – he tried once more. With a gurgle of blood and grating of bone, the blade slid free.

The detective hunkered down, panting. The tool clanked on the concrete floor; it was slimed and sticky in his grasp. For once, the all-consuming darkness was doing him a favour, Laycock realised. He didn't want to see that long steel shaft now coated with Craegan's red and black gore. He didn't especially want to see Craegan either – the bloke's left eye a raw, bottomless pit; or the shattered corpse of Barry Brunton – his chest cross-stitched with bullet-holes.

Then something else struck the chief-super... Brunton! Hadn't the young sergeant been carrying cigarettes for Grimwood? Cigarettes ... *and matches?*

Laycock wanted to jump up immediately, to hurl himself on the body and loot its pockets, but he resisted. That could prove fatal. While light might show him a way out, it might also invite another attack. Having said that, of course, it was uncertain how far into these entwined passages a flickering match-glow would penetrate. The detective listened again. The silence was still total. The thought began to occur to him that the killer might have left the air-raid shelters altogether. That would make sense of a sort. Wouldn't he be seeking freedom rather than an ongoing confrontation with the police?

Encouraged by this, the chief-super fumbled around until he found Brunton's feet and legs. Hastily, he worked his way up the body, grimacing when he encountered the coagulated pulp of the sergeant's chest, but not put off to the degree that he couldn't then rummage around inside the corpse's jacket. The cigarettes and matches were practically the first things he found, both stowed in the left breast-pocket. He extricated the smaller box, and shook it ... it rattled. Relieved, he opened it and took out a couple of sticks, then paused to listen. As before, no sound.

Laycock considered. His prime concern was getting out of this mess alive; but even if he managed that, he'd be in for a torrid time. Thanks to his bungling, they'd say, two officers were dead and one of Britain's most dangerous criminals now back on the loose. How he was going to explain it, he wasn't quite sure. He spent a moment wondering to what extent he himself was wounded. If he re-emerged from the tunnels with significant injuries, it would reduce the amount of ridicule they could heap on him, not to mention the blame; he might even be proclaimed a hero. Of course, the truth was that he wasn't wounded, apart from a broken nose and a few cuts and bruises. There might be something he could do about that when he got topside again, though he didn't much like the idea. Still, desperate times called for desperate measures. So thinking, Laycock struck a bunch of matches. For a second, the flare was astonishingly bright, dazzling him, but not to the extent that he didn't immediately spot Gordon Grimwood ... standing only a few feet away.

Laycock felt his jaw drop. In the sharp light, the maniac was ghostlike … pale as ice, smiling serenely, still spattered with the blood of the men he had slain. He was also carrying Craegan's gun, and now slowly raising and pointing it. Almost without thinking, the cop lunged out with the screwdriver – as hard and straight as he could.

It was about the luckiest moment of Jim Laycock's life. Grimwood, the Beast of Lancashire, an expert stalker and hunter of humans, had made only one mistake in his rapacious career, and now he made it again: a failure to consider that his prey might be armed. Even as he stood there, gloating, the steel spike struck his midriff and tore its way in, sinking to well over half its length.

The rapist's expression turned first to one of amazement, then to one of disbelieving pain. With a silent shriek, he fell heavily backwards, clamping the screwdriver hilt with both hands, though the tool was firmly lodged under his ribs. Only a feat of great physical strength would remove it, and Grimwood no longer had strength of any description. As he clasped the weapon, hot, dark liquid began to leak through his fingers.

Laycock tottered back, breathing heavily, nauseous with shock. For all the things he'd seen and done, he still wanted to block out this image of death by slow torture, to slap a hand to his face or turn away, or at least to close his eyes. But he did none of these. He was too numbed, too exhausted. Wearily, he slumped against the wall and struck a few more matches. He knew that at any moment these too would burn down and flicker out, and then he'd be in Stygian blackness again. But at least the danger was past. At least he needed only to blunder his way back to the surface. After this, he doubted anything would ever seem frightening again.

Then he was struck from behind. In the very middle of his cranium.

It was a terrible blow, delivered with such monstrous force that the detective knew his skull was broken even as he pitched face-down into the rubble.

The fact that two misshapen beings walked the dark, one of them female, was a shocking revelation. In Norse society, women were chattels and had no say in political events. The death of an adventuring hero like Aeschere at the hands of Grendel's mother was totally unprecedented...

"YOU... YOU DIED..." Laycock whispered as he gazed up at the thing that had dragged him over onto his back, "... in Broadmoor..."

She still clutched a half-brick, heavily caked with hair, blood and brain-matter. Clearly, she'd intended to use it again, but now there didn't seem any point. A piece of rag was burning on the ground by the policeman's head, though the light was rapidly fading from his eyes – which, horribly, were leaking blood from their tear-ducts. Red trickles were also visible from his ears. His entire body was frozen in a spasmodic twist.

Instead of dealing the death-blow herself, the apparition simply crouched there and watched; and even in the last seconds of his life, Jim Laycock had sufficient intellect to be appalled by the sight of her. Her once-human form was shrivelled and skeletal, and hung with the filthiest rags imaginable; her hair was a hanging mane of dirt-encrusted rat-tails, her raddled face a mass of warts and open sores. If there was any sanity at all behind her rheumy eyes, Laycock would have been astounded; but as his last vestige of consciousness slipped away, she gave some indication of that, for her gammy, toothless mouth curved slowly up into a hideous mocking smile.

Once the policeman had died, the hag moved along the passage and finally settled down beside Grimwood. She took his head into her lap and started petting it. The rag had now burned itself out, and total blackness again filled the passage. Not that Grimwood needed light in these circumstances. He'd had so few friends in his life that he would never forget their touch, their smell...

"You ... waited," he stammered. "All this ... time." Her hooked fingers were almost gentle as she clawed the hair back from his sweat-sodden brow. The simple effort of speaking was agony to him, but he was determined to try. "I... I told them, you know. I... I'm no murderer." He shook his head. "Never was."

He knew she'd be smiling kindly on him, fondly ... the fondness that only exists between parent and child.

He coughed up blood as she kissed him goodbye. "My lovely ... Kirsty ... Ann..."

FROM THE HEARTH
DF Lewis

ONLY THOSE WHO follow the story can understand how frightening is the road they tread. Susanna understood this when it was too late. Following the road, she found it became a tunnel where the sky was worse than Hell.

Today, though, she often wondered why the actual road where she lived was lower than the rest of them in an otherwise flat Essex town. Whilst standing at its top corner, she could still see a range of chimneystacks sloping down into distance. Perspective was everything. Even the past had perspective.

She was a wild-witted girl of whom advantage could easily have been taken, had it not been, in those more innocent times, for an over-protective step-father. An industrial working-class town where heads often nested in honestly Persil-clean pillows, heads that sweetly squeaked and squawked, pretending that their bodies only existed for fondling. Susanna's family was close-knit half the time, wildly ill-suited the rest. Dysfunction with a purpose. They tried to thrive on leisure, despite the work ethic that awaited them once they crossed the threshold of the front doorstep straight on to the blurred chalk of the road's hopscotch lines. Susanna's menfolk drew dole as if it were a throwaway sky-line where even angels (with oodles of self-righteousness) floated around painting pastel-shaded frescos upon otherwise ugly weather fronts.

Tom was her half-brother. Grizzled and grown-down to a tussock from a promising start as a stripling. Pamela her real mother. And, yes, her step-dad, Donald, the one with the wide whiskers and wraparound beer brims. His hat, too, was larger than life. Played the snooker balls as if they were dam busters. Which reminded Susanna that Tom was currently outside in the road, scuffing his best shoes with yet another game of football amid his gnarled cronies of childhood. Often kicking around a bristly youth called Hugger or, if Hugger were not available, a knurled mini-millstone – enough to jar even willowy calf-bones.

Susanna had only a few god-given graces. Anyway, lacking a finish to her breeding began to serve a purpose when her best friend happened to become a certain Lucy, a coincidentally separate individual, albeit one with sufficient similarity to engender inseparability. Lucy was a red-eyed droopy-lip of a wench who seemed rather resentful of having only one best friend in the shape of Susanna. Both yearned for the more meaningful companionship of the proud-looking sporties in an older class – those who wore gymslips like flags of war. After all, it was wartime, and the most patriotic spirit in those days resided within such middle-of-the-road communities.

Susanna and Lucy, therefore, by lack of other influence, were gradually attracted towards darker, direr affairs than polishing boys' faces. Susanna had inherited, through some miscegenate unaccountability, books and papers from step-dad Donald's attic, an attic that seemed deeply unvisited because nobody else knew of its existence by either angle of exterior roof or potential of perspective. Brother Tom and step-dad Donald had spoken of it, though, as if they suspected the existence of realms beyond man's understanding – spoke of it in barely audible words of one syllable (most of them mispronounced). Yet, with inadvertent intention, the two girls were somehow directed towards this attic where they were to discover mouldy documents speaking of worlds even lower than the basement – a dark sphere of imputed eeriness more in keeping with the Gothic Humours than the workmanlikeness of the local trades. Both girls were remarkably precocious as far as the written word was concerned, if not in the more spoken sides of their physical nature. The itches they needed to scratch they did more by reflex than salaciousness. Their singing in unison was perfect.

In any event, some particularly mouldy words in the attic's documents spoke of toad creatures harbouring themselves beneath the town's China Factory ... stating that some of the more decorative crockery was based on fitful sightings of these creatures, creatures that had recently drawn too near the surface. The fact of the factory workers' children being sent away, soon afterwards, was both a mystery and an all-too-clear sign that sirens were about to wail of war.

The toad creatures of which the attic's mouldy configurations told were nurse-like to the bottom of their Earthen natures – so much so, the two girls yearned to visit them and gain an inkling of how properly to nurture others. They did not want to grow up into the thrusting womenfolk they might otherwise have been destined to become during the more modern future.

At first, they delved along the road's alleyways that – according to the tracks the attic's tract told them to tread – traced a downward path, below the basement, to where the bravest toad creatures were said to prick their ears. Susanna and Lucy tried to crack jokes and enact a life of hockey-sticks and mild matriculation to ward off any encroaching eeriness. They had, indeed, since our first acquaintace with these two girls, become delegate Prefects at school – against the very base natures coursing through their inherited veins. Both step-dad Donald and brother Tom had, independently, long since vanished on imagined forays in North Africa or towards the Antipodes. Mother Pamela boiled soup interminably, often misrepresenting it as stew – a fact that caused Susanna to suffer from imputed anorexia before its time. Lucy, too, loved to suffer with her friend, and thus refused the more filling platefuls at her own home so that she could share the scraps and swill that mother Pamela dished up on faded and chipped crockery. This thinness of diet, it was reported, allowed the two girls to squeeze through gaps others couldn't even see.

There was a local belief that was so very local it was held solely in that part of the town, or even just in Susanna's road itself. Up was down. Down was up. Then was now. Now was then. Admittedly, it was the loose-lipped gossip of a belief that, perhaps, nobody had fully construed. This belief was often voiced abroad when digging the local allotment; probably in preference to War Talk proper, which, as primary sources maintain, often did cost lives during that inimitable make-do-and-mend era. It was as if Faiths grew and flourished from the very chimney smoke. The cleaner the flues, the more that clarity prevailed. The sootier, though, to the point where the smoke was close to becoming tangible curds of tar, crazy extrapolations were spoken with the straightest possible faces. The darker it was, the dafter the beliefs became.

It has already been known that there was a boy called Hugger – a village idiot with no village to call his own. He saw two extremely thin girls, but wondered whether he was seeing double because, in his eyes, different parts of the town shimmered out of perspective with each other and most roads *felt* as if they were already underground. He promised to accompany them on the final foray, after several dress rehearsals, to the very cellar where he told himself (if in different words) that the tops of some of the toads were embedded in the concrete like turnips.

How Hugger knew about the mouldy parchment in Susanna's attic was never satisfactorily explained – but that was because the girls forgot they had already told him to keep this a secret, there being a requirement for someone else to keep the secret to make it a better secret, a secret worth keeping. The more who knew the secret ... well, there was an optimum level before the secret was officially out. And there being three of them was certainly enough to make it a secret more secret than most. By leading them down, Hugger was merely re-enacting a story he thought he'd already been told.

Fear came from not being warned or even properly made to be afraid. Fear was strongest where there was nothing of which to be afraid. It could be sensed only in words – not in deeds, activities or even threats. The walls were black, the cold air they bodily negotiated even blacker. Yet their breath could be seen, as if the ghosts they feared were born from within themselves. The smell was that of parsnips, not so much parsnips that had gone bad as ones that had become strange healthy vegetables with a natural unwholesomeness that was ranker than mere putridity. Their feet felt cobbles through the runnelled soles, crag-hard muffins from a history belonging more to Victorian fogs than to the frost-graced wisps of youthful lungs. Their bootsteps, though, were slippered by black noise; even their voices were quelled by sounds that they knew were present by token of the wall's giveaway vibrations against their seeking fingers – yet sounds to which their ears were deaf.

And the sense of fear grew and grew, merely as the words grew and grew, as Hugger, in the guise of a sweep, led his water babies down to a deep cellar where chimneys-tops were rooted, with their pots sticking up from the ground primed to churn out cataracts of choking smoke.

"Hold my hand, Hugger."

At last, a voice had penetrated the suffocating silence.

Susanna could hardly see him, even before they'd hit the cellar proper and were still in the relenting gloom directly beneath the imputed floorboards. Lucy could hardly see her own face in front of her hand. Hugger could see neither of them – though he lived up to his nickname and gave them childish sooty cuddles to guarantee their presence. He had earlier shown them how to lift the trap that revealed the dizzy steps and cloying walls; wordlessly, he made them follow through ... a quest that, until they knew its meaning, held no meaning at all.

The attic documents spoke of toads, thought Susanna. Lucy even said it... with a short sharp laugh to relieve the impending terror ... but Hugger was uncharacteristically quiet, his hunched shape growing darker and darker as it led the way ... holding the sweet fingers he thought to be a girl's.

Earlier, even earlier than the opening of the trap, the three of them had gone into a huddle and discussed the quest. If this is being heard (as opposed to being read), one may already have overheard their mindless, middling lightness of laughter. The words were spoken in between, as if learned parrot-fashion from someone more omniscient than themselves:

"There seems to be a something I cannot get to the bottom of ... a horrid something that nobody can fend off."

Nobody at all could fend off a war, not even those well-meaning folk called by names she had grown to love as Donald, Pamela, Tom...

"Yes, yes, wars have angels you know ... many think they see them in the sky, as if the huge ovens bake birds blacker in readiness for flight as well as, as well as..."

"What's all that to do with the toad creatures, Hugger?"

131

He turned and spoke as if he spoke for the very first time: "The attic mould must have blotted the paper there ... you know, words can easily be mistaken for each other. Those people in the ovens you spoke of, they have to hit the road instead of staying where the evil squats. They're refugees, road walkers."

"*Road* creatures, then, Hugger? Not toad."

Susanna and Lucy nodded in unison at the enlightenment one of them had just voiced. The talk had gone on for hours before stepping out on the quest. Mother Pamela could be heard shifting beds upstairs. The monochrome snapshots of step-dad Donald and brother Tom in their gold-tooled holders glinted in the semi-blackout that the world still allowed.

Meanwhile, the trio of shadows – bordering on silhouettes – delved deeper into the bowels of the road. Hugger knew he was almost alone. His mind came to the forefront, if only by some false perspective. Always destined to be the protagonist, he drew sympathy and identification. Hugger was a hero, not an idiot. The girls were just two of the song-lines he followed. He loved their legs and the growing shapeliness of their being. He had watched them fondling each other, when they thought nobody could see. Love was often like that. He wondered, as a strange non-sequitur, about the aboriginal heart of the matter ... as he negotiated the lowest reaches that Mankind could ever reach without Hell itself kicking in.

The darkness was wet to the touch. Not so much darkness, though – more a negative radiance that shone from within the margins containing them. The two girls had re-established themselves with a growing provenance, relegating Hugger to a corner of their consciousness. The ground was littered with human heads, the blackness blurring their various racial leanings. Susanna somehow knew, without being told, that the rest of the bodies below the heads were embedded vertically below even this furthest reach of surface existence, their various legs stretched out in wide frozen stride or mean limp. The girls watched Hugger start kicking these heads to check how well the necks prevented them from becoming separate footballs. The resultant cracks, throbs, bleats and squelches thankfully filled the girls with more wholesome thoughts, visions even, of the toad creatures they'd originally hoped to see – honest-to-goodness horrors that would have made them shudder with mere fright or simple disgust.

Susanna felt herself to be alive and kicking for perhaps the very first time as a siren wailed far off. The first of many.

She heard Tom, Donald and Pamela scuttling to the basement air-raid shelter. But she stayed in the safety of her own bed, hugging her knees as if that would ward off an inevitable past. Flashes, as if passing under chimneys of light in an otherwise endless tunnel of nightmare, made her dark shape fitfully invisible. Lucy had failed to return to any degree of visibility at all, however. She never hugged her own curvy ley-lines. Had never been told the frightening story in the first place.

Listen, though, and you will hear your own black heart. You don't need ears for that.

NIGHTS AT THE REGAL

Jason Gould

IN THE THREE years I was employed by S_____ Enterprises, from April 1986 until I was thirty-two and anxious to get out of pornography, I made more than twenty deliveries to the shop in Hull; but if Rudkin hadn't been there that night, I would surely have lost my way within the riverside web of warehouses, sheet metal plants and bedroom-sized industrial outlets, whose ancient window displays of gaskets, valves and washing machine spares seemed to objectify a lingering need for the city to return to its blue-collar past. Rudkin wasn't from a working-class background himself. The only child of a disgraced University lecturer, so he'd once said as he proofed his monthly order, he'd had a privileged upbringing and a decent if ungratifying education. Often he would keep me chatting long after I was meant to be at my next drop-off in Bradford or Doncaster; but with Rudkin I allowed the business visage to lapse, because unlike the other traders he wouldn't haggle over price or think it clever if I returned to London with part-exchanges from which the most explicit pictures were torn. He was atypical of his field in that profit had no or little emphasis, and he was driven more – I thought – by a longing to guide. (I intruded one day during the ingratiation of a new customer: Rudkin was tenderly turning the pages in a copy of *Color Climax* that lay open on his outstretched palm, the glance he gave the man as each new spectacle was shown sufficient to say "I can take you there, and there, and there. Take my hand..." And – as if suddenly transfused by camaraderie – he would halt sometimes in mid-sentence to simper paternally at the backs of the browsing men, his face tanned a leathery orange by the gas burner he always had whistling and spitting nearby.)

I didn't feel entirely unguided myself as I was piloted through the industrial district to an event Rudkin claimed I would be senseless to miss. I kept up, but he was fast over the evening ground. Padlocks deadly enough to crush hands hung from factory doors, steel gates; sponge reached from a ripped seat in a fork-lift truck; light decreased across the compounds. The sky was pale, as though a group of buildings had been demolished recently. We were near somewhere by the name of Stoneferry.

In Hull in conjunction with my present job, and using a café on Lombard Street to embitter my taste buds with coffee brewed from heat and not much else, I'd recognised the lone diner two tables in front as Rudkin. He and his business had passed through my mind as the shaky regional train had taken me there, but I hadn't anticipated our days might collide. He was following agog the activity in the restaurant's kitchen by means of a door hooked back on greasy green hinges. When I said hello, he snatched off his spectacles as if they were impolite. Each time he glanced into the food preparation area – and he was distracted by the chatter of knife-edge on wood, the metallic ring of pan on stove throughout our conversation – he would peer through the spectacles but not put them on; and when we stood, our chairs scraping over the linoleum, he said as if in conspiracy, "You can see everything they do. Just the other day I saw someone spit in an apple pie," and in the exit in a vortex of noise and fume, his hand up from nowhere to encircle my forearm, "They don't know you're watching. I sat there three hours last week."

Witham Miscellaneous lay east of the river Hull, between and beneath a second-hand audio-visual outlet and the bromic window of a closed-down kosher butcher's. The building over the basement where Rudkin did business was no longer in use. Entry to the shop was through a narrow door best negotiated sideways; from over the road – or at moments of low cloud from the very pavement outside – the way in and down was expressly obscure: not for Rudkin the Soho-styled frontage: the tattooist's elaborate calligraphy, the Salome-esque silhouettes; sometimes there would be no suggestion that it was to here you should aim for pornography, though occasionally flimsy paper stars might be taped to the door, on them in biro: GAY/ TS, CP/DOM, AMERICAN IMPORTS. And from there it was down a flight of cold stone steps and through a second door, the top half of which was smoked glass up which pale tulips ascended. On the other side of that window human-like blots would browse absorbed, shuffling now and then from display to display or stretching up to pluck from an upper shelf a more costly item. An aura of air stepped in by a customer or sudden static on the radio would tug them up from between the pages. And then they would pay hurriedly, ill at ease and conformably English, and rush out.

I stood by while Rudkin used a key long and ornate enough to belong to a Swiss mountain chateau to unlock first the outer door and then, down in the ground, the inner. He ran his hand over a switch and magazine covers flashed intermittently. I'd spent only an hour a month there and that four years back, but once the strip light had settled the layout was familiar:

Twelve grey-brown carpet tiles, the cheap, bristly type put down in charity shops and second-hand furniture emporiums, were arranged in the centre of the floor like a zone from which to critique the surrounding delights; flaky cement sandwiched by scarlet brickwork was visible behind the wall-mounted aluminium shelves and between the topmost shelf and the ceiling, which was drilled in the farthest corner to receive copper piping through which gas or water had at some time passed; and at the far end – if my geography was accurate beneath the butcher's – a window cracked diagonally from upper right to lower left, an inch outside of which stood, bizarrely, a solid brick wall daubed in fleshy grey lichen, between it and the glass a choked, nightmarish space. Rung up with a sale of fifteen pounds was a cash register that had replaced the scuffed metal tin he'd used in the past, beside it folded open to keep the page a creased paperback by Louis L'Amour. The bedewed atmosphere was proof of the river's proximity, and so pervasive I pictured the stock floating ruined one morning atop two feet of silty sludge.

While he messed around with the gas burner, I idled along a row of magazines. The industry hadn't progressed much: the circumstances preceding the sex were as contrived as ever, the photographer's style when it got to the sex itself baldly journalistic. But amongst the imported hard-core were the glamour publications from the 1960s that Rudkin preferred. I'd asked him once where the attraction lay in these vintage titles, which though cheeky for their era were laughably tame for today. He'd responded by opening to the centrefold a pocket-sized black and white booklet printed on Holland Park Avenue in 1967. Rust from the staples had bled into the inner margins, which framed – on the left-hand page – a woman baring long, maudlin breasts beside wooden crates stamped PALE ALE, seemingly above or in back of a pub, and on the right-hand page several rowing boats and a fishing trawler bobbing coldly in a harbour beneath black storm clouds, the scene pondered from a window above a rain-soaked beer garden by a solitary nude. "My favourite photograph ever," Rudkin had said about it. "Who is she? Is she waiting for someone? Or is there someone in the room behind her? And how does her neck smell?" He was quiet. Then: "You know, sometimes I think I love her." And: "It makes me feel like I've woken from a dream and I want more than anything to go back." After that he was hopelessly distracted, gazing at each magazine I placed in his hands as if there were something else between it and his eye. I noticed when I drove by on my way out of Hull that he'd closed the shop after I'd left. This – and the sheer spiritlessness that befell his usually fatalistic Yorkshire face when he took out that picture, a spiritlessness invoked I thought by a need for more than paper when he put his finger to that page: for briny air, perhaps, into which he might reach, or be tugged – helped me understand a little his bewitchment by pornography. He had an urge that was more unmethodical than the simple urge to obsess habitually upon the forbidden: it was an urge rooted in (but not limited to) the eye: an urge that had huge designs on experience.

Three men arrived, then another two and finally a group of four. There was no friendliness between Rudkin and these men, and I wondered if their relationship were in some way contractual. They milled around best they could in the confined space. The strip light buzzed. Rudkin read his cowboy book. We were waiting, I understood. After I'd skimmed the introductory paragraphs to four self-published works of poorly written S&M, I began to wish I'd rejected Rudkin's offer and stayed at the hotel. But then a voice echoed in the stairwell outside. Rudkin looked at the gathered; they looked back. He took in breath and opened the door.

Staggered in slanting shadow between the fourth and fifth step was a man of forty-five or fifty, pleading in Greek to someone further up. The resonance of passing vehicles meant whoever was hesitant to join us had the door to the street held open. Twisting towards Rudkin, his shoes splashed by paint as if he'd been busy at an easel, the Greek expressed frustration and embarrassment at this eventuality by shrugging, and by swearing in a passionate, jagged accent. He called up again, his tone more gentle. At the lack of any reply I wondered if he actually had a companion, or if this were it and the event tonight was the spiralling of a madman's mind. I was wrong, however, because the velvety address enticed down from the safety of the surface the reluctant visitor.

She was around six years of age and, until it was impossible to maintain further, she hid her face against her father's hip. Because his thigh wasn't sanctuary enough the father had to bend now and then to reassure her in her native tongue, referring I imagined to her mother, a favourite doll, a song. When he did this she relaxed visibly. She even dared a peep at her surroundings at one point, though when her eye found mine I had to look away. In part it was due to where we were: decadence on all sides and she no older than my sister's girl Sophie. But it also had to do with the way she clung to him (and he to her) in this dank, unfamiliar place. I'd seen it in London in those fathers and daughters who flee the ash of their homeland to sit bewildered and broken in the espresso outlets of Oxford Street and Covent Garden, he in his only good shirt, she in her dead mother's pearls. But if I felt pity it was only toward her, coerced down here beneath this alien town. Toward the two as a family I felt the jealousy you feel toward people who seem to live life that little bit closer than you to some universal truth. Or I did later.

Before the dismal window at the back of the room Rudkin had put out a chair. The girl was walked to it now by her father, who crouched once she was seated. Caressing her hands, he leaned in and whispered in short motivational bursts. When he was done he squeezed her shoulders through her leaf-green anorak and slowly retreated, guarding her as he did with his dark, lazy eyes, and not properly unbending till he'd rejoined Rudkin and I and the rest of the onlookers. He stood at the head of the group, whereas I was comfortable at the rear. Shortly he issued to Rudkin a nod, and at the nod Rudkin announced, "No noise or movement now please. No talking. No-one must leave." Then Rudkin carried out some action that degraded the light in the shop to as if seen through a gauze.

For a lengthy period nothing happened. On the chair the girl closed her eyes, though she seemed nervous to do so; her head pillowed on her shoulder; her right hand lay over the left on her knee as if tethering it there. Fifteen minutes went by, in which the slackness that had affected her neck muscles spread down through the bulk of her body. But then for ten minutes more there was no change, apart from a fractional movement of the head that freed a lock of hair to drape across her face. Breath worked her chest, but the effect was almost indiscernible. The chair creaked as if she were accepting weight, or shedding it. And though there wasn't a lot to see, we stood transfixed by that sleepy Greek girl in zipped-up anorak and elasticated plimsolls, as if she were the immaculately attired corpse of some Victorian infant, as if Rudkin's shop were a parlour decorated in blacks and browns, and as if we – aloof and entombed emotionally – were the family in grief.

Behind me to the left I heard the scrape of paper as someone despaired of this farce and read a magazine. Before I could hush him (under the circumstances it seemed grossly disrespectful) an additional noise took my attention. I looked. The girl's left shoe was scratching the floor as the foot inside convulsed involuntarily.

Was why we were here beginning? Was rubber on stone the prelude?

I concentrated on that fluttering shoe; if you stared hard and didn't blink, the cellar and all its contents seemed to break away from the shoe and the floor around it like earth from a riverbank. On it crunched, the faintest of sounds. On, and on.

After some time I wondered if this was all, or if perhaps some element were awry. Was the girl about to slither from the chair, pale and mushy? Would we slip quietly away, heads down and collars up, while the father knelt over her and shrieked? I couldn't resist speaking to someone. I turned.

Where I'd heard someone fingering a magazine, there were only shelves and books. And on the middle shelf, the pages in the Christmas issue of *Black Tail* slowly turned. Each page lifted and teetered and finally unravelled like a glossy carpet of hair and skin. Breast and leg rolled by; columns of text, advertisements, cock-ends. No one was nearer than I and there was no breeze. I waved my hand over the pages, but it snagged no thread. The final page uncurled and the process was done. A black female Santa blew kisses from the back cover.

I faced forward again. At the side of the girl's head, an invisible source was dripping to the shop floor water seasoned by rust. The drops came in groups of three, divided by ten-second gaps. The crowd was silently impressed: it looked harder, a look I could hear. But the girl's face was unaffected by the advent of the liquid, and she blithely slept on; this proved the case with the father too, who was neutral but for a tiny smile when the first browny droplets bulged into view.

I watched the water percolate in, and I didn't question its genuineness. I found it more difficult to believe in the Greek and his daughter stooping to trickery than I did in a faulty tap that usually leaked somewhere else being made to leak into here. They lived at the front of too venerable a history to be charlatans; in a culture in which too much was sacred. It was the faith in myth, the deep respect for superstition and the prominence of the grandmother within the family that permitted this girl this gift. Of course, there would be something besides her lineage: something like a downy patch on her collarbone or swine at a nearby farm beserking wildly on the day of her birth. But even on its own, their nationality saved them from suspicion of foot levers.

Then, with the water pooling and their authenticity confirmed, footsteps were heard coming down from the street. I turned to the door, as did a handful of others, but whoever was there wasn't yet close enough to be seen. I was at the tip of the crowd now the focus had swung, and I would be first to greet the footsteps this side of the smoked glass and decorative tulips.

But their descent terminated five or six steps from the bottom. And then they were walking around inside the shop. They and the floor on which they walked was somewhere toward shoulder-height, though they were impossible to pinpoint solely by sound. After some aimless and clumsy trudging they found themselves a buoyancy, and they swept and circled from side to side and round and round as if waltzing alone in a silent ballroom.

Like a dog teased by a bluebottle, Rudkin followed the footsteps with his gaze, praying no doubt for a flash of ankle or twinkle of toecap. And when the dancer quit as abruptly as if the floor we were unable to see had been ice and the ice had gone in – and Rudkin hadn't seen a thing, only heard – he narrowed his eyes vindictively at the father. But the Greek didn't notice. He was too mindful of his girl:

Doughy, shroud-like cord floated above her lap from nostrils the size of pennies. It drew in the air a moderately-sized oval, which hovered as if on placid waters. Through it we witnessed – instead of the bookcase we should have seen – a varnished maple wood dance floor, and a stage. Autumnal leaves had blown in to litter the stage, where a solitary drum waited atop a steel tripod and a tasselled silver backcloth looked set to part for a torch singer, but didn't. At stage left water trickled down from somewhere high, clung to the rusted trellis-work of a window and then, too heavy, gave up and fell. Diamonds of plaster had torn from a wall split from ceiling to floor, dousing in dust a chandelier that – having decayed at the root – lay wrecked in a sea of other merry-making paraphernalia: pyramid-shaped party hats, coloured streamers, candid eye masks, cocktail glasses, cigarette cards. Where the dance floor met the encompassing carpet, a stocking hung limply over the back of a chair. Tobacco lay spilt from a snuffbox.

With no warning (and it seemed with no motive), the father began to berate Rudkin. He shouted in and out of Greek, repeating "This is more! This is more!" and jabbing a stiff finger at Rudkin's chest. But Rudkin paid no heed: he was fixated by the ballroom, towards which he was steadily drawn.

The Greek campaigned the others. He was desperate. He told them, "This has not been paid for. Be reasonable. You must not see." His face had declined from proud arbiter to swindled victim. He loitered indecisively behind Rudkin, as if analysing whether to attack the shopkeeper. He didn't, however. Instead he barged past and, as gently as his temper would allow, snatched up his daughter.

The ballroom wrapped itself around the fuming Greek as he

carried his child through the crowd, the decrepit columns and lonely stage adorning his face and hands like a tribalist's insignia. Finger-smudged fluting grafted leprously to the girl's left calf. Around her head, a halo of dust.

But when she awoke and discovered her father in a rage (and she in his arms), there was an eruption of tears. She squirmed, and kicked her legs.

Immediately the tableau was flung into runny mayhem, its structure and its definition lost to wakefulness. The walls, the ceiling and the floor were swept up in a wild wash. But it seemed that nothing in there was sufficiently solid to be smashed. Rather it all met and mingled, like watered-down paint. The colour to which it fused was blacky-brown, flecked by ash. And once it had fused it began to thin, and to disperse and vanish. It was simple, really: there was no longer an artist, or there was an artist but she was suddenly oblivious to her art, and because of that all this had to be put back on its palette.

The Greek turned sideways to fit his daughter's feet through the door. As he spun, the ballroom sprayed from his coat, showering a rack of magazines. Each dollop halved like quicksilver and faded like steam, and was gone. He dripped more on the steps as he left, with similar effect.

No-one spoke. The door swung pendulously on its hinges. By the empty chair, Rudkin pawed the space where the stage and the dance floor had been.

IN MY DREAM that night, shapeless people floated through a shapeless environment. Now and then an object might define: a fan belt beginning to perish at the edges, a metal tape measure, a bradawl. I opened my eyes. The hotel was hot. Through a tarnished brown grill set low in the wall a distant turbine hummed. I turned over. When I woke again the heavy green drapes were aglow in sunlight.

I don't think I was deliberately induced back to the shop that afternoon. I doubted the intent of the previous night had been to lure me in, if indeed there was anything into which I might be lured; though if it were bait, and if further uneasy evenings were planned for which I would be charged, then Rudkin would have assumed he was doing me a kindness, I'm sure, because he firmly believed there was no such thing as a good suppression.

But kindness or not, when I found Witham Miscellaneous closed I felt like the village pauper: I'd been up to the house on the hill, I'd peered inside (after the window had been wiped), and though I was awed by the splendour I'd seen I was now being chased away. Ashamed of the scorn I felt towards Rudkin – not for not being open but for rubbing his sleeve across that window in the first place (the girl had the talent, but Rudkin was the true spy here) – I pushed the door one last time, looked for any clue as to whether he might be back and, finding none, walked into the next street to an oily snack bar.

It was inevitable the ballroom should dominate my afternoon coffee. The nature of its unravelling suggested it to be no more than a humour in the head of a girl, which for reason unknown was exposed when she slept. But I wanted it to not be so: I wanted the method of its arrival to be deceptive and it to be a real dance hall, littered in the aftermath of a real dance. Sometimes we're all like Rudkin with his old black and white magazine, soothed by the rainy air of an afternoon he hadn't even breathed.

I was lost in speculation – who had caroused there? had fondling occurred by the cloakroom? and in the toilets: had there been discussion of who hoped to court whom later that night, or a feud perhaps, even a stabbing? – and I wasn't conscious that Rudkin had taken a corner-table. He had coffee to drink and he had his fingers in his open wallet.

"Ignoring me?"

He glanced up. He said, "One second," and while he totted up his cash I ferried my cup and coat to his table.

"I didn't see you," he said, putting away his money. Then, like a feverish adolescent, "What did you think?"

"About last night? Well, it was something. Really quite something."

"Seen anything like it before?"

"No. Never."

"Nor me. It was... shit... what's the word?" He drummed two fingers against his cup. "Pivotal. I reckon it was pivotal. For me, anyway." He rushed a mouthful of coffee, then admitted: "I've been up most of the night. I just sat in a chair. I couldn't get it out of my mind. And when I did drift off I looked down and my feet were on that old wooden floor."

"Who are they, the man and the girl? I mean, where do people like that come from?"

"Bath," he said, as if the city explained every uncanny aspect of them. "Not originally, of course. I'm not sure where they're from originally. Greece, I'd expect."

Probing why a Greek family from Bath might be associated with a porn-peddler from Hull might have offended, so I didn't ask. Rudkin was easily riled. He held dear the belief that the pornographer was the shaman of suburbia, and he was brutally defensive if anyone dared denigrate his cloth. He had in his possession a library of worlds; worlds of which everyday folk dreamed, whether they knew it or not. The reactionary, he said, objected more to the escape into these worlds by the unwashed and the uneducated than it did to the undressing of flesh. Flight of any order (liquor, narcotics, outlawed books) was of varying threat to stability. It made distinct to the poor man at his gate a world beyond the docile, the homespun; it made him think: what else have I accepted that I should have questioned? what else may not be so? And I saw in Rudkin an impulse to be the hero, a grimy hand in his as he led the proletariat to its dream.

Rudkin said, "He's an artist, the Greek guy, but no gallery will have him. They say he has no vision. He went for my throat when I suggested he paint his daughter doing what she does. It's one thing for her to be seen, another to see herself. Once her eyes are shut I don't think she's aware what's going on."

"Does she have a name?"

He shrugged. "In the adverts she calls herself Miss Mook."

"Adverts?"

"A few lines in the back of photocopied contact magazines. Her father handles the business side. He tells me they get a good deal of work in Germany, where they apparently pack out concert halls. Over there they call her Das Reiniger. The Purifier."

I was surprised she was famous, even if not in general society then in that beneath. Flawed as it was by its slip into unpaid territory, I'd understood our display the previous evening to be her début before an assembled public. But I'd made a boyish error. The watcher frequently misreads the loyalties of the watched: the man in purchase of erotic photography, his cousin of film, cousin to both of minutes in a peep booth; each feels the parade to be exclusively his own, when ostensibly it's for all, and in truth for no-one.

"I didn't realise they'd done this type of thing before," I said. "I thought last night was a first."

"We saw The Regal," said Rudkin. "I was digging around at the library this morning. By all accounts it was the hip joint in its day. Exclusive, expensive. Ordinary folk would wait months for their membership to be approved, then blow four weeks' wages in an hour. It seems some of the more well-bred patrons were connected with Freemasonry. Then in 1937 it closed after the local clergy said it was 'worryingly un-Christian', its atmosphere of a Saturday night 'orgiastic'. And a year or two later the Luftwaffe flattened it." He arced an eyebrow. "Wouldn't you say that was a first?"

I nodded, struck by how thoroughly saturated the shell of Rudkin's shop must be with the beat of that absent band. "I can't believe it was once really there..."

"Was?" he said, flirting with a smile. "What do you mean, was?"

THE PEELING AWAY was done when I arrived, and they were standing there in silent appreciation. Outlined to the same diameter, and with entrance at the same alignment, the dance hall loomed a short distance forward and to the left of the sleeping girl's head. And as before the water was falling droplet by baleful droplet, and the party was over and the band was nowhere to be seen. I thought about the time. It was later than last night by an hour, but nevertheless the moment into which she'd punched seemed to be the same moment as yesterday: the light on the walls hadn't dulled, nor had it ripened; the brickwork was no more denuded of plaster, the woodwork no more comprehensively wormed; and on the stage, the leaves that lay blown in from outside were no nearer crumbling. Nothing had altered, though I'd lived a day. But perhaps nothing ever did alter; perhaps it was always that moment there, regardless of when it was here.

It was a private theatre tonight, down beneath the community.

Only two others were present: the father, in love at the edge of the cellar with the glorifying of his girl; and now myself. In the café, Rudkin had said he'd scraped together funds for another event by taking to sale a hefty proportion of stock (the pricey, legally questionable imports; the nudism magazines too mildewed to open; a rare copy of *Vulgaire* he'd hoped to trade for a week in a Spanish villa: all had indeed vanished, the *Reader's Digest* volumes he stocked to dilute his main source of income spaced out to nourish the pared shelves). He didn't say how much he was paying the Greek, though he did say I was welcome to tag along free of charge. And though he attempted to house the invitation within the abruptness of an afterthought, as though he wouldn't mind if it were only the father, the daughter and he, I doubted it was so.

Soon we were able to hear the inside of the ballroom, as if the deeper the girl slept the more moth-eaten the cloak between here and there. Muteness had suggested The Regal to be stranded somewhere; marooned irreconcilably. But this suggestion was put off by the inflow of sound. The far-off cascade of water on water; the trapped, delicate silence; even – higher than was visible from our position – the occasional whisk of wing from rafter to rafter as if in some avian fracas: from all of this, dimension stirred and built, and we no longer had before us the flat definition of a place, but simply a place.

Rudkin moved to within an inch of the ballroom and fell like dropped silk to his knees. I followed and stood a yard behind, close enough to feel on my face the October sun that poured through those tall windows, over the maple wood dance floor and out into the murky shop. A scent of lavender-water seeped our way too, as though the dance – something lively like a polka, perhaps – had only this minute finished, the aroma still buffeting round the room. And I smelled cigarettes and gin. I was there, or as good as: a sequinned hip curved into my right palm, in my left the bird's skeleton of her hand; then later the chilly walk home through the gaslit town, her lips cold and thin yet fantastically erotic round the back of some damp Victorian terrace. It may have been uninhabited, but out of that dance hall swam lives.

And so we were – I standing, Rudkin kneeling; I swirled in shadow to the waist, he to the shoulder – when flesh slapped against wood, somewhere in the ballroom, as if a monkey had dropped barefoot from the ceiling.

Was it the clientele? I wondered. Were they near? Was the cigarette smoke calling to life the lungs in which it had coiled? Was talk of housing conditions or of issues at the dockside about to rouse, bringing with it the lips through which it had passed? Would every fingerprint inspire a finger, every wineglass a hand?

But the revellers weren't ushered forth, reared by their smoke, their words, their touch. In no place was the dust removed to the underside of a brogue or the heel of a stiletto; nowhere did fine particles of plaster sprinkle down the walls, brushed by a ghostly shoulder. No-one was mustered. I was certain I'd heard a noise, however. I wanted to speak to Rudkin, but the shop felt too completely focused on the dance hall. Nevertheless, I whispered, "Did you hear something?"

Rudkin was too seized to reply. I was toying with the possibility that I'd offended him by talking, when he said, too rapt to turn, "Can't you see him?"

"Who?" I said. "Can't I see who?"

"Him just there, to the right of the stage." He was whispering passionately. "Look closely. This is what it's all about."

A minute went by before I was able to pick him out, simply because he wasn't there to be picked out, only his shadow. He eluded our line of sight by less than a yard, his shadow itself grainy and vague: a shadow cast at a time of day or at an angle not conducive to shadows.

My bloodstream quickened. Back in my youth I would have been on my knees beside Rudkin, gulping down the archaic air. But I was suddenly very unrelaxed and anxious about my involvement. I looked down at the top of Rudkin's sun-yellowed head. I wasn't like him. By character I wasn't a snoop: I didn't roam the streets of my hometown, propelled by a kind of pseudo-satyric inquisitiveness. I was accustomed to (perhaps comforted by) the surface of things. Rudkin chancing upon an open cell door after a lifetime of incarceration would fly instinctively, I – as many more like me – would slam it shut. Though it was the truth it made me feel, at some idealistic level, unadventurous and stupid.

I was about to back-step and quietly depart when Rudkin reached inside, sunlight racing up his arm. Dust wheeled around his hand. The ballroom seemed to shift and then settle, even in its remotest corner. Catarrh thrummed in the girl's chest. But she was still; as was her father.

I grabbed Rudkin's shoulder. I said, "Are you crazy? What the hell are you doing?"

"I must," he said. "I must see him. I must see his face. His shadow is all I've ever seen. And he and I need to speak. We have much to discuss."

"There's nobody there," I said. "It's an illusion." I looked again. The shaded area had darkened, as if at my challenge. If he were real, it wasn't my place to know who he was, to know from which high ledge he had sprung to stand there so still and watchful. But all the same, I said: "Who is he?"

"He's my oldest friend," said Rudkin. "He and I go back a long way." He turned to me; I bent. "When I was a boy he lived in my house," he said quietly. "My father had in his study a locked drawer, where he kept illustrated volumes of de Sade, and some original footage from the Grand Guignol. Also in there was my favourite: an envelope of drawings made in 1921 over seven nights at Aleister Crowley's Abbey of Thelema. I remember as if it were yesterday stealing the key and sneaking in to look through those pictures. They showed sex mainly, heterosexual and homosexual, and metaphorical sacrifice. But the one I really adored depicted Crowley on a carpet of white petals fellating a man dressed as a horse. Oh I could look at it for hours." He turned back to The Regal. "And he was there in all those pictures. Well, his shadow. Thrown across an altar or ottoman."

First Rudkin rocked forward onto the balls of his feet, then he stole sideways into the ballroom like a thief through a floating window. The girl cried out in her sleep, convulsed on the chair. It was momentarily ambiguous which half – the half in the shop or the half in the ballroom – was the real Rudkin. Split thus, he said to me, "Look for him in the background of any pornographic film or photograph, and you'll find some trace of his shadow." Then he smiled at me, as if in goodbye. But the ardour in his face wasn't enough to eclipse a small, underlying sadness. (Thinking later, I wondered if he'd glimpsed the shelves and the slough of magazines and was suddenly worried – too late in the game – if this would be as sweet an experience as it had been a conceit. Or maybe it was merely vanity; maybe he was gutted by a sense of professional ineptitude at having to abandon me here on this, the dreaming side.)

I strode backwards through the mean light and was out and up the stone steps before he'd fully hauled himself in. Out in the street I staggered free of the doorway. I walked, making my way through the riverside web of warehouses and sheet-metal plants toward my hotel. And in the bedroom-sized industrial outlets, parts for obsolete appliances hung fastened to perforated hardboard. A void crashed with a waterfall's ferocity through the ventilation slits in the second-hand televisions. In the musty tiled confines of the kosher butcher's, rust spread across the slicing machine. And beneath the ground, where I expected to hear Rudkin screaming or laughing, there lay the elite silence of a world as hidden to ours, as ours was to it.

EMPTY STATIONS
Nicholas Royle

GARETH SANGSTER, FREELANCE hack and sometime actor, was sitting in front of a computer screen in the office/spare bedroom of his Stoke Newington flat. He was staring just past the screen at the rear windows of the houses in the next street. He wasn't watching anything in particular, just passing the time, seeking distraction from an unfinished review. A press release lay on his desk next to the keyboard. He'd read it a dozen times. He'd seen the film he was trying to write about only the night before in a Wardour Street basement. But something about it resisted his attempts to get it down.

He knew what it was. It was the fact that he'd seen the film a hundred times before, and read the press kit as often. The studios went to the trouble of giving them different titles, but they were all the same movie. The script got a minor rewrite and the actors ghosted through ninety minutes without breaking a sweat.

The phone rang, shattering his reverie. He picked it up and listened.

"Where?" he asked. "When?"

He hung up and went back to looking out of the window. He was wondering if his life was about to change. Or if Ash had fired the starting pistol for another wild goose chase. You never knew with Ash. He could be right, he could be wrong. Most of the time he was wrong.

Gareth looked at the screen. He knew he should shut the machine down and go out to meet Ash, but a phrase had entered his tidy mind and he decided to write it down before he forgot it. The phrase proved to be the key to unlocking the piece and his review wrote itself in less than ten minutes. He emailed the review to his editor, then selected 'Shut Down' and left the flat while the machine was still finishing up.

MOST LIFE-THREATENING situations that cannot be blamed on the random concurrence of unrelated events are reached as a direct result of people delving too deep into their own obsessions. The time the alarm bells should no longer go ignored is when two people's crazy desires are indulged at the same time and one of them shows all the signs of being quietly mad.

The alarm bells would have been ringing to wake the dead and Gareth should have heard them, but for some reason he had his head stuck up his arse. He always had had where Ash was concerned.

He picked up a black cab on Church Street and allowed its fluid acceleration to propel him back in his seat as the gates to Abney Park Cemetery flickered past the window. Whenever he passed the great Victorian boneyard, a still image of its fabled subterranean catacombs would light up like a silent movie behind his eyes.

Gareth's obsession was with lost London films. He'd been in one, of course, which was how the bug bit him. When he was doing stage acting, appearing in fringe productions and living hand-to-mouth in a squat in South Street, Mayfair, he'd agreed to take a part in Harry Foxx's *Nine South Street*. The conceit – that the film would feature a bunch of Mayfair squatters playing themselves – appealed to him. He liked the fact that the director wanted them to improvise around a basic thriller plot that was already in place. He also liked the director. It was Harry Foxx's first film, but the tyro seemed confident beyond his experience.

Since its initial, extremely limited release, *Nine South Street* has never been screened. While other British independent films of the same era, such as Richard Stanley's *Hardware* and Vadim Jean's *Leon the Pig Farmer*, would enjoy an occasional afterlife at the Watermans or the Riverside, *Nine South Street* simply disappeared. Its only scheduled network TV broadcast was postponed due to a live football match going into extra time, and it was never reprogrammed, so Gareth Sangster's only screen performance went unseen by most of the world, including its casting directors and independent producers.

Years later, when attempts were made to locate prints of the film for a revival at the NFT, none was unearthed. Even the negative had vanished. Ash, who had been Gareth's co-star in *Nine South Street*, was less concerned by the disappearance of the film, since he'd had no acting ambitions in the first place, despite being a talented mimic. Ash was squatting in South Street at the same time as Gareth and they had formed a relationship, in spite of personal incompatibility, based on their shared interest in film. They went to movies together, making the most of the Lumière, the Electric, the Scala, while they were still in business. Mostly they saw British films from the 1960s and '70s – Nicolas Roeg, Lindsay Anderson, John Schlesinger. They caught Skolimowski's rarely screened *Deep End* at the ICA, and *The Shout* at the Roxie. Gareth watched Malcolm McDowell and James Fox with the concentration of a counterfeiter staring at legal banknotes, then reproduced their tics and mannerisms in his fringe work.

"It's not the same as what you do," he explained to Ash. "It's not impersonation, but reinterpretation."

"Tell that to the judge," Ash replied in his best Bogart.

And, so, when Gareth and Ash encountered a tall, long-haired stranger prowling around the disused corridors of 9 South Street – a forbidding ex-office building they squatted with a dozen or so others – they were only too happy to buy his story about scouting for locations for a low-budget film. The three of them shared a bottle of Stolly that Harry fetched from the off-licence in Shepherd Market and the idea for the film was born.

For Gareth it was the perfect opportunity to fulfil his dreams. Ash was less clear about what he wanted out of life. South Street was his first base in London and he'd only been there a couple of months, having moved south from the West Midlands, where, he claimed, he'd been the drummer in a band. He'd quit before they'd got a recording deal and then, as soon as they started to acquire a cult following, had been written out of their past, he said, airbrushed out of rock history, but Gareth soon learned to treat whatever Ash told him with caution. The Midlander drank heavily and did a lot of drugs. When they had first met, Gareth had been slightly in awe of him. Despite being a year or two younger, Ash was astonishingly dissolute. He maintained his various expensive habits by stealing books and CDs, which he sold on to second-hand dealers. He never paid for a meal in a restaurant, and so never visited the same establishment twice. Later, when it became clear that unreliability was part of Ash's character, Gareth could never quite erase the power of those earliest memories.

Consequently, when Ash called to report a lead in the search for a lost London film, Gareth jumped.

The cab cut through the top end of Barnsbury and hit the Cally Road a few yards from the tube station that bore its name. As he paid the driver, Gareth spotted Ash peering up and down the street from just inside the station entrance.

"Are they after you again?" Gareth asked.

"It's no joke, man," Ash insisted. "Anyway, I don't think I was followed. On this occasion."

"Ash, who the fuck would follow you?"

Ash looked pale and unwell, fish out of water. "You might," he said.

Gareth shook his head in exasperation.

"Come on," Ash pressed him. "We haven't got much time."

They took the stairs and within moments were waiting on the westbound Piccadilly line. Gareth noticed, in the sickly gloom that prevailed on the tube platform, that Ash didn't look so pale. He was also less tense than he seemed on the streets these days. Increasingly, it seemed, they hung out underground – travelling by tube to basement bars or preview theatres beneath Wardour Street. Getting from the tube to the venue was always something of a dash. It was one reason why Gareth didn't see as much of Ash as he used to.

It had started as an interest in the city beneath the city – London under London, like the book by Trench and Hillman, one of the few books Ash had stolen and not offloaded the next day. The interest had gradually eclipsed any others, apart from film: he combined the two by being selective about which cinemas he went to. Out went the Gate and the Phoenix, in came the Lumière, the Metro, the Renoir – cinemas where the auditoria were located below ground level.

Once on the train itself, Ash seemed to glow with vitality. He even started grinning at Gareth.

"Stop that. I don't like it," Gareth said. "Tell me where we're going. Is this a wind-up?"

Ash leaned forward. "You know how sometimes late at night," he said, "you're waiting on the tube platform and an empty train goes by without stopping? No lights on. It barely slows down, just passes through the station as if it weren't there."

Gareth nodded.

Instead of continuing, Ash sat back and crossed one leg over the other. He was grinning again. Gareth looked away. The train was pulling into King's Cross. He thought about getting off and leaving Ash to head off on his own, but then he remembered he felt the same impulse most times they saw each other and he never acted on it. When the doors closed and the train set off again, Ash crossed the carriage and sat next to Gareth. He had to shout to make himself heard over the din of the train's progress through the tunnels.

"Just as there are empty trains that go through 'our' stations – your stations and my stations, everybody's stations – without stopping, so there are other stations where *these* trains –" he pointed at the carriage floor for emphasis – "go through without stopping. Empty stations."

Gareth's nose was close to Ash's mouth, but for once he couldn't smell alcohol on the younger man's breath.

"Empty stations?" Gareth said, humouring him.

"Empty stations."

"You mean disused? Like York Way, British Museum, Wood Lane?"

"No. I mean empty. These stations have never been used. At least not by the likes of you and me. These stations are not on the network. They're off the map."

"I suppose you've found a way to get out at one of these stations?" Gareth couldn't keep the sarcasm out of his voice.

"You just have to get on the right train. You have to get on one of the trains that stops at those stations. Some of them stop at empty stations as well as normal stations. Some only stop at the empty ones." Ash indicated the rush of light that signalled their arrival in the next station.

"And you've done that, I suppose?" Gareth snapped.

"No, I haven't. But I know a guy who has. He lives in the tunnels."

"Yeah, right – and here we are at Russell Square. I've seen *Death Line*, Ash. Do us a favour and stop bullshitting me, OK? Just piss off!" Gareth jumped to his feet and stepped smartly between the closing doors, leaving Ash in his seat with a strange, sad little smile on his face.

GARETH MARCHED OFF up the platform, angry with himself more than anything for allowing himself to get sucked into Ash's paranoid fantasies. The train accelerated past him. He looked up in time to catch a smeared glimpse of Ash's face through the last window, his features as blurry as those of a corpse behind heavy plastic.

Gareth watched as the train slid into the tunnel. Its red light burned until the first bend had been navigated.

He reached the end of the platform, glared at the unbroken wall and cursed. He'd been so wrapped up in his anger, he'd managed to miss the exit. He turned round and looked down the full length of platform. There was no exit sign, but that didn't mean anything, as half the stations on the network were falling apart. He started walking back down the platform, paying more attention to his surroundings. He must have got confused when he'd been talking to Ash, because this didn't look like Russell Square. In fact, he couldn't see the station's name anywhere. Halfway down the platform, however, he found the exit. It was still unsigned, but it appeared to be a way out, so he took it.

The corridor led away from the platform and turned a corner. Faced with a flight of steps, Gareth climbed them rapidly. The dull echo of his footfalls disturbed him. He'd noticed a lack of posters on the walls – but then some stations were like that, in parts at least. There were no other people in evidence apart from himself. He moved faster. At the top of the steps, the corridor went left, then right – and then it stopped. It didn't run into a rough concrete wall or massive steel doors. It didn't end in barred gates, scraps of litter idling in desultory circles on the dusty, unattainable floor beyond. It ended in a perfectly ordinary, perfectly grouted, green-tiled wall. There was a subtle bevel where one wall joined the next, just as there would be if it was a proper wall, if it was supposed to be there.

The effect was like that of an amputation on a living limb. It was a dead end.

Gareth touched his fingers to the cool tiled surface. He was aware of no particular sensation. But a strange feeling was growing inside him, in his stomach and creeping down into his legs. It was fear.

He walked back to the platform, forcing himself not to run, but he passed no other opening on the way. He checked up and down the platform, but there was no other exit as far as he could see.

Movement on the track caught his eye. Moving closer to the edge, he peered into the suicide pit, the space between the rails. He saw it again: a tiny fragment of darkness detaching itself from the background and scuttling away, a mouse.

Then Gareth felt the displacement of air on his face. He looked up but there was nothing to see. The rails began to whine and the turbulence increased. Suddenly, pushing air out of the tunnel ahead of it, a train burst into the empty station at speed. Gareth staggered back from the edge, waiting for the train to stop. But it didn't. It didn't even slow down. Once he had realised it wasn't going to, he started waving his arms in the air and shouting. Not a single passenger caught his eye or reacted in any way. They seemed to stare right through him. Almost as if they were staring at the dark rushing of the tunnel wall.

He watched the red light of the disappearing train with an emptiness growing inside him that felt like death.

ASH TOLD THE police that London was built not on clay, as most people believed, but on celluloid. Some of the deeper tube lines bore right through the stuff, he said. Key locations in significant films were not picked at random: location scouts went looking for spots where the material ran close enough to the surface to affect the atmosphere.

His witness statement was not worth the tape it was recorded on.

It had been me who had dragged him into the enquiry after Gareth's girlfriend had called me to say he was missing.

Gareth, he said, had gone looking for a copy of a lost London movie starring Terence Stamp and Theresa Russell. Ash was one of the few people who had seen it. Since it bore no credits, it was impossible to say who had directed it. The presence of Theresa Russell suggested Roeg, but the style was too laid-back for him. Ash suspected the hand of Jerzy Skolimowski, although he couldn't say why, and in any case the police didn't give a fuck. They were going to charge him with wasting police time, but when they realised that they would have to get psychiatrists' reports and all that carry-on, they let it drop and Ash was a free man.

Gareth, however, was still missing. His girlfriend was inconsolable. Couldn't I do something, she wanted to know. I'd known Gareth almost as long as she had. Surely I had some idea where he might have gone, where he might have buried himself. I told her I'd do my best, but what did I have to go on? Not a great deal.

I checked out the big homeless areas. I rode the tube system – every line, each station. Once I thought I saw the back of his head at Archway, but I lost him in the crowd and later convinced myself I'd been mistaken. I didn't really know Gareth as well as his girlfriend thought I did. It was more a professional relationship, and a sporadic one at that. I commissioned film reviews off him and various longer pieces. But her need impressed itself upon me.

One night, in the early hours, the phone rang and it was Gareth. At least I thought it was Gareth. It was hard to be sure. His voice sounded a long way off, obscured by static and interference. He kept breaking up. But I managed to pick out the name of a tube station before the line went dead. Russell Square. I was down there at 5am, first customer through the gate. I prowled every corridor, bumped up and down in the old lifts. I peered into airshafts furred with years' worth of dead skin. Nothing. If I'd been hoping to get, at the very least, a sense of Gareth's recently departed presence, I was disappointed there, too. Dejected and worn out, I slumped down onto one of the blue metal seats to wait for the next train. On the seat next to mine was an unlabelled, scuffed video cassette.

I took the tape home and played it. There was nothing on it but static. If I try really hard, after a dozen or so viewings, I imagine I can hear Terence Stamp's voice (the laconic London drawl of *The Hit*, rather than the forced Cockney caricature of *The Limey*) struggling to make itself heard over the interference on the soundtrack.

Or I convince myself that the snowy picture is about to resolve itself into a tasteful interior shot of Theresa Russell's naked back.

Times when I'm still stuck in front of the screen way into the quiet hours, the bottle on the floor beside me more or less empty, I kid myself the voice I think I can hear is Gareth's, but then I remember Ash's talent for mimicry and reach for the remote. Stop, rewind, play.

THE STONE MAN
Derek M. Fox

MIKE BRADLEY LOVED to scare others less fortunate than himself.

One summer day back in the fifties, with both of us totally unaware that a storm threatened, Mike came up with a pearler. "The Stone Man will get you!" he said, dark eyes levelled at me, the suggestion of a grin tickling his lips. He'd do it purposefully, so no-one really knew whether he was fibbing or not.

Some of his so-called scares were pathetic anyway, but if you were less fortunate and perhaps less educated, they made you wary.

Mike and I were born in October, same day, same year, and in the same nursing home in adjacent beds, so naturally our mothers made friends. Like she took me to visit them, and they visited us: a sort of comparing baby growth time, get the picture? We exchanged presents and stuff on birthdays and at Christmas. As we grew, Mike and I were encouraged to write to each other, most amounting to naff all. B-o-r-i-n-g.

Differences emerged as we matured: Mike leaned towards the sciences – I guess you'd call it esoteric with his books on the weird and wonderful – whereas I was more artistic. I suppose the only real thing we came to have in common was the Stone Man.

Who is he? You might well ask. At the time I wanted to think he was something from one of Mike's books. He wasn't. To answer some of it, mostly conjecture you understand, I have to explain a few things – not least how Mike's dad seemed to me.

When Mum and I visited, our respective dads would be working to earn the proverbial crust. This left our mums with their woman talk, such crap as how they expected their proud offspring to grow up. You get the gist. Suffice to say me and Mike were pretty much on a par education-wise, so he didn't need to prove a thing to me, or vice versa.

Generally, we were left to our own devices, and considered anything and everything that our eleven-year-old minds latched on to. But always, during visits to their place, I would watch the clock, or surreptitiously glance at my wristwatch, wary of five p.m. – the time Mike's dad came home. I willed Mum to go for the half past four bus, but she never did. Nor could I tell her why, 'cos it risked a ticking off for being cheeky to my elders.

In those days, it was easy to see Bradley Senior's resemblance to a horror comic cover. Odd how we tend to see such likenesses in artwork, even in movies. Not to put too fine a point on this, Lionel Bradley scared me, what with his widow's peak and dark, heavy brows planted above eyes the colour of jet. And his downturned, tight-lipped mouth just had to hide fangs. He didn't say much to me, no loss, and I reckoned he didn't much care for kids anyway, not even his own son.

Lionel and Hermione Bradley, and Mike of course, like us, were an ordinary family residing in an ordinary suburb (in an avenue no less) in an equally ordinary town, whose outskirts were full of smoking chimneys and dour backstreets.

Complexion-wise you might term Mike and me "fresh", our hair the same mousey colour, mine a shade darker, but there it ended. He had a square jaw and tended to slouch when he walked, whereas I, being more round-faced, not fat, and a head taller and proud of it, tended to pull back my shoulders to emphasise the advantage.

That summer of '53 was hot, storm-warning hot. Given the Queen had been crowned on a rainy day and Everest had been conquered on a cold one, it kind of made up for earlier inclemency. Whatever the weather, all seemed right in our world – until the Stone Man came uninvited and ruined it.

We Turners had no pretensions to being better or worse than the Bradleys. We owned our own house, Dad had a reasonably paid job, and life was largely uneventful. To say all kids have their head in the clouds isn't too broad a statement. In hindsight, I believe I was a little more imaginative than Mike, this asset accentuated in my drawings, our differences becoming more apparent as we grew up together, yet somehow apart. Thinking about it, maybe my sketches leaned a tad towards the macabre, yet in no way were half as disturbing as the ones depicted in his books.

That third Tuesday of the summer hols saw us sitting on their well-maintained back lawn, not even a weed daring to mar the precise borders. We'd eaten Spam sandwiches for lunch swilled down with orange squash, and played Monopoly. Boredom set in – certainly on my part. Mike had bought Park Lane with loads of hotels, and yes, I kept landing on it, my assets rapidly shot.

I'd actually been winning but he was a poor loser, and we fell to arguing until Hermione brought us to heel. That said, I let him win rather than fall prey to one of his many moods.

"Right, what's next?" I asked, contemplating his dad's perfectly circular rose bed where blackfly dared not tread.

"Yes Chris," Mike said, "we should do something." He considered this, then clicked his fingers. "I know, we'll visit the tunnel."

"Tunnel? What tunnel? Didn't know there was one near here."

"It's on the other side of those trees." He pointed beyond their garden gate to a narrow pathway, running a fair to moderate straight line through a patchwork of allotments, garden sheds, half-filled water butts and cris-crossed canes where peas and beans grew.

"Is it a long tunnel?" I ventured.

He opened the gate. "Goes on for miles. Dad says not to go there on account of the trains."

"Trains?" Daft question. But then I hadn't heard any trains in all the times Mum and I had visited. Even if there had been, why didn't Bradley Senior trust Junior to avoid trains? Maybe there were trains whose sound, like most things, grows on you, so much so you forget they're there.

"The tunnel slopes underground." Mike pointed. "See where the embankment rises, and all that ivy and grass and stuff kinda hangs? There's a culvert as well," he explained. "Dad told me it's where the run-off goes when it really rains and the river floods." He paused, then added: "It's been dry for weeks, so no problem."

I checked the sky, certainly not as blue as earlier. "What's so special about the tunnel?" I ran to keep up, as he hurried down the path.

"Don't go on the soil," he warned. "If any of the old codgers see you trampling on their gardens they'll go loopy."

I glanced quickly around, not a soul to be seen.

"Just because you can't see 'em, doesn't mean they aren't there." He stopped abruptly and turned. I cannoned into him – those eyes, as dark as his father's, meeting mine, an unspoken question behind my own.

"They hide," he said quietly. "See all those sheds? They watch from there, sorta guard the tunnel. If we put a foot on their soil they'll have us."

His tone was quietly menacing, urging me to run, an uneasy thought jogging with me, conjuring opaque eyes leering from behind summer-dusted windows that reflected acres of garden and bean rows and shimmering sunlight.

"They won't ... won't ... hurt us?" I tried to sound calm. Hell, I was bigger than him, and took comfort from the fact that it's usually the smaller ones they pick on first. Hopefully. "They won't, will they?" I nudged him.

It won a shrug. "Dunno, haven't been down in ages."

Reticence spiralled. And when he followed up with "The Stone Man will get you," that capped it.

I grabbed his arm. "Who's ... who's the Stone Man?" Another noncommital shrug. "Mike!" Then the penny dropped. Or I thought it had, fear thrown skywards on a few high-pitched decibels of humour. "You're funning me."

Silence. His eyes registered passive images. I loathed horror comic eyes even if I had drawn a few in my time.

The hour was on hiatus: soundless, windless, apart from a yipping terrier confirming that something lived beyond this expanse of static plants and geriatric labour. Time and distance merged, heat-haze shimmered close to where the path ran between two recently creosoted sheds, an aromatic smell was pungent in the static air. Beyond them, a haphazard regiment of silver birches grew ramrod-straight, listless.

I wished us back on the lawn, but said nothing, annoyed with myself for suggesting we do something else. Right then I would have felt happier feeding money into Michael Bradley's Monopoly account.

And I didn't dare think about spying eyes, as cold, as penetrating as stone. Or Mike's dad's eyes. Or the single eye of a tunnel hiding a Stone Man. You see, that kind of made it worse because I hadn't seen him ... yet.

"You are having me on, aren't you?" I needed the confirmation.

His grin was condescending. "And you're scared."

Saying it with such conviction as he did convinced me that inside the tunnel, there lurked something darker, not easily guessed at.

In our earlier years we'd been just two kids playing with each other's toys, but that day things changed. Whether or not he was jealous of me for some inane reason, I never did discover. I didn't have any more toys than he did. Until then, I suppose we more or less saw eye to eye. Ah! A joke? Except for his crazy moods, the way he tried to belittle me and others. I really hated that.

Monopoly ceased to be a game, more a sinister dare. A different CHANCE? So, do I pass GO? Collect £200? That day I defined £200 as saving face.

We stood amongst the birches, gorse and broom like two dabs of oil on a watercolour painting, mere splashes of colour amidst waist-high grass. Still nothing moved except us, the ground falling away as we crested a slight rise. Below us the sombre, down-curved mouth of the tunnel belched hot air.

One foot perched on a rickety fence, thumbs hooked into trouser pockets, Mike looked towards it. "See where the culvert disappears underground?"

"Not really," I said, seeing only a narrow defile barely discernible in the shadows.

On a sigh, and grinning like he'd scored another point, he said, "They found a body there."

The words cut runnels down my back. "Body?" I echoed. "Who? When?"

"Last winter. Dad said it had been hit by a train, but I sneaked a look in the local paper. It said: 'Police are regarding the death as suspicious.'"

Call me thick if you like, but I said: "What's that mean? I didn't know there were any trains. Thought the line was disused."

"Chris!" He sounded exasperated. "It means the police don't think it was an accident."

"What was it then?" I asked, wondering if I really did want him to tell me.

The birds stopped chirping when he said, "Murder." The allotments remained deserted; the sun had moved round, diffused rays deflected off house windows. I looked away, the after-glare affecting my vision.

And in the tunnel mouth, amidst the duller shades, I just knew something stirred. It looked huge and awkward, a sort of grey shape, movements jerky. Only shadow images, I told myself. Yeah, shadows of vegetation hanging from the top bank of the tunnel. A cool breeze stirred the grass, another threat in my void of self-doubt. I distanced myself from Mike's puzzled frown. "The St... Stone Man." I jabbed a finger towards the grey-black mouth of the tunnel.

He thumped me on the shoulder. "Come on, scaredy cat, let's take a look."

The invitation held a dare, and I didn't want to lose face. But why had that cornflower-blue sky suddenly gone AWOL, replaced now by heavy, threatening clouds?

My enthusiasm had bottomed out. Very unsure, I reluctantly followed Mike and was relieved when he skirted the dark culvert's maw beneath the tunnel, where a rusted grating fell away into nothing. Had he seen the shape too, and daren't admit it?

Whatever the reason, I was pleased to follow him up the bank. He squatted and touched the dulled, rusted rail track. "Sometimes you can feel a train coming."

There are no trains, I reminded myself, yet felt compelled to touch it. And Jesus! I swear it vibrated, a bit like a load of drums beating the same monotonous rhythm in the distance. Like the footsteps of a giant drawing closer.

"Dad used to work on the trains," he said.

I hadn't known that and said so.

"One time he tested the wheels, banged them with a hammer. If one was cracked it sounded different. They'd change it to stop accidents."

"Not murder then?"

"Don't talk daft, Chris."

"They got stations on the Monopoly game," I said. "There's Fenchurch Street, and Mary-le-something..."

"Bone. It's Mary-le-bone Station."

"Yeah, that's it." I didn't like the way he said *bone*. Bodies have bones, that much I did know. And they'd found a body, Mike had said – a murdered body.

But there weren't any fucking trains. Not on this line.

I wondered if Bailey Senior had anything to do with the body. He used to work on the trains. With a hammer.

Touching the line with my foot, I jerked back. It still thrummed, clouds had gone darker in that lowering sky. I turned to see Mike at the tunnel mouth. "You shouldn't stand there," I yelled as I ran to join him.

"We're okay." His eyes glared. "Go and stand by the culvert if you're scared."

Venom sat in that last phrase, posed more questions: Should I stay and see what happened? Or leave him there with only shadows for company?

He went in, actually walked inside the damp, dark, dripping mouth of the tunnel, his shape there one minute, gone the next, his voice, distorted some, echoing: "If you don't come in, they'll get you on the way back."

Get me? Who'll...? The guardians in the sheds, that's who. I followed him in, urged by the first heavy spots of rain. I mean, I did wait right up until the last minute.

What made me go, I don't know. Scared of getting wet? Scared of leaving him, of being on my own and still feeling the dull drumbeat of vibrations never diminished, never any louder, but there?

"Mike?" I walked carefully, a hand touching damp, tacky walls smothered with a type of furry growth undetectable in the waning light. I pulled a face, mind conjuring all sorts of weird stuff. I mean it could have been anything from scalps to dead rabbits. I took some comfort in looking back towards the tunnel mouth. Grown smaller, sure, but as long as I kept it in view then everything would be fine.

"MIKE." It cannoned off tunnel walls, the hollowness sounding real bad. Only the echo warbled. "WHERE. ARE. YO-O-O-U?" The last word rushed back like a train whistle.

Then I heard it: the breathing. I know I did.

Clamped to the tunnel wall, I looked back, the distant entrance flaring purple and yellow like the eye of some god-awful beast. I put my heart and soul into a real belting scream, my voice high, reedy, and very scared.

Tentatively I reached into the dark with my foot, felt contact with the line, its vibrations having taken on a new timbre, the sound surging through my body like an electric shock. Noise climbed, grew excruciatingly loud, smothered suddenly by a loud crack that surged down the tunnel, the vast enclosed space one big echo-chamber of light, sound ... and movement.

The dark lit up and I saw Mike's screaming face some ten feet from me; saw his flesh tear, any fresh sounds absorbed by whatever other noises soured these already corrupted walls. And in that effervescing light, I witnessed something defying description, perhaps a thing from my own warped imagination, or maybe out of one of Mike's books. Here was stone that rippled, and ... Christ! It drew breath, and its footsteps vibrated on the rails, mashed the gravel that lay between them.

I tried to run – the stones, the damp and what I took (hoped?) to be moss making it difficult, my trousers torn, knees grazed as I stumbled towards the distant tunnel mouth in that invading, embracing twilight. A yell of despair and fright caught in my throat, a mere bubble of breath accompanying me as I fought to reach safety. Stones tumbled, bounced, walls ruptured. A cascade of earth threatened: I dodged, skipping with ungainly speed to the far wall. One toe caught the line, sent me sprawling, a worse fall prevented by the slimy, dank stone – mineral? Or animal? Wincing at grazed hands, I kept on zig-zagging – aware that something dogged me, mental vision overburdened, ears tortured with an amplified blat of noise, all else choked in a cacophony of threat.

Words and phrases thudded in my mind: *No trains. Disused.* So what did follow me? What had I discovered in this dark place? As God's my witness, my saviour, any-damned-thing, I prayed I wouldn't end up like Mike ... torn to shreds. I closed my eyes briefly against the image and made it worse.

A handful of displaced air shoved me. The scream... of a whistle?

Or of victory? I could hear the rain, the thunder, still see a disembodied face floating behind – huge, distorted, a face hewn from stone. My words, indecipherable even to myself, were snatched away, melded into a silent yelling.

"Oh please ... please ... let me live. I don't wanna die... Let. Me. Live." I stumbled backwards, not daring to lose sight of a vision barely seen in the shadows.

Birds whistled and squawked above, their flapping wings adding to the hell of the tunnel. And yes, Mike was right: it did slope, the gradient indeterminate in my breathless, scared state. It seemed as though I climbed upwards out of some ink-black hole, desperate to escape the bad dreams that, even today, still haunt me.

I heard something give, the rending brittleness of age-old metal. Voice suddenly rediscovered, I yelled, my cry shredded by the thunder. I slid, carrying pain and noise with me, my arms entangled in ivy, sharp tendrils scourging face and arms, shirt sleeves flapping against skin in some desultory round of applause. A jutting branch, growing from stone, fetched me a nasty crack on the head. Thunder. Lightning. Cries. Nothing.

Blood on my hand as I touched my head. I whimpered and sat up, a grizzled view of clouds far above me, my vision hazy – and a new sound hard to pinpoint, its cause made very apparent as water cascaded down the sluice, soaking me to the skin.

I tottered, thoughts submerged in a wash of sound and drab light, and the memory of that awful other noise. A train whistle? (No trains!) So ... what? In the tunnel?

Like some drowned item of clothing slung into a weir, I crawled amidst the gross, evil-smelling shadows underneath the tunnel. Arches rank with mildew sprouting weeds, the grey stone cold, my palms stinking with deposits that oozed from its cracks.

This wasn't Park Lane with its fancy hotels. Maybe it was the Old Kent Road, with rotting tenements and things that crawled and scurried in the shadows where light never fell.

And maybe it really was the haunt of the Stone Man. The man with the hammer. The man with eyes as hard and black as deepest night.

Mum told me once, in answer to one of my curious growing-up

questions, that souls don't die, that when a person dies their soul waits to be reborn. A great believer is Mum.

But what of monsters? Do their souls, like ours, wait to be reborn?

The gloom entrapped me, and I realised I didn't want to meet the soul of that body they'd found last year. So why did I ask the bloody question?

The sluice's roar became a living thing I hated. I was alone, swallowed into a ground from which stone walls the colour of dead men grew, and forced to think about what had really happened in the tunnel.

I called Mike's name again, rewarded only by a cold wind surging into the opening. Time seemed pointless; my only need was to get out, into the rain and the world, and normality. I tried to stand and collapsed, my right leg unable to bear even my slight weight.

In waning light, as vegetation raged across the mouth of this... this monster, I made out a livid gash from knee to ankle. Had I done it? Or had something else? Something that lived under here? A thing with claws?

I yelled: "M-I-C-H-A-E-L-L-L-L." Echoes surged, emphasising the *ell... ell... HELL?*

And it rained. Despite my earlier thoughts, time now became all-important. The day had ceased to be bone dry, the sluice engorging, more water, the flow intensifying, the– What had Mike called it? Culvert! And that posed an even greater threat as water swirled around my knees, old leaves and a thousand gorse needles floating on a rising tide.

Faces on glass shed windows; sunlight-emblazoned houses, all jeering: *You've passed GO, but you can't collect any winnings! Nobody wins. Ever.*

Pictures in Mike's books of gargoyles etched from stone. Ancient paintings discovered on cave walls of beings long since extinct. Oh Christ, let it be that way!

This tunnel was man-made, that much I did know – but it didn't prevent another horrendous, worrying thought: Who or what had been the models for such hideous creatures? Might they be the acolytes of the Stone Man?

More stone cracked, showered down. I had to get out, a kind of madness adding more damning cries as I attempted to re-scale the slope, hampered by the remains of an eroded grill caught in the branch that had nearly rendered me unconscious. I could have drowned, might still drown, if I didn't manage to climb the slippery stone. Clumps of soil came away in my hands, my smooth-soled shoes unable to find purchase, the pain in my leg a hindrance. I shrieked, called out for Mike, only to realise he wasn't coming. No-one was.

Petrified, I managed to swish to the opposite side, knowing that I walked beneath the lines above. With eyes rooted on the dark, soulful hole where the sluice, culvert, whatever, angled into a wide Y shape that boiled with water and outflung spray, I grabbed at creepers, praying they wouldn't give as I made my slow, tortuous way across, the tide swirl an ever-present threat.

Surely there had to be another grill. But then, if the rain...? Fresh terror warned it would be the same, but I had to attempt to discover another exit. My heart rattled, I hurt and I was scared. But I wouldn't cry. If Mike heard me I'd never live it down.

To some, friendship can be short-lived, and to me ours had died because I now knew what Mike's intention had been when he took me to the tunnel. His talk of bodies and bones and a man with a hammer...

Perhaps he realised I'd let him win that stupid Monopoly game and didn't like that either.

A sound! Breathing. Exactly as I'd heard in the tunnel. Had you been there, I swear you would have heard it.

The in-flow gushed, marooning me between one grating and the hole I had blindly fallen down. I clung to the stone, clawing for handholds against its onrush. I traced patterns in the stone, the dim light momentarily throwing up a recognisable face carved there, maybe one I had sketched and left to wonder how it came to be there. Diffused light erased it. At the opposite end, a mountain of dead branches and other nameless detritus had tumbled down, sealing off any escape in that direction. Above me the storm shouted, leastways I hoped it was the storm and not some infernal beast imbued with a semblance of life on cave walls when man first came to be.

I wanted Mum. With that need uppermost, I turned with difficulty.

The water had reached my thighs, smells of age and nature and drowned creatures making me nauseous. Something floated past, brushed my legs, wan light reflected in cold, dead eyes.

I yelped, my horror comic drawings given screaming life when something big and grey rose up out of the water, great feet parting the tide as it shambled towards me. All I saw was a mass of grey: stone-grey arms reaching, long fingers hooked, open mouth calling, the grey-white of teeth. I backed off, me and a dead rat butted up against the dead-fall. A sickly sweet aroma punched me in the face.

"They found a body," Mike had said. "Souls wait around," Mum had said. Honest.

The scream? Had it been Michael? Or me? Or just the train whistle as it left Mary-le-bone?

Night-dark eyes were projected from a putty-coloured face, partially consumed by reflected water shadows. He had got me. The Stone Man. Mike had said he would. Now he would punish me, keep me inside his tunnel for eternity. He reached, grabbed...

As I reached and grabbed at the nearest thing floating past me. I hefted it and started beating him, screaming for him to "LET ME GO. Mike's fault. He ... brought ... me ... here."

I hit out, bits of flesh and dark stuff spraying out, and instantly realised that I was clutching Mike's severed arm...

I recognised the colour of his shirt sleeve. I was hitting the Stone Man with the soggy end, like a joke I heard years later, and seeing only a bestial face covered in blood.

Then everything went total black.

WE HAD ALL the sobbing, the praises, but mostly I remember the smell of creosote.

Footprints in muddy soil.

Figures in glasses looking as if they were peering from behind a multitude of shed windows, all of them clapping, laughing. Acolytes.

I've often wondered if they were welcoming a new disciple to their fold.

They told me Bradley Senior had saved me from the flood, and died because of it. Hailed as a hero, they said. At least it warranted a big spread in the news.

I'm consoled by the fact that me and the Stone Man do have one thing in common – we're heartless.

They said that when the train hit Mike he would have died instantly. A terrible accident.

No suspicious circumstances.

All lies, media talk. Most knew that Michael Bradley is still down there with his dad. A double sacrifice? See, I traced the outlines of Mike's face in the stone. Might even be his soul. So had I drawn his soul? Unconsciously wished him, or maybe both of them, dead?

Today I avoid the railway; I don't go out when it really rains. Thankfully, I have understanding parents.

I still like to draw Mike. And big monster engines wearing his face. My interpretation has bared teeth, and dark grey stone eyes ... exactly like the ones I glimpsed in the lightning's flash that day in the tunnel. And in the culvert. Looks great on the latest cover I'm drawing for *Monster Monthly*.

Poor Mike longs to shake the dice, collect his two hundred smackers. Well, let him wait. Bastard loved to scare the unfortunates! They say God never pays his debts in money.

And let me say: There are no trains in that tunnel. Not now. Not then. Nor will there ever be, because they dismantled it ... stone by stone. Shame about the mysterious deaths...

As I said, the Gods never pay their debts in money. That fact was emphasised when I saw a grey stone-clawed hand reach out and tear Bradley Senior's head off.

Whatever the thing was, it shoved me out.

TO WALK IN MIDNIGHT'S REALM

Simon Bestwick

MARBAN: Have you thought why ... we don't see them more often, the dead?
BRAC: Well –
MARBAN: Because of the pain of dying, brother.
Which is like a wall.

Howard Brenton, *The Romans In Britain*

DUSK WAS FALLING as I slowed the hired Land Rover to a halt on the bleak, unwelcoming mountainside, listing badly with only the grip of its tyres to anchor it in place. The coming night lay like a grey haze or screen of gauze over the flat sides and lichenous spars of slate protruding through the long and wiry grass.

All around spread the Llandegla Moor; the lights of a small town glimmered in the distance. Gathered densely at the foot of the mountain, directly below, a thick conifer wood bristled against the descent of the sun.

Things rustled in the undergrowth, and I flashed the torch I'd brought around sparingly, never sure what was the low wind in the bushes and what the movement of small animals. Or what might be ... other than those.

Clouds gathered, and the wind bit cold, and I wondered, not for the first time, what the hell I was doing here, in this place. It could still be dangerous, here in the Gwynedd heartlands; the mountains were an easy place to get lost, to die of exposure.

To hallucinate? Perhaps that explained John's letter, but it had never seemed like the ramblings born of a drug-induced haze, or even of a dream. It was too coherent – and besides, if things hadn't happened as John had said, then what had become of him and his companions, out here on the bleak mountainside?

I didn't know. But it occurred to me that there was little room for doubts now. I should have thought of that before removing his body from its coffin. A bribe to the undertaker had substituted something – *hopefully* some*thing*, but I wasn't eager to press the point further – in his place for the cremation, and so now, as far as anybody was concerned, John Baxter was only a fine rain of ashes, strewn from another Welsh mountainside, for he'd loved this land like no other place and no other person, except perhaps me ... and one other.

All of which would make life very difficult if I got pulled over for speeding or something. The Gwynedd constabulary don't tend to have that much to do at the best of times, and if they discovered John's shroud-wrapped body in the back of the Rover... At times like this, I was very glad both our parents were no longer around. Some things you really don't want to have to explain.

What had possessed me to make that promise – and, more so, to *keep* it? In the cold light of day – or even in the dimmer one of the early evening – it seemed ridiculous, what I was planning to do, and why. At least, if I was rumbled by some nosey copper, I wouldn't go to prison... *Now, Mr Baxter, let's not have any trouble; just go with the nice men in the white coats...*

I shook my head to clear it, and poured myself a coffee from my Thermos. It had to be said there were better ways to spend a weekend.

I was glad the shroud was securely wrapped; he'd be starting to go off a bit by now. Still, at least the rigor mortis ought to have worn off.

Did I really think that events would turn out as he'd suggested? I looked at my watch and saw that it was almost ten o'clock. In two hours I'd find out first-hand. Without wishing to sound cynical, I wasn't holding my breath. Still, I reflected, John seemed to be doing that for both of us, and I fought to suppress a wild outburst of laughter. It escaped my compressed lips as a sort of farting noise, and that did set me off. When I calmed and quietened down I felt much better.

But what was I going to do when, come the dawn, I was confronted with the prospect of the disposal of my brother's mortal remains? I'd never considered the problem, however strange it might sound; I'd been too caught up in trying to plan out his last request. The authorities would never have allowed it, hence the subterfuge. I was very close to my brother, and his death had distressed me deeply. Feeling guilty for it, even though I bore no responsibility for his death and had had no opportunity to prevent it, had come naturally. That, of course, is what had possessed me to honour this mad request – fraternal love and devotion, and deep sorrow.

But still it seemed unreal, until I touched my thick jacket, just over where I knew the inside pocket lay, and heard the crackle and rustle of folded paper. Of course. The letter.

It had come to me the day after John's death, courtesy of his bank manager, who'd been instructed to hold it for him. He'd had, obviously, no idea whatsoever of its contents. Best, John had thought, to keep the whole thing between the two of us; certainly no whiff of it to the solicitors. God, what a three-ring circus they'd make of it then! I'm no solicitor, but I can imagine what impact a letter like this would have had. All the distant relatives with a glitter of avarice in their eyes, swarming like termites to chew off a piece of the action. Not that John had had a great deal. Ten years in a factory, then a back injury and a juicy pay-out that left him without the need to work again. But he was a working man, had always been. I was the shy, bookish one; he'd been the footballer, the fell-walker – and, of course, the mountain-climber. Well, less a climber than a camper. He liked to walk, to explore, and he especially loved places that were unfrequented, rarely visited. Like this mountain; a busy road wove across the Llandegla Moor, and nearby there was the clay-pigeon shooting club. Even here, there was activity, but not on this mountain; it stood alone and unregarded, even shunned, and for no reason that I could ascertain.

But I digress. Yes, John was a working man, even when he couldn't work. And so he'd set out and found work. Volunteer shops like Oxfam, then later on to a local FE college. He was a good carer, good with people, and that was how he'd ended up with the rehab crowd.

Again, strictly volunteer work, helping out at an inner-city drop-in for addicts and working women, then in a clinic for the same kind of people, holding hands and wiping away tears. But he'd been good at what he did. After he died, I cleared out a few of his old drawers, and found them crammed full of cards and notes, covered in writing that was often spidery and clumsy, but always clear in the emotions it sought to convey. Thanks, gratitude, affection. Even love. I cried that day, long and hard. I didn't throw the cards out. I have them still.

Some of those people came to the funeral. They hung back, diffident and shy, as if afraid of being scourged, driven out with whips, clubs and the occasional judicious use of a shotgun. By then, of course, I'd read the cards, and welcomed them. John wouldn't have minded; hell, he'd have been over the moon, so let Great Aunt Sourpuss turn up her nose. I even invited them to the wake.

I heard a lot of stories about John there, some I'd heard before and some I hadn't. There were funny ones and there were not so funny ones. The one that was the unfunniest of them all – and everyone knew it – was Tricktrack's.

I said that there was love there. That was where John had found it, that kind of love, for the first and only time in his generous life. Found it and lost it. Tricktrack.

Tricktrack had been about nineteen, a good ten years younger than John, but that had never mattered. One of those people who come to you so battered and broken by bad luck and bad life that if they were a car they'd have been written off long ago. Most people write them off too.

But John never wrote anyone off as a human being in his life – well, apart from Margaret Thatcher – and he wouldn't write off Tricktrack, even when everyone else had. Tricktrack had been foul-mouthed and violent at times, sometimes not even needing to be strung out to do it. Abused at an early age, she was ferociously aware of the effect her body could have, and on a number of occasions she'd stripped and come on to social workers and people like John. Most of them ran like hell.

Not John, though. John had stood his ground and taken it all. Her screaming. Her anger. Her provocation. Even her blows. I remember thinking of my brother as a rock, one against which all life's troubles broke like the raging sea without harm, a shelter and steadying prop for me when I was embattled. He'd been like that for Tricktrack too.

Even John had never known her real name. She had never volunteered it, and John, loath to damage their emerging friendship by probing too deep or hard, had never asked. Tricktrack was her name, to him, to others, and even to herself. Whatever nightmares lay in her past – and I dread to think what they might have been – they'd tainted whatever name she might have been given. It lay in a bin of broken glass, rusty syringes and starving rats, and she wouldn't reach down for it at any price.

But that was fine by John. Bit by bit, he brought her out of her shell. She came to trust him, and to depend on him. And he, in his turn, came to care for her as for nothing else in his life. Damaged and dangerous, but still fighting on, never giving up. It earned his respect first, and then it earned something more.

I don't know when he realised that he was in love with her. But I know that others weren't slow to spot it. They kept him with her, didn't transfer him, because no-one else could handle her. Hell, there was no-one else who'd even stay in the same *room* as her. The oddest of couples they made, the rail-thin teenage hooker with the short spiny coxcomb of red-dyed hair and eyes of midnight black, and the big gentle volunteer worker, but they worked. At least they did until Tricktrack started to feel the same way about John.

John had never put a foot wrong with her, on that all were agreed. He'd known how he felt, but at the end of the day, he'd known what to make such a move would mean. But Tricktrack had never seen life in such complicated terms. Whatever she had, she'd fought for; whatever she wanted hadn't been subtly gained. So she made it quite clear to him, in no uncertain terms, that she wanted them to be more than friends.

And my brother, of course, my big kind unselfish brother who'd never willingly harmed a soul, who put her before his own gratification – my brother turned her down, rebuffed her. Gently, but a rebuff is a rebuff.

Tricktrack was inconsolable. It was more than being told that they couldn't be a couple; it was the fear that she'd cost herself the only friend she had. Perhaps she was thinking of the effect of her less sincere come-ons in the past. Whatever the truth, that night she disappeared from the clinic, into an icy December night. John was out looking for her till the crack of dawn, looking everywhere he could think of; but in the end it was someone else, unhindered by hope, who found her last resting place.

Tricktrack had drained a full bottle of vodka, stripped naked in the freezing, windblown night, and jumped off a bridge into the river. The river had frozen over, though, and her rail thin body hadn't the weight to break the ice. Instead, she'd broken her back and lain there, paralysed. Whether shock or the cold killed her first, no-one seemed sure. It hardly mattered. It only mattered that they found her there, just under the lip of the bridge, in the cold and rosy dawn; frozen to one pale cheek, a single perfect tear.

JOHN HAD BEEN devastated by Tricktrack's death. Not unnaturally, he'd blamed himself, though he was never sure for what. Should he have responded to her advances? Would that have saved her? Could anything have?

The year and a half that followed had been dark. I'd been there for him as best I could, but at the end of the day the real battle wasn't going on anywhere near me, but miles away, in some twist of neurons or dark recess of the soul. Depending on who you asked.

What he needed, if anything, it was concluded, was to get away from it all. Two of our friends decided to take him on a camping trip to Wales. They were taking him away for two reasons: one, to give me a break, because I was wearing myself to a frazzle doing whatever I could for John; second, because although they both got on with John, me, and even each other most of the time, Derek Lane and Ken Stokes were never going to see eye to eye. Ken was a Catholic priest, a faith within which our family nominally resided, while Derek lectured in psychology and anthropology at the university. The point was that their positions were miles apart. I had the feeling it might bring John out of his gloom, if only long enough to bang their heads together when they started pitting their beliefs against one another's.

Ken and Derek, you see, both agreed that it was their duty as John's friends to help him come to terms with Tricktrack's death. A break in the Great Outdoors, confronting the Ancient Majesty of Nature and so forth, might be just what was needed to put things into a context of some kind. But, to Ken, the point was to help affirm John's belief that Tricktrack existed still, in another form and in another place; that her life hadn't been pointless, made to count for nothing. She was happy, cared for; a new star in heaven, safe in the bosom of Our Father, and so on.

Derek, on the other hand, regarded notions of the afterlife as a dangerous fantasy, a superstition used to cow people into submission in this life, the only one you got. Coddling John with fairy tales, in his view, might be a good defence mechanism temporarily, help him to heal – but his eyes were as beady and watchful for John as a shepherd's for a newborn lamb. With Ken as the ecclesiastical crow. He wasn't steering John into the Church's fold if Derek could help it. Derek would much rather John came to terms with the fact that Tricktrack was dead. She didn't exist any more; it was that simple and that brutal. It wasn't fair, but fairness was just an idea humanity had created and tried to impose upon the world as best they could. John should live in the here and now, not spend his days mooning after some impossible, non-existent reunion with his forever lost beloved.

As you can imagine, it promised to be a magical mystery tour, though I wouldn't be surprised if Derek hadn't planned it to become a bit of a shouting match. Nothing like a bit of the old shock treatment. Ask any psychologist.

Well, in the end ... but I'm getting ahead of myself.

The sun was almost gone now, and the mountainside was no longer visible. I didn't relish the thought of sitting alone in the dark, and so I turned on the small light inside the cab of the Land Rover, unzipped my jacket, reached inside and pulled out the letter, unfolding it with a soft rustle. And, in an effort to understand his story and my own, to see once more what had brought us both together for the last time, here, on this edge of mountain and night, I began to read.

MATT, *THE LETTER begin.*

By the time you read this I will be dead.

Sorry, little brother. Always wanted to write that. Talk about a once in a lifetime opportunity, eh?

I had a check-up a week ago, and all's apparently well, but for all that I don't expect to be around much longer. I don't mean I've got any plans to kill myself either, so don't worry – but then again there'll be nothing to worry about when you get this, will there?

What I mean is, I've seen something that I don't really think I was meant to see, that I don't think any of us are meant to. But it's done now, and I can't complain. I just wish I could find a little more comfort in the prospect of my own pegging it.

But anyway, don't think from this you're to go chasing after suspicious circumstances, because you won't find any. All I know – in an entirely instinctive way – is that sometime in the near future, I'm going to die. Nothing human will have anything to do with it, or even anything malign, I think. It's far more complicated than that. You need to understand that. Derek and Ken didn't, and...

Oh, God, you're thinking. He did them in, didn't he?

No, little brother, nothing like that, although the thought of belting the pair of them with a shovel did have a certain appeal after a while.

What do you know? I have to keep reminding myself of it, because I've never really kept secrets from you before. Let's see.

We went camping in Wales, didn't we? Out near Llandegla. Only I came back; they found me half dead of exposure on the Moor, hardly remembering anything. Ken and Derek...

Anyway, it was all supposedly a tragic accident. But it wasn't.

It really happened like this.

IT WAS EARLY afternoon when we arrived at Llandegla and stocked up on a few little extras in town – fresh fruit and a couple of rabbits from the local butchers – before heading on to the mountain, with Derek and Ken conducting a non-stop chattering match every step of the bloody way.

Don't get me wrong, there was nothing acrimonious about it. They just chattered and quoted and argued and counter-argued nineteen to the dozen. I began to think that maybe it was some sort of comedy double act. It did start to wear after a while, though.

Still, once we set up camp and had a good brisk walk to whet our appetites, things improved greatly. When night began to fall, we set up a fire and I set to work on the rabbits. You know me – never go far without a few good herbs for cooking with. That, a little of that Navy Rum Derek was so fond of in the coffee and a couple of big bars of Bournville Dark for afters – well, Tricktrack always used to say that men were just little boys, but taller and with hairy dicks. Never really grow up, and I suppose it was a bit like when we were all kids and used to go camping. Remember that? But I don't want to go off on a tangent about all that, pleasant though it might be.

We were all well-mellowed by then – for 'mellowed' read 'pleasantly pissed' – but not sleepy; if anything we were wider awake than we had been all day. It was just that none of us were sure what the hell to do about it.

"How about a sing-song?" suggested Ken. Derek groaned loudly.

"Like what? *Onward Christian Soldiers*? *Hark The Herald Angels*?"

"Wrong time of year. Bloody heathen."

"Children, children," I put in. "Play nice."

"S... S'alright, John," said Ken, drawing himself up with bleary dignity. "I'm a forgiving soul, and I forgive Derek. He knows not what he does."

"After half a bottle of Lamb's Navy issue I should bloody well hope not," said Derek. "And nor should you. Ought to be ashamed of yourself."

I brewed black coffee, and we drank it down. Things started to level off a bit after that, but then the cold began to seep into our bones as the fire started dying. We'd piled up a respectable supply of dried bracken and deadwood, but we'd thrown most of it on at the beginning to create a hearty blaze and now it was on the wane; there were only a few twigs with which to fuel the flames.

"Well," I said, "unless someone wants to get us some more firewood, I think that's about all she wrote for the night. Unless you want to retreat inside one of the tents and help me kill this bottle of Lamb's?"

"To hell with that," said Derek, winking at Ken. "No offence, padre."

"Arse," said Ken.

Derek blew a raspberry. "Sling us a torch, you bastards, and I'll go a-gathering."

I let him have the torch without a fight; I knew from experience that trying to talk Derek out of anything, especially when drunk, was like trying to beat the tide back with a stick. He wandered off, singing something that sounded vaguely blasphemous as he went.

Ken slumped back on the ground and giggled. "Think I should tell him about the ghosties?"

I laughed. "That'll really impress him." Then I blinked. "What ghosties?"

"Oh..." Ken waved a hand vaguely. "Some local legend. Supposed to come out on the mountain by night or something – or was it live inside it? Can't recall offhand."

I shrugged, and squinted off into the dark. Parts of Derek were faintly and intermittently silhouetted by the bobbing light. "Derek!" I yelled. "You all right?"

"Not been grabbed by the ghoulies, I hope," Ken called, and fell back in fits of laughter.

"Fine," shouted Derek. "And no jokes about whether or not I'm getting any wood, please."

"Just watch your step out there," Ken rejoined, having composed himself again.

"Yes, mother," Derek shouted back. "Don't worry, I'm fi–"

Right on cue, there came a squawk of pain and fear, and a loud crashing and clanging, receding into a far distance. Too far for my liking. In the same instant, the torch beam flickered upwards and was gone.

"Derek?" I shouted, rising unsteadily to my feet. "Derek? You OK?"

No answer.

I looked over at Ken, and he rose to his feet too. We both shouted "Derek" again, and once more he gave no answer. I dug up another pair of torches, and taking one each, we made our way towards the spot where we'd last seen and heard him.

We almost followed him down the hard way. The hole he'd fallen through was so thickly overgrown that you normally wouldn't see it until it was too late. Fortunately Derek had thrashed a very clear trail to it, and the vegetation was pretty well beaten about. All we needed to do was flash our torches, and we found ourselves with a perfect view of a hole about four or five feet wide, plunging down like a curving water-slide into the living rock of the mountain.

"De-rek!" we yelled. A moment later, his voice called back up to us.

"I'm OK! Come on down! You've got to see this!"

Ken and I exchanged glances. I know what you're thinking, Matt – *what?* In the dead of night, up on a mountain in the middle of nowhere, I was going to venture down a big hole in the ground? Never mind that Derek had fallen arse over tip down it without apparently doing himself any harm; you must be shaking your head in disbelief right now that I could do something so stupid.

But I was half-cut (we both were), and it all seemed a laugh, just as it had when we were kids and did crazier things than this for the hell of it. Remember – no, better not. I'll go off down Memory Lane for page after page if I'm not careful. And, of course, I had a big what-the-hell attitude. I felt no great fear of death, or incentive to carry on; that hadn't changed since Tricktrack's death.

So, of course, we climbed into the tunnel and began to make our way down. It was a tricky business; there were a few jagged edges sticking out of the walls. I looked closely but couldn't see any blood. With the amount of alcohol Derek had taken, he could probably have lost half his arms and legs on the way down and not noticed a thing.

But there was no blood, and Derek, when we found him, seemed to be in perfect shape, a few minor cuts and bruises aside. In fact, he was hopping around like a monkey with haemorrhoids. "Look at this!" he said. "Look at it! What a find!"

Ken and I shone our torches about, joined quickly by Derek's, which had somehow survived the bumpy descent into the depths of the mountain. I swear I heard the click as Ken's jaw dropped open. I managed to restrain myself to a low whistle of astonishment.

The cave-tunnel that we'd followed down opened out into a great bell-shaped chamber, the walls of which were carved like nothing I'd ever seen. A strange and eerie medley of images and shapes. There were bas-relief carvings, and there were full, three-dimensional statues; elsewhere there was what looked like a mosaic, and another painting in a style that appeared almost to be *al fresco*. All the statues had been hewn from stalagmites and stalactites or other protrusions of rock.

They ranged across cultures and times: from Ancient Greece and Egypt, across to the Saxons and the Vikings. Some were oriental in appearance; others owed a lot to the architecture of early Christianity. A few even looked modern. But all were linked by common themes: they were, without exception, deeply morbid and sombre. The carvings represented Anubis, or the Harpies or Gorgons of myth. A bat-winged, fork-tailed, goat-headed Satan leered with very ungoatlike fangs from one particularly convincing-looking image.

"Jesus, Mary and Joseph," whispered Ken, and for once Derek didn't have anything to say to that, even if he heard it in the first place. He was too busy inspecting a few carvings in the shadows of the cave. "Come here, you two," he called. "Don't think I've ever seen anything quite like this before. What d'you make of it?"

We squinted. The carvings seemed to make abortive, abandoned attempts to represent some sort of giant, looming figure, grotesque and inhuman to look at. It's very hard to describe, largely because the detail was so vague. But it was big, you could tell that from the little human stick-figures placed in terrified relation to it, and from what it was doing to them it looked pretty unfriendly, to say the least. Just take it from me, Matt, you wouldn't want to meet it on a dark night.

"What is this place?" Ken was shaking his head. "I've never seen anything like it."

"Pretty damn fascinating, you must admit," said Derek. He flashed his torch further along the wall, to light upon another tunnel. "Come on. Let's explore."

"Explore?" protested Ken. "Shouldn't we wait until morning?"

"Why?" Derek gave his devil-may-care grin. "Not scared, are you?"

And that was that, wasn't it? Ken wasn't going to turn down a dare like that. The more I think about it, the more convincing Tricktrack's theory sounds. And me, of course ... well, I was game for anything.

Torches casting long yellow cones of light ahead of us, trawling the dark, we advanced into the tunnel.

CRAZIER AND CRAZIER, I know, Matt. In the end it keeps

coming back to Derek's motivations. It was he who gave the whole expedition its impetus. His daring Ken to follow. Why would a sensible, rational man like Derek lead such a foolhardy, madcap (drunken) expedition, in the dead of night, into tunnels apparently unexplored for years?

Well, Tricktrack's theory goes some of the way. It was fascinating, even to us; to Derek, it was a goldmine, and like a kid on Christmas Day, he found waiting to open his presents impossible. And, of course, there was the distinct possibility he might have hit his head on the way down.

But I think there was more to it than that, now. So convenient, wasn't it, in the light of future events, that Derek should find that tunnel gaping under his feet when he did? I know you're supposed to wait till the count of three before happenstance becomes enemy action, but in this case I think I'm entitled to make an exception.

Something down there wanted us to find it. Or perhaps it wasn't something, but someone...?

But I'm getting ahead of myself.

THE TUNNEL RANG and echoed to the drip of water, a noise that rang louder still as it widened out into a cavern. Stalactites and stalagmites curved and thrust like fangs. Even here, they had been carved into new and grotesque shapes. Demons of Assyria, and ancient Babylon. The dread Bel-Marduk of the Sumerians. All carved, somehow deathlessly, in the limestone, despite the constant soapy gush of water over the surfaces. New ones grew, but the old were never lost, and the tunnel was never too crowded to navigate. Mystery. It's a drug, and as with any other, once you're hooked, you can't let go. No more could we.

Even when we heard the hoarse, rasping sound of breathing, one that seemed to come from all around us, and dared not shine our torches in what we thought was its direction, because we were all – even Derek – terrified, against all reason, of what we would see.

"What is that?" whispered Ken.

"Echoes," suggested Derek. Ken laughed harshly.

"The wind, then." Another laugh.

"Will you shut up?" Derek snapped. Laughter again; Derek, mood turned suddenly ugly, grabbed a fistful of Ken's shirt. "Ken, just–"

"Derek–" Ken said softly, swallowing hard. "Derek, that wasn't me."

"Then who–" I began, and Ken flashed his torch round.

The circle of yellow light from the torch fell on it and we all grew still. For long moments we all stared. There was no doubt in our minds; we could see it with cinematic clarity. Head, shoulder, arm, an extended hand. The hand was mostly red; flaps and fragments hung down from it like peeling wallpaper. In places the bone gleamed white.

The head was a nightmare, and there was little of a face even worthy of the name any more. The head no longer had its original shape and in places had split.

We faced an impossibility. It could not be alive, much less capable of movement, but we could hear its hoarse, stertorous breathing, and the rattling moan that came from its throat. From the shadows beside it came a laugh, hoarse and asthmatic. Derek's torch flashed towards it and pinned another face in its beam. This one was pallid and horribly bloated, almost to the size of a beachball, mouth and eyes all but swallowed in the pulpy-looking flesh, spotted with patches of greenish mould.

We could still hear the breathing. It was louder still; it seemed to come from all around. Ranks of shadows were packed together, behind the ones in plain view.

The beams of our torches began to rove, faster and faster as even the tiniest sounds brought a response. And everywhere they went, fluttering through the cavern like pale moths, they alighted on another face. One looked like a coloured guy at first, till I saw that it had been burned almost to charcoal. Borne on its shoulders was a child whose face I can't get out of my head even now. I don't even want to think of how that child must have died.

Died, yes. As we stood contemplating one another, the two groups, there could be no doubt, no ambiguity. They were all dead. And yet they stood. They walked. They saw.

One of them took a hesitant step forward. An incoherent sound escaped Derek's throat.

Then they rushed at us.

They moved clumsily but not slowly, like the zombies of films. They might lumber a little and paw when they meant to grab, but hell, I thought with insane humour, if you'd been hit by a sixteen-wheeler truck and dragged halfway along the M6, I think your hand-eye coordination might be a little off too, don't you?

What I want desperately to convey, and *can't*, however hard I seem to try, was the sheer *madness* of that scene. I was glad – I think we all were – that we only glimpsed the briefest details once their attack had begun. The only weapons we had to fend them off with were our torches, which were sturdy, but a blow smashed the bulb on mine within minutes.

Cold, wet stone pressed against my back: the cavern wall. We were all shouting and screaming; my throat felt raw and hot. Derek stopped yelling, his torch blinking out; the dark figures swarmed in to clutch at Ken and me.

Then Ken's torch died, breaking as it struck something that made a soft, unpleasant noise. An exultant howling, an avid rush. We were both screaming, weapons braced in throbbing hands for the final assault.

Then light! Bright and beautiful, coming from a heavy torch swinging from above, blazing into my eyes as its butt-end thudded into the forehead of one of our attackers. Clutched in one of Derek's hands, the other grabbing mine. "Come on!" he roared. I held tight as he hauled, bracing my feet against the wall and climbing up it before he practically flung me bodily onto the ledge he'd reached, legs locked round a stalagmite. Then he lunged down again, to grab Ken and pull him up to safety. A couple of *them* tried to crawl after us, but with their co-ordination it was nothing doing, sad to say, so sorry.

Opening my mouth to deliver what would hopefully be some sort of witty remark, I tried to lean back against the wall and pitched back through it instead. Derek and Ken scrambled over and pulled me back to my feet; I'd tumbled into another tunnel leading from the ledge. Quickly, before the living dead things behind us could master the climbing of the walls, we ran down the tunnel, the beam of Derek's torch the only light to guide our way.

"COME OUT TO Wales, they said," I puffed later, as we staggered round yet another bend in the tunnel. "We'll go camping, they said. Get bladdered, have a laugh, they said. Take your mind off things, they said..."

"John," gasped Derek, halting, hands on his thighs, and gulping air, "I know this isn't an easy time for you, and you're in shock, and you've been through a lot – but having said all that, will you please shut the fuck up?"

"I don't suppose," Ken broke in before I could try mustering a comeback, "that anyone's got the slightest idea where we are?"

"About half a mile under..." I began, and suppressed a burst of hysterical laughter. I knew that if I started I wouldn't ever stop, and then someone would probably end up braining me with a torch. "No," I said soberly. "Derek?"

He shook his head exhaustedly. "No. So many twists and turns back there... Besides, I couldn't even tell you where in that cavern we found this tunnel. We're completely lost."

"If you've any more good news..." I groaned, and shut up.

"W-wait," Ken croaked, lifting a hand, and we paused, our own breath rasping in the echoing tunnel. "Do you hear that? What the hell is it?"

The noise was a low roaring, like a vast furnace, or a charging army.

"Oh Christ," I moaned, "not more bloody zombies."

The others ignored me. "Sounds like ... water," said Ken finally. "To me, anyway. What do you think, Derek?"

"Guess so." Neither of them asked my opinion. I could hardly blame them, as all I'd so far offered had been lame jokes.

"What d'you think? Try and follow it?"

"Why not? Least there's a chance of a way out that way."

And so we decided to follow the noise of the falling water – which was a good thing too, as the tunnel forked a minute or two later. All the time, we kept flashing our torch back down the tunnel, dreading the sight of squirming, clawing shadows spreading along the wall behind. We saw none.

At last, the tunnel showed its ending. Slate and shingle spread beyond it; that and space, and the glimmer of black water. We ventured forwards, towards it all.

THE TUNNEL EMERGED onto the shores of a vast underground lake, so huge the beam of Derek's torch barely penetrated a fraction of the distance. He'd brought a change of batteries, and that strengthened the beam; but still, it couldn't go far, and both mine and Ken's torches were beyond all hope or prayer of revival. What it revealed, though, was more than enough.

Stalagmites and stalactites met and merged in the lake. Its floor wasn't remotely even as far as I could tell, but plunged and rose at random, giving way from ankle-deep shallows one moment to a plunge all the way to Hell's bowels the next.

Derek prodded the lake's edge with the torch beam. Shallows, gravel-bottomed, yawned abruptly away out of sight. A huge pallid fish, eyeless, flopped wetly from the shallows and was lost in the dark.

The glimmering surface of the black subterranean lake stretched on forever, or it seemed to. I wish I could describe to you, again, what it was like, I wish I could make you visualise how dark it was. It wasn't a dark where your eyes could grow accustomed to it; *there was no light* down there, except the faint flicker of the torch, the brief blaze of a match in comparison to how long this place must have lived in endless midnight, without relief by moon or star. It was a blackness that made your eyes physically hurt as they strained against it like horses trying to haul a mountain, and in doing so it was maddening, literally *maddening*. I understood why the creatures down here (the living ones at any rate) would go blind in this dark; it was their only chance of sanity. Things plopped and shifted uncomfortably as the beam played over the water. Light was a wounding aberration now, down here. Something white wriggled and thrashed above the water, a vast columnar thing. God, what was it? Only when Derek's beam shone on it did we realise: it was a waterfall, dropping directly from the ceiling hundreds of feet above (yes, that too was out of the torch's range) to crash into the lake's blackness.

We felt dwarfed, reduced, and very afraid down there; Derek tore away from the sight, sweeping the torch-beam along the huge chamber's walls. They were high and striped with ledges, linked by rough paths hewn from one to the next.

"Want to try going up?" I suggested.

"Might as well," said Ken. "Least we know we want to go that way."

As long as we didn't end up under Bala Lake, I thought privately; I wasn't that good a swimmer. But I didn't say anything.

"OK," said Derek, turning, "now ... let's..."

He grew still as he turned, and his face paled. I opened my mouth to ask him what was wrong, but he raised a hand. Then I heard it too: the slap and flounder of hands and feet on stones.

Derek pointed his torch into the tunnel, and the beam flashed onto their faces – dozens of them, rushing forwards out of the dark onto the shore.

There was only one route away from them. The three of us began scrambling up the hewn paths in the chamber walls.

But the things that blundered, lumbered and lurched in the black and dripping warrens beneath the mountain came after us, and they were fast. They leapt and hopped and dived like grasshoppers; some scrambled to their feet again, others were trampled, and some tumbled over the edge to drop on the spiny shingle below. But they only had to get lucky once...

As the path narrowed, we had to break up into single file, me leading, brandishing the torch, Ken behind, and Derek bringing up the rear. And that was when one of the zombies caught Derek and brought him down, tackler and tackled rolling from the edge of the path.

Crying out, Derek clung grimly to the edge, swinging in nowhere. Below, the throng of horrors on the shores of the lake roared forward, hands upstretched in grasping anticipation of their prize.

For a long moment Derek swung in space, knuckles white, as we ran towards him. The creature's claws gouged deep through his clothes and into his skin, blood welling up.

We were almost there when – I'm sure – he smiled at us, and let go.

Perhaps it was the sight of the dead walking, his having plunged into a world where logic was a forgotten word, his own faith in reason and science cast to the four winds and lost; perhaps he didn't want to live in such a world. Or maybe I imagined the smile, and the weight of the clinging zombie simply dragged him down.

When he landed among the living dead there was a terrible cracking and crunching and splitting and ripping as they leapt on him. I didn't want to hear, but I had no choice.

More of them crouched on the path, dead eyes watchful in their stupid ways. I saw nothing human there: only dullness, greed and hunger.

Ken and I tensed as they readied themselves for the final rush.

"No!"

The cavern rang to the cry, and the living dead recoiled as though in terror.

The voice, cold and high and ringing, scattered greyish-white, blind-eyed bats from the unseen cavern ceiling as it spoke once more, now in a strange and unknown tongue. And the living dead quailed and shrank back.

Pale bare feet the colour of stone crunched in the grit beside me. A sort of cloak or cape was all their owner wore. The legs were long and slender, the body slender too, or what I could see of it; its upper part was in shadow.

The figure pointed, and the zombies scattered at unbelievable speed, like swarming rats, disappearing back down the tunnel from which they had emerged. Only the pathetic, mangled ruin of Derek's body remained, lying far below.

"Derek..." I croaked, numbly. He had been a good friend for a long time, as well you know, Matt. And he'd saved our lives, back in the cavern.

The figure laid a cold and comfortless hand on my shoulder; then, as Ken and I turned, it beckoned, and turned away from us. We followed it up the path. As we went, I saw that there were one or two others, silent, with it. I could see little of them.

At length we came to a cave, burrowing into the wall of the great chamber and, according to what the beam of the torch revealed, furnished into a room. Rickety wooden chairs and a table, on which rested an old miner's lamp. The figure we had followed picked up a box of matches that lay beside the lamp, struck one and lit the wick. The glow rose warmly and began to fill the room. The figure kept its back to us. It was small and thin, the cape covering the rear view of it from neck to ankle, though from what I'd seen it had gaped wide at the front. The hair, though ... what was it about the hair?

"It's good to see you again," said the figure in a voice that rang cold and dull as lead. And then it turned around, and the sight drove the breath from my lungs like a blow.

"Did you miss me?" Tricktrack asked.

THE BRONZE-RED coxcomb of spiny hair lent the only colour to her new appearance. Her eyes were still midnight black, of course; so were her lips and her nipples. The rest of her body, naked but for the cape fastened at her throat, was pale and smooth as alabaster. I wondered if this was how she'd looked when they found her that morning, her last tear trapped on her face.

Ken was mumbling. Looking over at him, I saw that his eyes were glassy and he was shaking.

"A touch of culture shock," said Tricktrack in her cold, empty voice. "He'll get over it." She smiled at me – sort of. There was no fluency to it, as though she was making her face do something long forgotten. "Did you miss me?" she asked again.

My eyes filled with tears, and her mouth parted. "Of course I did," I answered.

She reached a hand out, fingers trembling, and gently brushed and lifted the first falling tears from my face. "Warm!" she said wonderingly.

"What is this place?" Ken said suddenly. "Is this Hell?"

Tricktrack gave a bitter laugh. "Hell? There is no Hell. There is no Heaven. Only this. People make of it what little they can."

"Are all the dead here?" I asked.

"All that I know of."

"Why here? Why under a mountain in Wales?"

"That isn't where we are," she said dully. "It's just – a place where worlds touch. A gateway from your realm to ours."

"What's it like?" I asked after a little longer. "Being ... dead, I mean?" Maybe not the most sensitive question to ask, but none of it seemed real any more.

"Cold," she said. "Very cold. I don't just mean..." she gestured at her body. "I mean..." her hands rose to touch first her left breast, then her forehead. "Things are not the same here. Things are ... cold. Cold like stone."

Ken was gazing at Tricktrack in horror. She reached out to touch his arm; he recoiled. "I'm sorry, Father. Not what you were expecting, is it? You thought death would be better than life, only to find it's worse. Or, at best, much the same."

"Those things..." I began.

"We were all like that once," she said. "I was. You will be too, one day. It all comes here, even the ashes. Takes shape again. The newborn are always confused, angry, violent – half healed, full of appetite still. And jealous. They envy the living. Their heat, their capacity to feel."

She no longer sounded like the Tricktrack I had known, and I told her so. She bowed her head, then turned to cup her hands around the miner's lamp. "The heat," she said. "The light. We see it so rarely. Only on special occasions. This qualifies."

Was it my imagination, or did her shoulders shudder? I reached out and rested my hand lightly on her shoulder. "Is this it?" I asked her. "Is this all there is?"

She turned, and in her eyes welled two large black tears. "I don't know," she wept. "Hold me, John. Make me feel alive again. If only for a little while."

And I could do nothing else. She was cold, cold as ice, and I wondered as I clasped her to me if she would drain the life from me, vampire-like, till I was cold as her, and I realised that I didn't care.

"John," she said. "My John. Through all the cold I dreamt of you."

"Hush," I whispered, and let myself warm her, so that I could feel as though she'd never left. I stroked her hair. "I dreamt of you too, my love."

"Love? Do you mean that?"

"You know I do."

"No. The dead know little more than the living. I know only what you tell me and what I can believe."

"I love you, Tricktrack."

"And I love you. So why didn't you...?"

"My job, remember? I didn't want to hurt you."

"You failed, then."

"Tricktrack..."

"Ssh. I don't blame. I'm beyond blaming here. Ssh."

"Why am I here, Tricktrack? Why? Did you bring me?"

I pulled back to look her in the face. Despite her dark tears, it was capable of little in the way of expression. She shook her head. "No, John. Not by intent, at least. Call it a joke if you want. Fate's joke on us." She reached up and touched my face. "When I'm with you, John, I think I can remember how it was to be alive."

Her hands began to unfasten my shirt. "Make me feel alive again, my love. Love me my love. Love me John."

And I couldn't refuse her again.

AFTERWARDS, WE LAY together. Her body almost felt warm again, but not quite; it held only the heat it had absorbed from mine. It could generate none of its own.

But for all that, it had been good. Better than good. We were in love, after all.

She kissed me with her black lips, and her dark tears ran once again. I offered her a handkerchief and she dabbed them away. "Thank you," she said. Then she shivered and rose, and put her cape back on. "Now you must go."

"Already?"

"The living cannot stay here long. This realm will claim them for its own; that is its way. I pray it isn't too late for you." She bit her lip. "John, I'm sorry. I should have thought—"

"It wouldn't have made any difference," I said. "I would have stayed anyway."

"But your friend..."

Ken! "Oh Jesus," I said, and began to dress.

I TRIED TO take Ken's arm, but he shook me off. I don't think he could accept what I'd done. I could hardly blame him; I was having a hard time getting my head around it myself.

We left the cave and walked out onto the ledge. Tricktrack carried the miner's lantern, and its glow carried far, falling on the glittering, depthless lake below.

I looked around the deserted chamber. Deserted? No, not quite; something was moving below, at the foot of the wall.

"Derek!" I shouted. "Tricktrack, it's Derek, it looks like he's–"

Tricktrack's hand fell on my arm. "No, John. I'm sorry. He belongs here now."

Derek lurched upright, and his dark, sunken eyes found me. His jaws yawned wide, and a bloody snarl crept forth. Tricktrack crouched, and her body seemed to lunge, another eruption of that unknown tongue baying from her throat. Derek cringed back, and looked up at me one last time in mingled bewilderment and sorrow. Then he turned, shoulders slumped, and disappeared into the tunnel down which the zombies had gone.

I sagged, heavily. Tricktrack squeezed my arm again. "Come on, John. Let's go."

"Sure." I let out a long, weary sigh. "Come on, Ken–" I began, and stopped.

Ken stood very still on the edge of the wall, leaning out as though into a wind only he could feel. "Ken–" I said. "Ken, no. Don't. Come on, mate. Come back–"

He turned and looked at me. In that look there was no judgment of me, no contempt; only the deepest and most profound grief I've ever seen. Ken had always been a man of strong faith: the promise of Heaven, the threat of Hell. When a faith like that is broken, nothing remains. And there is nothing that can be said.

And so I said nothing. I only exchanged that last glance with him; and he turned, and stepped out into space.

The spell broken, I ran to the edge as the splash echoed and called his name. But he never came up again; the lake's surface was as smooth as black glass. Behind me, Tricktrack's head was bowed, her face pillowed in her hands.

DAWN WAS BREAKING when at last she led me from a cave entrance on the flank of the mountain. We kissed for one last time.

"I can't come any further," she said.

"I understand," I replied, though that was a laugh.

"I almost remembered there," she said. "How it felt."

"Will I see you again?" I asked.

"Not until you come to me."

I remembered Ken. "How long will that be?"

"I don't know, John." Her face was placid, emotionless; already the coldness of death's estate was settling on her once more. "If you were there too long, then sooner or later it will come. But it should be swift, and without pain."

"I suppose that's the best any of us can hope for."

She gripped my hands tightly. "When that time comes, John – soon or far away – come to me. Or have someone bring you. It's vast, what lies beyond. I would search for you, but it could take years. Or forever. Have someone bring you here, to this place."

"I will."

"I'll take care of you. I'll nurse you through being newborn. I've been there. Only promise that you'll come to me."

"I promise. Where else would I go?"

AND THAT, LITTLE brother, is more or less it. I'm almost certain now that I did spend too long in that netherworld, and that sooner or later, it'll happen. As she said, it should be swift and painless.

I know that when it comes, I need to be with her. Perhaps we can make each other feel alive now; that or come to love what we have. Perhaps with time, you come to appreciate the transition, accept your new state for what it is. I don't know.

Whatever happens, Matt, promise me one thing. That one way or another, you'll bring me to the mountain. Don't let me be cremated. I don't want to be piecing myself back together from the ashes. One way or the other, get me there, to her. Please.

With love,

John.

AND SO ENDED my brother's letter.

Two weeks after the date on it, John went to Devon for a fishing weekend. He went out on a boat with his rod and line to go after tope or skate, I forget which. Out of nowhere, on a millpond sea, a freak wave came and carried him overboard. No-one else had been harmed. The tide brought him in that evening.

And here I was now.

I looked at my watch. 11.50 pm.

It was time.

I opened the back of the Land Rover, and lifted John out. Cradled in my arms, I carried him down the slope into the little dell he'd specified. Among a thicket of trees and bushes and creepers, no doubt beautiful by day but just plain eerie by night, a flat wall of slate rose. I laid him down before it.

11.57.

I made my way back up the slope to the car, and looked down.

12.00.

The wind roared. The slate darkened into shadow. And in the shadows, something glowed. Something like the lights of fires.

Inside the wall?

The fire danced and threw shadows; the picture cleared. The fire, I saw, played on the wall of a cave, a tunnel. It was advancing towards the open ground of the dell. There was a tunnel, where before there had only been a blank wall of stone.

I wanted to run. But I couldn't look away. I had to know.

She came out, silhouetted and half-lit by the torches blazing in the hands of those who followed her. I could see little of them, save that each carried a burning brand, and that between the six of them they carried a bier.

She wore only the dark cape, fastened at her throat; beneath it she was naked, her body stone-pale but for the black nipples, lips and eyes, and the red of her hair. She knelt beside the body and tenderly unwrapped it, and gazed down at my brother's blue and pale face. She leant down and kissed his mouth, then nodded to the six.

She stood as they came forwards, thrusting their torches into the ground as they set down the bier and lifted John's body onto it, arranging it with tenderness and care. Then they picked up their brands once more and hoisted the bier to their shoulders, their backs turned to me.

Before she turned to follow them, she stopped and her eyes met mine, lit by the reach of the pallbearers' fire. In that moment, I saw her love for him: that even through the cold silence and reptilian numbing of death, her love had survived.

Perhaps that's the only real salvation. Not in prayers or devotions, in hymns or commandments. Certainly not in judgments or intolerance. Only in our love for one another; that alone endures.

Before she turned and followed the others, and John, back into the place from whence she'd come, she smiled – after a fashion – and bowed deeply to me. I bowed back, and our tears ran together: hers black, mine clear.

Then she followed them into the dark, and their torches faded and there was only shadow; and then the shadows scattered from the emerging moon and there was only slate.

But I often remember her like that, and that solemn procession. And I remember something else: the sound of a great roaring over the sound of the wind, like that of the great waterfall crashing into that black and bottomless lake, in the heart of midnight's realm.

ABOUT THE EDITOR

Joel Lane lives in Birmingham. His tales of supernatural horror have appeared in a variety of magazines and anthologies. A collection of his short stories, *The Earth Wire*, was published by Egerton Press in 1994 and won a British Fantasy Award. His other publications include a collection of poems, *The Edge of the Screen* (Arc, 1999) and a novel set in the world of post-punk rock music, *From Blue To Black* (Serpent's Tail, 2000). His second novel, *Your Broken Face*, is due to appear in 2002. Current projects include a crime anthology, *Birmingham Noir*, and a book-length study of horror fiction in the twentieth century.

CONTRIBUTORS NOTES

Born in 1971, **Simon Avery** lives and works in Birmingham. His short fiction has been published in the anthologies *Cold Cuts 3*, *Last Rites and Resurrections*, *Watch Fire* and *The Tiger Garden*, and in the magazines *The Third Alternative* and *Crime Wave*. He is currently at work on his first novel, *Final Fling*.

Simon Bestwick was born was born in 1974 and lives in Timperley. About fifty of his stories have been published or are forthcoming in various magazines and anthologies, including *Nasty Piece of Work*, *Sackcloth and Ashes*, *Enigmatic Tales*, *All Hallows*, *The Dream Zone* and *Strange Seas*. Several novels are currently doing the rounds with agents and publishers. Six of his stories have received honourable mentions in *The Year's Best Fantasy and Horror*, and his story 'Love Among the Bones' was nominated for the 1999 British Fantasy Award.

Ramsey Campbell lives in Wallasey, Merseyside. He was presented with both the World Horror Convention's Grand Master Award and the Horror Writers Association's Bram Stoker Award for Life Achievement in 1999. His books in the field of supernatural and psychological horror fiction include the collections *Demons By Day-*

light, *The Height of the Scream*, *Waking Nightmares* and *Ghosts and Grisly Things;* and the novels *The Face That Must Die, The Influence, Midnight Sun, The Long Lost, The One Safe Place, The House on Nazareth Hill* and *Silent Children*. He has edited several anthologies, including *The Far Reaches of Fear, New Terrors* and *Meddling With Ghosts*. His novel *The Nameless* has been filmed as *Los Sin Nombres* by Spanish director Jaume Balaguero. A new supernatural horror novel, *The Darkest Part of the Woods*, has recently appeared.

Pauline E. Dungate lives in Birmingham, England, and is a teacher at the local Museum and Art Gallery. Her stories have appeared in UK anthologies such as *Skin of the Soul, Narrow Houses* and *Swords Against the Millennium* and US anthologies such as *Merlin, Victorious Villains* and *Warrior Fantastic*. She has been a runner-up in a crime writing competition two years running, and the stories have appeared in one of the region's leading newspapers. She has won prizes for poetry, and has also written numerous articles and reviews under the name of Pauline Morgan. She is one of the leaders of the Cannon Hill Writers' Group. Her other interests include gardening, cooking, truck driving and bird watching.

Paul Finch is a British-based former police officer and journalist now turned full-time writer. He earns his bread and butter writing for the TV crime series *The Bill*, but is a great fan of the horror and supernatural genre, and produces short stories whenever time permits. His first hardback collection of stories, *After Shocks*, has just been published by Ash-Tree Press, and a second collection is due shortly from Silver Salamander Press. A story of his has recently been optioned for feature film development, and Paul is currently working on the script. He lives in Lancashire, northern England, with his wife Cathy and his children, Eleanor and Harry.

Derbyshire author and creative writing tutor **Derek M. Fox** spent six years in amateur dramatics as an actor and producer, and steered three theatre groups towards producing comedies and thrillers. His own play, a story of the war years, will be staged this year. Derek has had numerous stories and articles published; his first novel, *Recluse* (1996) was followed by *Demon* (1998). A collection, *Treading on the Past*, won excellent reviews, and a story in the anthology *F20* earned an honourable mention from Ellen Datlow. *Heart of Shadows: Lord Byron & the Supernatural* (Blackie) was launched at Newstead Abbey in April 2001. Having completed a talking book version, he is now writing the follow-up, *Sinister Quartet*. A collection, *Through Dark Eyes*, and a horror thriller, *Jackdaw*, should hit the markets later this year. His well-received story 'Teeth' was issued on CD in September, 2001.

Jason Gould was born in 1971 and lives in Hull, where he works in website design. A number of his short stories have been published or are awaiting publication in a variety of magazines and anthologies, including *The Third Alternative, Year's Best Fantasy 2000* (edited by Steve Savile and published by Cosmos Books), *Crimewave* and *Albedo 1*. 'Nights At The Regal' was inspired by those bookshops that appear every now and then in the backstreets of northern England, trading science fiction and horror paperbacks from the 60s and 70s alongside the latest pornography imported from Denmark and Germany.

John Howard was born in the latter half of the last century in St Helier (the other one). The child being father to the man, the effect of being brought up in the Chiltern Hills within easy sight of West Wycombe has left its mark ever since. He is a long-time contributor to the science fiction and horror small press.

Tim Lebbon is the author of several books in the genre of supernatural horror: *Mesmer, As The Sun Goes Down, Faith in the Flesh, Hush* (with Gavin Williams), *Naming of Parts* and *White*. The latter has won a British Fantasy Award and been optioned by a London film production company. *The Nature of Balance* has recently appeared from Leisure Books, *Until She Sleeps* from Cemetery Dance and *Face* from Night Shade Books. Other new novels and collections are in the pipeline. His work has appeared or is due in *Year's Best Fantasy & Horror*, *Best New Horror*, *October Dreams*, *Cemetery Dance*, *The Darker Side*, *Subterranean Gallery 2* and many more.

D.F. (Des) Lewis (born 1948) formed the Zeroist group in 1967 and was a Company Pension expert for 22 years until 1992. He has had over 1300 stories published worldwide (in titles such as *The Year's Best Horror Stories*, *Best New Horror*, *Stand*, *Orbis*, *Iron*, *Panurge* and *London Magazine*) until he retired in 2001 and is now the *Nemonymous* Tsar. He was awarded the British Fantasy Society's Karl Edward Wagner Award in 1998. He has been married for over 30 years and has two grown-up children. Des is a member of Storyville.

After learning that 'astronaut' was an impractical career choice, **Mike McKeown** studied astrophysics at university. This stood him in good stead for both his first full-time job as a warehouseman and his brush with designing home computer games in the 1980s. When not concocting fantasies, he now works as a manager for an IT services company and edits a monthly science fiction fanzine for a coven of his co-workers. Mike is married with two young sons and lives in Cheshire.

Nicholas Royle is the author of four novels – *Counterparts* (1993), *Saxophone Dreams* (1996), *The Matter of the Heart* (1997) and *The Director's Cut* (2000) – and more than a hundred short stories. He has edited eleven anthologies, including *Darklands* (1991), *The Ex Files: New Stories About Old Flames* (1998) and *The Time Out Book of London Short Stories Volume 2* (2000). 'Empty Stations' was originally written for *Beneath the Ground*, but appeared first in *Ambit*. Nicholas Royle lives in Shepherd's Bush, West London, with his wife and two children. He is currently working on a new novel, *Straight to Video*.

David Sutton was born in 1947 and has been writing and editing in the fantasy and horror genre for a generation. In recognition of his devotion and achievement in the field, he was honoured with the British Fantasy Special Award in 1994. After editing the small press magazine *Shadow* in the 1970s, he went on to co-edit the British and World Fantasy Award-winning magazine *Fantasy Tales*. Recently he has edited *Voices From Shadow*, an anthology of non-fiction drawn from *Shadow*, and written the booklet *On the Fringe for Thirty Years: A History of Horror in the British Small Press*. Anthologies he has edited include *New Writings in Horror and the Supernatural* (two volumes), *The Satyr's Head and Other Tales of Terror*, and jointly with Stephen Jones, *The Best Horror From Fantasy Tales*, five volumes of *Dark Voices: The Pan Book of Horror Stories* and five volumes of *Dark Terrors: The Gollancz Book of Horror*. His short stories have appeared in many publications, including *Best New Horror 2* and *7*, *Final Shadows*, *Cold Fear*, *Taste of Fear*, *The Mammoth Book of Zombies*, *The Mammoth Book of Werewolves*, *Skeleton Crew*, *Beyond*, *Shadows Over Innsmouth*, *The New Lovecraft Circle* and *The Merlin Chronicles*.